PRAISE FOR

Eliza Starts a Rumor

T0028891

"A smart, engaging treat for *Big Little Lies* fans. The perfect summer read!"   —Katie Couric

"A funny, poignant, very topical romp through some real-life issues humans deal with every day. In every town. Throw this one in your summer beach bag, you'll devour it in short order."
—Lee Woodruff, journalist and *New York Times* bestselling author of
Those We Love Most

"Jane L. Rosen is a sparkling, original voice. With hilarity and heart, she takes us into . . . the picturesque Hudson Valley where life is anything but perfect. Secrets are revealed, grudges form, forgiveness is found, men come and go, but through it all, divine friendship endures in this glorious read."
—Adriana Trigiani, bestselling author of *Tony's Wife*

"A compelling examination of the shared female experience. I couldn't put it down."
—Jo Piazza, *New York Times* bestselling author of
Charlotte Walsh Likes to Win

"Exquisitely written, compulsively readable, and brimming with charm, *Eliza Starts a Rumor* is everything I look for in a book. Jane L. Rosen has a forever fan in me."
—Emily Henry, *New York Times* bestselling author of *Beach Read*

"Warm and funny and utterly of this moment. . . . The magic of Jane L. Rosen's novels is that they reveal the cracks in women's facades just enough to let their true strength shine through. I loved it."   —Jamie Brenner, bestselling author of *Summer Longing*

Also by Jane L. Rosen

Nine Women, One Dress

Eliza Starts a Rumor

JANE L. ROSEN

BERKLEY

New York

BERKLEY
An imprint of Penguin Random House LLC
penguinrandomhouse.com

Copyright © 2020 by Jane L. Rosen
Readers Guide copyright © 2021 by Jane L. Rosen

BERKLEY and the BERKLEY & B colophon are registered trademarks
of Penguin Random House LLC.

ISBN: 9780593102091

The Library of Congress has catalogued the Berkley hardcover edition of this book as follows:

Names: Rosen, Jane L., author.
Title: Eliza starts a rumor / Jane L. Rosen.
Description: First edition. | New York: Berkley, 2020.
Identifiers: LCCN 2019059334 (print) | LCCN 2019059335 (ebook) |
ISBN 9780593102084 (hardcover) | ISBN 9780593102107 (ebook)
Subjects: LCSH: Domestic fiction. | GSAFD: Humorous fiction.
Classification: LCC PS3618.O83145 E45 2020 (print) |
LCC PS3618.O83145 (ebook) | DDC 813/.6—dc23
LC record available at https://lccn.loc.gov/2019059334
LC ebook record available at https://lccn.loc.gov/2019059335

Berkley hardcover edition / June 2020
Berkley trade paperback edition / April 2021

Printed in the United States of America
1 3 5 7 9 10 8 6 4 2

Book design by Laura K. Corless

For my mother
"I'll be looking at the moon, but I'll be seeing you."

Above all, be the heroine of your life, not the victim.

—NORA EPHRON

PROLOGUE

Eliza Hunt had always been a fan of the sisterhood. It was the reason she became a Girl Scout—well, that and the Thin Mints—and why she joined the women's chorus in high school even though she couldn't carry a tune. It was her impetus for pledging a sorority in college when frat boys made her nervous, and why she worked at a female-run marketing firm after graduation. Eliza was completely happy to be traveling through life in the company of her girlfriends, until one fateful night across a Greenwich Village bar, when the boyfriend that she wasn't even looking for appeared.

Eliza and Luke were engaged within the year, married in the next, and pregnant with twins shortly thereafter. Soon, the Hunt family of four moved into the house Eliza had grown up in, a traditional Colonial in Hudson Valley, New York, where they quickly settled in for their happily ever after. Or so she thought. It wasn't long before Eliza found herself longing for the safety net of female friendship. She missed the camaraderie, support, candor, advice, laughs, drama, and encouragement that one gets from being in the company of other women. Eliza missed the sisterhood.

She joined a mommy-and-me group, started playing round-robin tennis, and spent a lot of time at the local playground, but these interactions all left her longing for more. When she came up short, she set out to create a solution of her own. Inspired by the traditional bulletin boards at the library and supermarket, Eliza took the concept of posting things into the twenty-first century, creating an online source for exchange and support that, like most modern resources, can be carried around all day, right in your pocket. She named it the Hudson Valley Ladies' Bulletin Board.

Creating and moderating the bulletin board immediately felt like a gift to Eliza—just what had been missing in her life. After the local newspaper ran a piece featuring her and the bulletin board, its membership quadrupled.

It turned out that the ladies of Hudson Valley weren't alone in their digital love affair. The newspaper reported that women in communities from Manhattan to Mumbai were also banding together online to commiserate over their pelvic floors, the glass ceiling, and everything in between. What began with sharing recipes and doctor recommendations morphed into an electronic soapbox where women could shout their innermost truths and fears from computer-generated rooftops. Children, careers, fashion, love, orgasms, money, and men were all fair topics for endless, lay-it-on-the-line discussions. Women holding one another's virtual hands through the joys, the frustrations, and the traumas of life. It was a tale as old as time, from the biblical menstrual tent to the quilting circle to these modern online hives—female bonds help solidify happiness.

And Eliza *was* happy—for a very long time. The article featured a photo of her leaning against her desk, looking smart but casual in a crisp white blouse, pencil jeans, and ballet flats. Twelve years later, it still sat in a frame beside her computer. The last time that she looked at it she had cringed. She barely recognized the smiling, fresh-faced woman in the photo. She was quite surprised that no one wondered where that woman had gone.

CHAPTER 1

Eliza Hunt

Eliza Hunt sat in the parking lot of her local Stop & Shop. Her neck was soaked in sweat, her hands trembling uncontrollably. It wouldn't be long before she'd have no choice but to curl up in a ball on the front seat of her car and give up.

She looked at the curved bold font of the familiar bright purple sign and read it out loud: "STOP & SHOP." Such simple instructions, yet she felt as if her body were weighted to the front seat of her car, pinned down by fear.

She refocused and tried talking herself out of the car: "Eliza. The twins are coming home from college for the long weekend. You need to walk across the parking lot and buy food for them."

Nothing.

She had already attempted to will the panic away with calm breaths in and out, in and out, a method she had learned from the psychiatrist who treated her during her first bout with agoraphobia some thirty years earlier. It hadn't helped then, either. She pried her feet out of her sneakers, peeled off her sweat socks, and shoved them under her now-drenched underarms. Thankfully, the sweat socks lived up to their name. How did I get here? she asked herself. She knew the answer, but as per usual, she didn't have the strength to address it. She stared out at the familiar market she had been in a thousand times and yelled, "Get out of the damn car, Eliza!"

Still nothing; the fear was mounting, not retreating.

At this point in her life, Eliza knew the Stop & Shop so well that she could direct someone to aisle nine for beverages and aisle five for Preparation H as deftly as the store manager could. She knew that if she could just get midway down aisle four to her old friend, a box of chocolate-covered Entenmann's donuts, she could ingest enough sugar, and derive enough comfort, to hold the panic at bay for the duration of her shopping. Growing up, she had kept a similar box under her bed, hidden from her mother, who didn't allow sweets in the house. Whether she was suffering from anxiety, rebelling, or just looking for a remedy for the teenage blahs, they always did the trick.

Eliza closed her eyes and pictured the familiar blue-and-white box, with the clear window on top, visualized herself opening the side tabs and scoffing down one, or two, or four. She imagined her first bite—the distinct segue from the hard chocolate shell to the soft, vanilla cakey inside, channeling her mind and spirit into the exquisite sense of anticipation.

"Focus. Focus on the donut, Eliza."

Before she knew it, she was out of the car and standing in aisle four, three donuts in. They had the desired effect, and she took a few deep breaths to seal the deal. She pulled the socks out from under her armpits, threw them in her purse, and yanked out her shopping list. She was good to go.

Half an hour later, with her cart overflowing, Eliza stepped in line at the checkout counter. There she was instantly distracted from her fear of exiting the store by a lively conversation between two young mothers ahead of her. One, who had a baby strapped to her chest, was helping the other, who had an unruly toddler strapped in the seat of the cart, unload her groceries. As the toddler's mother placed one item on the belt, the toddler took another off and threw it back into the cart. It was entertaining, and Eliza was in no rush to go back outside.

The mother of the baby said, "I was up all night reading that epic thread on the local chat group. Did you see it?"

"Of course I saw it. It was like a train wreck."

"I just don't understand how these women spill everything. I mean, 'My husband has erectile dysfunction, please help'?"

"At least she wrote that anonymously. All those women who answered with their expert advice, you can only imagine that their husbands have issues in that department as well. I mean, my God, my husband would kill me."

They both laughed. Eliza did not. She found their conversation very alarming. Eliza reviewed and approved every post that went on the Hudson Valley Ladies' Bulletin Board, and the one that these two were discussing was unfamiliar to her. She redirected her anxiety and butt right into the women's conversation.

"Not to be nosy, but I couldn't help but overhear. Are you referring to the Hudson Valley Ladies' Bulletin Board?"

"Oh, no. That dinosaur bores me to tears," the woman with the toddler answered. The insult registered on Eliza's face and the other woman seemed to notice and proceeded to sugarcoat her response. To Eliza it felt more like arsenic.

"That one is more for *your* generation. There's a new site called Valley Girls that's more relevant, you know, *for us*." Her high ponytail did a pirouette as she motioned to her just-off-to-the-gym outfit.

Eliza looked down at herself. She was wearing the shirt she had slept in and sweatpants. She couldn't remember the last time she had on leggings, let alone jeans. She vowed to shower and blow her hair out before the kids arrived home. And to put on an actual outfit.

"Valley Girls?" she asked. "When did that one start?"

"A few months ago. More dirty laundry, less how best to wash it."

Eliza pulled back her cart and slid it toward an empty register. All thoughts of her recent panic were temporarily banished by new fears. Was the bulletin board becoming irrelevant? Would it wither and die? She couldn't let that happen—especially not right now. Checking those posts and watching the attention they received had become her biggest connection to the outside world and, as pathetic as it felt to admit it, her only emotional high, save a phone call from her kids.

Suddenly, she couldn't get home fast enough, and for once, not just because of her agoraphobia. She had no idea how she would do it, but she would not allow these sleek millennial mommas to make her site obsolete.

CHAPTER 2

Olivia York

The anniversary gift was due to be delivered by ten, and Spencer, Olivia's husband, had promised to be home from his run in time for its arrival. He often miscalculated the length of his runs, adding on miles and subsequently time. It was doubtful that he would be at her side for the big reveal. Standing alone with the deliverymen was not how Olivia had pictured this moment.

On hearing the sound of wheels on gravel, she texted Spencer, They're here. If he were home, where he should have been, that text would have included at least three exclamation points. Her lack of punctuation matched her mood. Olivia was disappointed. All of the romance she'd felt when first hearing of his imminent surprise was replaced with annoyance. The doorbell rang. She brushed off the gloom and answered it with a genuine smile.

"Right this way," she directed the two men, with a mixture of nervousness and excitement, as they carried a large crate through the front door. It had been just six weeks since Olivia and Spencer had moved to Hudson Valley with their beautiful baby, Lily, but it already felt like home. She loved everything about the house right down to the lovely name of the street, Evergreen Lane, where she had resolved to bring up her family. Actually, "resolved to" made it seem as if Olivia was not fully embracing this move. That was not the case. Though it had not been her idea, Olivia York took on this transition in her true, hopeful fashion, as she did most everything that came her way.

A born and bred city girl, she had no idea how to live in the country. Even calling it the country as opposed to a suburb of Manhattan was apparently incorrect and made her husband laugh every time she said it.

It had been Spencer's plan all along to move out of Manhattan: grass for the kids to play on, fresh air, the promise of a golden retriever or a standard poodle or some combination of the two. It was the way he'd grown up, and the offices for York Cosmetics, his family's multilevel-marketing company, were based nearby. Olivia knew that even a reverse commute couldn't beat the hop, skip, and jump it would now take for Spencer to get to work. As a freelance graphic artist, Olivia could work from anywhere. She felt selfish insisting they stay in the city forever, though it had always been her preference.

Olivia thought she'd have a few good urban years while Lily was still tiny before Spencer broached the topic of moving. But the first time she walked into the glass house that jutted out from the mountainous banks of the Hudson, perched at the perfect angle to see for miles in each direction, she wanted nothing more. By the time they saw the master bedroom, its windows set to capture every hue of the ever-changing foliage, the choppy currents, the passing ships, she was sold. Spencer was no fool. He knew his art history–loving wife would not be able to resist living within a Hudson Valley landscape any more than Monet at Giverny. When they returned to the city after seeing it for the first time, she stopped at the magazine stand and grabbed the latest issues of *Architectural Digest, Elle Decor,* and *Country Living.*

Olivia directed the men to hang what they confirmed was a painting over the living room fireplace. She suspected it was a piece from some up-and-coming artist she'd admired the last time she'd dragged Spencer through the galleries of Chelsea. She hadn't imagined that he was even listening to her, let alone noting her favorites for an anniversary gift. Spencer did have a way of doing things that took her by surprise. It was one of the reasons she had fallen for him in the first place. Since she was a real planner, being with a free spirit like Spencer had taken her out of her comfort zone, and she liked it.

When the deliverymen removed the painting from the crate, revealing the canvas in all its glory, Olivia was . . . speechless. Spencer had had their wedding portrait reimagined as a modern version of Botticelli's *Birth of Venus,* with the two of them standing on a seashell in a calm sea.

Olivia was suddenly relieved that Spencer wasn't home so she could take it in unobserved. To say Olivia wasn't a fan of the trend of repurposing classic paintings into pop art was an understatement, but Spencer didn't know that. And, she reasoned, there was no denying the romance of her husband's gift. It wasn't what she'd expected, but it was infinitely more personal. The early Renaissance painter's rendition of the goddess of love had been a highlight the first time Olivia had dragged Spencer through a gallery—the Uffizi in Florence—and the gift was obviously a loving homage to their Italian meet-cute.

Olivia and Spencer had met in their junior year abroad on a train in Italy. She was traveling with her suite mates from Wellesley and was buried in a novel, *A Room with a View,* which she had chosen in part because it was set in Italy. She was just the kind of girl who would match her book with her travels. She didn't notice the dark-haired, blue-eyed American across the aisle watching her. In all fairness, there was often someone looking at Olivia.

Olivia was very beautiful. She wasn't perfect; her nose was a bit long, her ears could probably have done with being pinned back when she was a child, but she had that thing—that thing that propelled the likes of Carolyn Bessette-Kennedy and Julia Roberts into the spotlight. Like them, her beauty seemed to emanate from her smile and continue down her perfectly tanned frame and colt-like legs.

Growing up in New York City, Olivia had felt as if the boys were everywhere that she was. One smile, and there was never one who didn't ask for her number, who didn't call, who didn't call again—but more importantly, never one who she cared enough for to call back. The attention overwhelmed her, so much so that when it came time to go to college, she only applied to all-girls schools. It wasn't that she didn't like men, but she liked books more and she knew she would get to the men part eventually. Eventually came on that train to Florence.

When Olivia returned to her seat after a bathroom break, she found Spencer sitting in it, refusing to get up until she agreed to accompany him for a drink in the bar car. There was nothing especially distinctive about Spencer. In Olivia's world, handsome, educated, wealthy, sporty guys with an entertaining undercurrent of immaturity were a common entity. There was really no one reason why Spencer had succeeded where others had failed. Maybe it was timing, maybe it was Florence, maybe it was the romance in the book she was reading at the time—the story of a somewhat serious young woman falling for a free-spirited young man—or maybe a combination of them all: a perfect storm.

She went for the drink, then dinner, then the rest of her time in Florence followed by a sunflower-flanked drive down the Tuscan coast to Porto Ercole. She was not one to deviate from a plan, nor to ditch her friends, but somehow she got caught up in Spencer's deep blue eyes and the way he undressed her with them. By the time they reached the coast, she had fallen in love for the very first time. And, as it turned out, Olivia loved being in love. She especially loved the promise of it—being "taken" felt quite satisfying on many levels.

After their semester-long European courtship, they dated long distance throughout their senior years. She traveled to visit him at Duke for his formals; he met her in Boston, where they barely left their hotel room. By graduation they were pinned, two years later engaged, and six years later inhabiting their new home in Hudson Valley, with Olivia staring at the campy wedding portrait while their baby slept soundly in her nursery.

The two men stepped back to see if the painting was straight.

"What do you think?" one asked, bringing her back to the moment.

She took a beat. It was a funny combination of classic and modern, like her.

"I love it," Olivia decided, right there on the spot.

"It's a real nice picture, lady," one of them said with sincere appreciation.

As Olivia escorted them out, a station wagon filled with a gaggle of babies pulled up to the house. She watched from the doorway as the woman she'd been expecting—their mother—stepped out. Olivia was pretty sure she was still in her pajamas. She went up to greet her.

"Hi!" she said, excited to possibly make her first suburban friend. It was obvious from the woman's response, "Yeah, hi," that she was not similarly interested. Her tone and the three babies strapped into car seats, two of whom were crying, made it quite evident that she was not in the mood for small talk. Her attitude, her attire, and the fact that she was selling Olivia her barely used Thule Urban Glide jogging stroller, all pointed to the fact that Olivia might never see this woman again, except possibly at the pediatrician's office.

They exchanged the stroller for the agreed-upon hundred dollars and the woman was on her way.

"Nice meeting you!" Olivia tried again.

"Yeah, bye," she scoffed at her, as if it were Olivia's fault that she'd given up on jogging.

Olivia had found the notice for the prized stroller on the Hudson Valley Ladies' Bulletin Board, which she'd joined the same day that they had closed on the house. There, she was happy to discover the source for everything she needed in her new life. She had no way of knowing then that it would also provide the seed for its destruction.

CHAPTER 3

Eliza

Eliza dropped her grocery bags on her kitchen counter and rummaged through them, carefully pulling out the frozen food and perishables before collapsing into a heap on her kitchen floor. She had made it through her shopping list and was thankful for that. But every bit of strength she'd summoned at the supermarket seemed to have declared mutiny and turned against her on the car ride home.

It would have been so much better for Eliza if her husband, Luke, knew what was going on, but she had made every effort over the past few months to cover it up. She certainly had practice. This may have been her first major flare-up since high school, but in the years in between, she'd still preferred the safety of home—often using the excuse of having something in the oven. It was hard to know if she loved to bake and loved running the bulletin board or just loved how they tethered her to her kitchen and computer.

So though it wasn't unusual for her to be a bit of a homebody, hiding it all was like a job in itself. Her go-to list of fun things to do on weekends was substituted with a list of well-crafted excuses. She perfected the facade of the busy housewife coming and going—placing her tennis racquet by the front door on the days of her usual game and putting the things she bought online in old shopping bags strewn on the floor of the bedroom closet. Sometimes she would have to turn to illness: a stomach bug, a bad headache. Those were easy to pull off because both were actual symptoms of her anxiety. All she needed to do was come close enough to the estimated due date without a good excuse and she would soon find herself massaging her temples or vomiting into the toilet.

At first she missed Luke, really missed being close to him. For as long as she could remember they had looked forward to the empty nest phase of their lives. They loved being parents, but they also loved being alone together. They were lucky that way, lucky that the spark hadn't fizzled and that they truly liked each other's company. But lately she resented having to answer his solicitous questions, resented his unintended part in making her feel pathetic. When that happened, when she started wishing he would just leave her alone so she could stop dealing in excuses, that's when she worried that she had done irreparable damage to her marriage and her family.

Eliza had held on to the notion ingrained in her since childhood that mental health issues were not to be spoken of. Though she was smart enough to know that being in a constant state of fight-or-flight was not good for her health, mental or otherwise, she never did anything about it.

Back when Eliza had missed four months of high school, the first time her agoraphobia rendered her nonfunctional, her mother pretended she was home with mono. Her daughter's bout with mental illness, though it manifested itself differently, was the first time Birdie Reinhart had seen a glimpse of herself in her child. There was no way Eliza's polished, stick-thin mother, with her shiny golden hair, would have admitted that her daughter, who did not receive her skinny gene or her shiny gene, had only inherited her crazy gene.

From the day Eliza was born, Birdie would stare at the chubby baby with brown eyes and dark curly hair and look for some reflection of herself, but none existed. Eliza inherited her looks from Birdie's Jewish mother, while Birdie was an obvious by-product of her Protestant father. She had even changed her name from Bertha to Birdie at age eighteen, officially transitioning from Jewess to Wasp.

Back in high school, thankfully, Eliza's problem departed as quickly as it had appeared. One day she woke up, got dressed, and went to school. Just like that. She never discussed with the psychiatrist, or her parents, or her best friend, Amanda, what had brought it on in the first place. In fact, none of it was ever mentioned again.

Years later, when Eliza met Luke, and he set about falling in love with her every flaw, she didn't reveal that one. She wondered now, if she had been truthful from the outset, whether she would still be lying there in hysterics on her kitchen floor. As it had nearly every night since the twins' high school graduation, the memory of the commencement ceremony took hold.

On that beautiful June day, Eliza had sat in the high school auditorium enveloped in a particular sense of pride she had never felt before. She had been prepared for it by other parents, who'd told her, "There's nothing quite like watching your children graduate." She was thrilled to be experiencing it for herself.

She had waited impatiently for the ceremony to begin, anticipating the pomp and circumstance to come. Luke, equally excited, sat by her side. He put his hand over hers, squeezed it tight, and smiled at her with nothing but love in his eyes. It was common for him to look at her like that. He had no way of knowing how much it meant to her. She had a much harder shell than her husband did. Of course, she loved him and the twins with all she had, but she tended to keep her own heart behind a wall—a very tall wall. She was beyond grateful that Luke had persistently leaped over it, and on that day she had personally dismantled more than a few bricks—her heart felt more open than she had ever remembered.

Commencement was taking a while to begin. She imagined the kids lined up in the hallway of the high school trying their best to be quiet, but too hyped up to stand still. "Imagined" may be the wrong word; a better choice would be "remembered." Eliza had graduated from the same high school as her children some thirty years earlier. She had lined up in the same hallway where they stood now, as she and her best friend, Amanda, rearranged the line so that they could march down the aisle together.

Eliza looked down to see Luke fidgeting with the program, rolling it between his palms like he was shaping dough. She took it from him; she wanted to keep it for posterity. She straightened it out, bending it in the other direction, then pressing it flat on her lap. She opened it up to read, first turning to the page that listed the students. There they were: her graduates, Kevin Hunt and Kayla Hunt. As she silently read their names, she could almost hear the voice of the principal calling them up for their diplomas. She imagined the cheers as they each made their way across the stage. The anticipation was palpable both in her mind and in the room.

She turned to the order of events, glancing through what she already knew. The principal's remarks would be followed by speeches from the valedictorian, a girl she had known since the kids were in kindergarten, and the salutatorian, a boy who played lacrosse with Kevin. She was eager to hear what they both had to say: smart young minds ready to take on the world.

She turned to the next page in the program, a special dedication. As she read it, she began to shake. She tried to steady her hands in her lap but seemed to have no control of her own body. The program dropped to the floor, and Luke bent down to pick it up. As he went to hand it back to her, she saw panic in his eyes.

"Oh my God, Eliza, what's the matter?"

Sweat poured out from under her arms, soaking the lavender A-line cotton dress with cap sleeves that she had worked so hard to fit into. She could feel the heat radiating from her scalp at the point where her hairline met her neck. Beads of sweat rolled off her upper lip and landed in her lap with such frequency that it seemed as if the roof was leaking. Her heart was literally shaking inside her body and she couldn't seem to catch her breath, as if she was always one step behind it.

"Eliza, are you OK?" he asked in a panicked voice. "Should I get a doctor?"

Eliza looked down at the now melon-shaped circles of sweat under her arms.

"No, I'm OK. It's just a hot flash." She constructed her first outright lie to him on the topic.

It shut Luke up, as anything associated with menopause or menstruation always did. The first familiar notes of the graduation march began and all eyes, including Luke's, turned to the auditorium doors. They swung open, revealing the graduates entering two by two.

Eliza didn't hear a word of the speeches, didn't relish the photos of her children in the montage. She sat, dazed and confused, as Kevin and Kayla walked across the stage to collect their diplomas. She stood when the audience stood, sat when they sat, clapped when they clapped, but didn't hear a word of the commencement program.

As she stumbled out of the high school and into the June sun, she was only grateful that they had come in two cars. She slipped away from the crowd and got into hers alone. She locked the doors and drove down the block from the school, where she turned off the engine and screamed so loudly and so uncontrollably that she wondered if she might die. Wondered if her heart would explode right there, right on the spot.

Now, as she lay on the floor of her kitchen drenched with perspiration, just as she was then, she heard the loud screams once again. It took her a moment to realize that they were coming from her own mouth.

CHAPTER 4

Jackie Campbell

Jackie Campbell was a creature of habit. No matter what was going on at the office, he made sure to be on the 5:49 train out of Grand Central in order to be home for dinner with his teenage daughter. Tonight would be no different.

"If Obama had dinner with *his* girls, then I can certainly manage to have dinner with mine," he would say when the notion seemed impossible.

That's not to say it wasn't difficult—Jackie often felt like he was doing loop-the-loops trying to be in two places at once—but their dinnertime ritual remained sacred. It was all about connecting with his daughter, Jana, even when she had no desire to connect with him. Never was that more true than right now.

Jackie had always worried about the day Jana would get her period. The first time he held her, alone in the nursery after the reality began to set in that he would be raising her on his own, the thought ran through his head. Through the unbearable shock and his streams of tears he actually thought, *What will I do when she gets her period?* And he was right to worry. It was as if she went to sleep one night a rough-and-tumble toddler and woke up a young woman. A young woman who suddenly looked very much like her mother. That part of it Jackie loved. To see Ann's face again, and sometimes her smile, that was a gift he would never tire of.

But yesterday morning when his assistant interrupted his presentation on the current risk appetite for currency trading with a call from his housekeeper, his fears felt warranted.

"Jana's friend has arrived," the housekeeper announced.

"Well, tell her that Jana's in school," he answered, annoyed by the silly interruption.

"No, no, Mr. Campbell. I found a few pairs of Miss Jana's dirty underwear in the garbage. Her lady friend has arrived, and I think you need to buy her supplies."

"Oh. Oh," he repeated aimlessly. And then again, "Oh."

"If I could give you some advice, Mr. Campbell?"

"Please do."

"Don't get tampons, sir. Just pads. Tampons lead to sex."

Jackie felt the room spin around him as he thanked her and hung up. He repeated her warning again in his head, replacing his housekeeper's voice with the voice of God: *Tampons lead to sex.*

When his meeting was over, he went down to the drugstore, where he purchased every kind of pad on the open market: maxis with wings, ultra-thin scented minis, super-absorbent overnights, and various-sized liners with names like Always and Ultra and Stayfree and Poise. If his mother were still alive he would have delegated this entire situation to her. Today he missed her even more than usual.

He arrived home that night with his triple-bagged purchases and stood at his daughter's door. He paused before knocking, reminding himself that he was a grown man: accomplished, formidable, and possibly even brave. Though he didn't feel very brave at that moment. He knocked gingerly.

"Come in, Daddy," she said.

So far, so good.

"Hi, baby girl." He sat down on the bed. "I'm very sorry your mom or Grammy is not here to talk to you about this, but we always get along pretty well, don't we?"

She shook her head yes.

"So, I bought you some things that I think you may find helpful."

He nervously opened the treasure trove of sanitary napkins. As he did, he wished he hadn't gone so overboard. Lucky for him, she laughed.

"I don't need all that, Daddy. I went with Ivy after school and bought a box of tampons. I'm good now."

"You can't use tampons!" he shouted with an urgency one usually reserves for reporting a fire in a theater or, more likely for Jackie, a catastrophic drop in the Dow Jones. Her face immediately morphed into her "you don't know anything, and I hate you" look. Jackie tried to backpedal, but he knew from experience that once her ship of adolescent contentiousness sailed, it didn't return for days. He took a breath.

"I'm sorry I yelled. I hoped you could start with these."

He opened the bag.

"Any of these." He pulled out the ones with wings. There had been nearly a year somewhere between three and four where she had insisted on wearing her sparkly fairy wings every day, even over her pajamas. He pictured her sleeping on her belly with her little tush in the air and those wings sprouting from her back like a butterfly.

"These have wings," he said, hopefully.

It was clear that she got the reference but didn't find it funny.

"Ugh, Dad, you're being so extra! I'm not a child. I know what I'm doing."

But you are a child, he thought, *and what the hell does being "extra" mean?*

She retreated into her phone as if the conversation was over, a tactic that always infuriated Jackie. He retreated into his overwhelming need to control everything that he could, ever since the uncontrollable had happened to them.

The box of tampons sat right out on her desk. He knew he had two choices: to leave and let her have her way, or to take them and insist on his. The voice of God came back: *Tampons lead to sex.*

He grabbed the box of tampons and placed the bag of pads on her bed.

"You can use these until you're older," he said without once pausing for breath. And got out of her room as quickly as his feet allowed.

CHAPTER 5

Eliza

It took nearly an hour before Eliza peeled herself off the kitchen floor and dragged herself upstairs. If it wasn't for the thought of Luke and the kids finding her there, she might not have had the will to get up. She took her now-sacred bottle of Valium that they had bought for kicks on a trip to Mexico years before from the medicine cabinet, and emptied its contents into her hand. There were only four left. Over the past months those pills had felt like little life rafts to Eliza. She bit off half of one and washed it down with water from the faucet. *When I get down to one*, she swore, *I will reach out for professional help.*

In the shower, she pictured the water washing off the ugly remnants of the outside world. She stayed in there until the Valium kicked in. The hot shower and the drugs left her feeling duly calm and collected. As she dried off, she made a bargain with herself in the bathroom mirror: "You don't have to leave the house again all weekend. Put on your happy face. Your kids are coming home."

She was thrilled to have her babies home for a few days. It was the perfect amount of time, long enough to make sure they really were as happy and settled in as they claimed, not too long to raise suspicion. Kevin would never notice, but Kayla was very attuned to her mother.

The thought of a full house lifted Eliza's spirits and gave her something entirely separate to focus on. Then she remembered there was another thing that needed her attention. She grabbed a snack and dashed to her desk.

When things first got popping with the bulletin board, Luke constructed an office area for her, a cozy spot at the end of her upstairs hallway big enough for a desk and some bookshelves on either side of a bay window. It wasn't a real office, but running the bulletin board wasn't a real job either. Still, Eliza had painstakingly set it up, choosing just the right books and photographs to fill her shelves. She surrounded herself only with things that made her smile: a first edition of *A Tree Grows in Brooklyn* that had been a gift from her treasured grandmother for her sixteenth birthday; two glitter-covered, tiny handprints pressed into clay made by the twins in preschool; a Hollywood snow globe she had bought as a souvenir the one time she had visited her best friend, Mandy, who had moved out to Cali after high school.

A treasured, awkward school photo of her twins and the "first look" shot from her wedding sat front and center. The photo of Luke, smiling from ear to ear under their wedding canopy, was probably the first thing she would grab if her house was on fire. Their wedding photographer had been so entranced by his joyous expression that she forgot to turn her lens toward the bride as she was escorted down the aisle by her parents. When the proofs came back without the classic shot, her mother was furious. "How could she miss such a thing?" The photographer explained that she had honestly never seen a guy so excited to marry a girl before and got caught up in that. Occasionally she would still catch Luke looking at her that way. It should have made her feel loved, but it left her feeling guilty.

She turned on the computer and tapped her fingers impatiently as it booted up. Thinking about Luke and all she had kept from him sometimes stressed her out more than the issues at hand. As usual, she put it all out of her head and embraced the diversion. She was beyond curious to see the site that the women at the Stop & Shop were talking about: her competition.

Good thing you left the house, Eliza, she praised herself silently. *It could have been months until you got wind of Valley Girls*. For obvious reasons, running the Hudson Valley Ladies' Bulletin Board had meant more to her in these past few months than it had in years. Before her agoraphobia kicked back in, she had even toyed with the idea of passing the torch to a younger mother, one who was more qualified to moderate a debate on the virtues of the Citi Mini stroller versus the Bugaboo Cameleon versus the Peg Perego versus the ultra-luxurious Mima Xari. After all, they were possibly forking up as much money to perambulate their babies as she had for her first car. But now it felt like her only safe window to the outside world. There was no way she was giving up the one environment she had control over.

The computer hummed, and she quickly typed in "Valley Girls" as if someone was looking over her shoulder. *A stupid name for a site for stupid girls*, she thought, as it came right up. She had to answer a few questions to be approved by the moderator first.

Do you live in Hudson Valley? *Yes.*

How did you hear about us? *At the Stop & Shop.*

Do you agree to abide by the rules of Valley Girls?

Eliza read through the rules. The last one, *What happens on Valley Girls stays on Valley Girls*, made her laugh. *The two women at the Stop & Shop must have missed that part*, she thought, as she replied, *Yes*.

Luke texted, checking in on her:

Hey, sweets. Are you sure you don't want to come to the airport?
I can swing by and get you, no problem.

She wrote back:

I wish I could, but I still have things to prepare for the party tomorrow, and I'd rather have dinner waiting. I'm sure the kids will be starving by the time they get home.

You're the best mom.

Luke's text made her feel even worse. She knew that the best mom wouldn't have had an excuse, more like a lie, prepared in advance for this exact situation.

As she put her phone down, a message appeared on her computer screen:

Welcome to Valley Girls.

She got down to business.

After just a few months, Valley Girls already had a thousand members, and there was definitely a younger, hipper vibe to it than she was used to. Keeping it current felt like the antidote to her own fleeting relevancy. She found the erectile dysfunction thread that the women were freaking out about at the market. Penises in general seemed to be a big topic of conversation, including opinions on the age-old question, does size really matter?

There was a lot of talk about sex: anal sex, oral sex, bad sex, good sex, too much sex, and not enough. The names of positions and sex toys were thrown around so knowingly that Eliza wished they had a glossary. She had to google the Rabbit Habit, the Hovering Butterfly, the Trick or Treat, and the Dirty Sanchez. She wished she hadn't googled the last one, having just eaten.

It felt to Eliza like there was a lot of grandstanding going on—women posting things just to get attention. There were also plenty of basic posts—asking for advice on the best breast pump or summer vacation spot with the kids. It wasn't all Hudson Valley Girls Gone Wild, like she had thought it would be, but it was clearly much more salacious than her site. Their cover photo showed a valley between two snowcapped mountains, or, if you looked at it differently, breasts. Hers was of an actual bulletin board.

Most of the more titillating posts were written anonymously. And those got tons of comments—epic threads, they routinely called them. There hadn't been an "epic thread" on the Hudson Valley Ladies' Bulletin Board since Hilary Winters accused Trudy Summers of bribing the high school tennis coach with her famous apple pie. At least that was what Eliza thought it was about; her daughter insisted it was a code word for sex.

She wasn't about to change the tone completely, posting about foreplay or fellatio, but she needed to come up with something that wouldn't be discussed openly at back-to-school night. How could *she* create an epic thread?

The phone rang, startling her, as many previously innocuous noises had been doing lately. She answered before looking at the caller ID. If she had done so, she would have let it go to voicemail.

It was Nancy Block, one of the four players in her monthly bridge game and the only one that she considered to be more than an acquaintance. Eliza hadn't played in a while and had taken to texting in her excuses and not answering calls regarding them. Nancy's voice sounded strange and Eliza immediately addressed it. "Hey, Nan, are you OK? You don't sound like yourself."

"No, actually, Eliza, I am not OK."

Eliza took a deep breath. She had heard so much awful news lately: cancer, kids in rehab, parents with dementia. Getting older seemed to be bringing a whole new set of issues. She really cared for Nancy; she braced herself for the worst.

"What is it? What's wrong?"

A heavy sigh on the other end confirmed that bad news was coming. "I guess there's no other way to say it. *You* are what's wrong, Eliza. You have no respect for our bridge game, or for me for that matter!"

Eliza began to shake. She was totally caught off guard and that was one of her worst triggers. Thank God for the Valium already in her system or she may have found herself right down on the floor again. Her bridge game was her last bastion of real-life social interaction. For the first Tuesday of the month she would bake pecan sandies (Nancy's favorite), oatmeal raisins (Mara's favorite), and gluten-free chocolate chips (for Dana). She would shower, do her hair, put on something other than sweatpants, and sometimes even a coat of mascara and lipstick. Even with all of that, for the past three games she couldn't make it out the door. She knew it was so wrong to cancel at the last minute—obviously they couldn't play without her. She was ready to apologize and say something resembling the truth, when Nancy threw salt on the gash that she had inflicted. "We are done with you and your excuses. You are no longer a part of our game."

As if her harsh words weren't enough, her tone was caustic.

Eliza could not remember being spoken to that way before. And where was the empathy? Where was "Is everything OK with you?"

Eliza barely managed an "I'm sorry, Nancy, I really am . . ." when Nancy interrupted her apology with a final blow, "Whatever, Eliza. Maybe you should take up solitaire!"

The line went dead, for which Eliza was mostly grateful. She understood Nancy's disappointment. No one was more disappointed with Eliza than Eliza. She was filled with anger but wasn't even sure at whom to direct it. She was angry at her "friends" for not seeing her disappear before their eyes, and she was angry at herself for not having the strength to overcome this thing. And on a much simpler level, she was angry about losing something else that she really enjoyed. She had already given up her weekly tennis game with the excuse of plantar fasciitis. The tennis ladies had at least cared enough to send bath salts and a foot-shaped ice pack. She felt completely isolated from the outside world, raising the stakes even higher on the value of the bulletin board in her life. She asked herself again, *What can I post to create an epic thread?*

She stared out the window for an answer and, just like that, one appeared.

It wasn't the first time that Eliza took notice of what was going on in the house next door. Albeit for different reasons, she was sometimes as bored as housebound Jimmy Stewart in the movie *Rear Window.* And while she didn't use binoculars, the new neighbors had yet to install window treatments. Between that and the angle of their houses, hers being slightly uphill from theirs, Eliza could see a whole lot from her desk window—specifically the comings and goings of a certain gentleman who was most definitely not Mr. Smith.

At that very moment, while she was staring out the window, Not-Mr.-Smith approached the front door and rang the bell. But this time Mrs. Smith didn't let him in. Eliza could see her look out from her bedroom window and decide not to answer it. Not-Mr.-Smith went from patiently ringing to incessantly banging, while Mrs. Smith went from calmly ignoring him to pacing back and forth like a prisoner on death row. He finally gave up and left.

Eliza opened up the Hudson Valley Ladies' Bulletin Board and began typing:

> **Anonymous:** I just moved here from the city with hopes of starting over after an affair that my husband knows nothing about. The man I was having the affair with followed me here and keeps showing up at my door. Today I pretended I wasn't home. He was banging so hard it scared me. I've told him I want to end things, but he won't have it. I know it's wrong to cheat. That's why I want to break it off and start fresh. Please only comment with constructive advice.

She read it over. *Pretty scandalous*, she thought. She pressed Post and waited. It didn't take long before the comments began rolling in.

> You reap what you sow.

> Do you think he can get violent? Call the police.

> I empathize with you. I've been in that boat. Maybe ask to meet him in a public place where he can't go crazy and explain that you want to recommit to your husband.

> That's a good idea.

> I agree!

> You don't say if he's married. Is he married too?

That's a good question. *Is Not-Mr.-Smith married?* Eliza wondered. The phone rang, startling her again. It was Luke on speaker.

"I got them!

"Hi, Mom!"

"Hi, Momma, see you soon!"

The sound of her children's voices, along with the excitement of the impending epic thread, put Eliza in the best mood she had felt in ages.

CHAPTER 6

Jackie

The 5:49 train pulled into the station, and Jackie Campbell got on and took his usual seat. Within a few minutes, his two commuter friends, Skip and Lee, arrived. Skip was really just a circumstantial friendship for Jackie. Skip grew up with Lee, which was ironic because the problem with Skip was that he never really grew up. He and Jackie were polar opposites, as Jackie was born grown up. They never would have been friends without the link that was Lee.

Lee was more than just a commuter friend. Jackie and his late wife, Ann, had met Lee and his wife, Charlotte, when they were newlyweds living in Park Slope, Brooklyn—back when they were poorer and happier. It was no surprise that when Lee moved his growing family to the suburbs, Jackie chose to raise Jana in close proximity. They were all heartbroken when Ann died, and Lee was painfully aware of the inequality of their burdens. He did his best to help his old friend when he could.

"How did it go with the crimson tide?"

His best wasn't always very tactful.

"Do we have to talk about this again?" Skip protested.

Jackie ignored Skip.

"Not well. Very badly, actually."

They both leaned in as they sensed that Jackie was about to whisper feminine hygiene words. They were right.

"She already had the *tampons*, so I had to take them away."

Skip groaned. "I don't envy you, man."

The three men sat back in their seats and just breathed.

Soon Lee leaned back in.

"You were around plenty of women at the office today. You should have asked one of them about it."

"Yes, because talking about a woman's privates in the workplace is a wonderful idea."

Skip nodded. "I agree. Not cool. *I'm* even feeling a little violated right now."

Lee laughed. Jackie didn't.

"OK, do you want me to ask Charlotte? I mean, granted we have boys, but she is a woman."

"Thanks, but I need someone with teenage girls. The other day on the way to school she asked me if her eyebrows looked bushy. I didn't know what to say. Was she looking for bushy? Is bushy good or bad? I swear, I need a consortium of women to make it through these teenage years!"

Lee put his hand on Jackie's shoulder in solidarity, but it was Skip who came up with the solution.

"I got it!"

They both looked at him skeptically, waiting for a joke.

"Join that Hudson Valley Ladies' Bulletin Board."

"That's a great idea," Lee agreed. "Charlotte is on that thing all the time."

Skip opened up his phone to Facebook and showed Jackie the page, as his face was registering nothing.

"Look. Are you on Facebook?"

"Barely. I have an account, but I never check it."

Jackie pulled it up on his phone. Skip took it and searched for the group.

"Here. Can I sign you up?"

"To a ladies' bulletin board? I don't think I'll be accepted."

"Actually, you will. Your profile picture is of Jana as a baby, and your name is Jackie. Finally, a good reason to have a girl's name."

Jackie shook his head. Skip laughed. "Don't go all 'Jackie Robinson was my dad's hero' on me again. It's a girl's name and you know it."

"This coming from a man named Skip. Here, Skip, come on, boy!"

Skip ignored him and typed into his phone. A few seconds later he handed it back.

"Here, done. Just wait for them to accept you, and you can ask thousands of women your lady parts questions."

Jackie stared out the window while he waited, his thoughts calmed by the marathon of foliage whipping by. The green leaves gradually being taken over by reds and oranges and yellows the farther north they traveled.

By the next stop Jackie's request to join was approved. By the following he had carefully crafted his question:

My 14-year-old daughter got her first period. Should I let her use tampons?

As they pulled in to their station it posted.

"It's up!" Jackie announced.

They congratulated themselves on their success and went their separate ways.

CHAPTER 7

Olivia

Olivia lay in bed counting sheep. It was late, and she knew the baby would be up in a few hours, but she was wide-awake. Spencer was sound asleep next to her. His chest rose and fell and rose and fell as if taunting her.

Olivia usually liked to watch Spencer sleep. She liked to see him sedentary, as it was so rarely the case when he was awake. Spencer was always on the move. He would routinely wake up with the sun and run six or seven miles before Olivia had had her first sip of coffee. He was very fit, and it usually turned Olivia on, but she was currently so far from her naturally thin figure that she found herself resenting him. It was hard to picture getting back in shape. She looked down at her swollen breasts and post-pregnancy tummy and sighed. It didn't seem right that Spencer got to parent Lily equally with zero physical sacrifice.

Olivia had started running again, too, even before getting the jogging stroller. She loved finding new trails at every turn, such a different feeling than running in Central Park where she knew every path by heart. But it hadn't yet seemed to make a difference with the baby weight.

"It's only been a few months!" Spencer would say when Olivia complained about her body. "I don't even notice it," he'd insist.

That is true, Olivia thought. Spencer didn't seem to notice her body anymore. Even when he finally returned home that morning and she jumped him, covering him with kisses and thanking him for the painting, he laughed and swatted her off.

"I'm so sweaty, Olivia. Stop, I'm gross."

The rejection stung, and the sting registered on her face. He noticed, placed a kiss on her forehead, and pulled back to look at her, his blue eyes were sparkling like those of an expectant child.

"Do you love it? Are you surprised?"

She did love it, more for the effort than the aesthetic. She was also thinking that the old Spencer wouldn't have cared how sweaty he was if sex was on the table. He would have jumped her right back. She was thinking about that again now, while tossing and turning.

She was well aware that she and Spencer had only had sex once since Lily was born. It had been too early and way too painful, and when she couldn't finish, he was very understanding. She knew that her body was healed by now. She had reached her hand inside after a somewhat erotic part of the novel she'd been reading had stirred her. Everything was in working order internally, but she didn't feel attractive. Being a new parent was taking its toll on her libido and, surprisingly, Spencer's as well.

It's probably normal, she thought. It would be a great post for one of those parenting groups she was on, but she worried hearing other mothers respond that their husbands were all over them, and vice versa, would make her feel worse.

Olivia found online forums addictive. She was still a member of an Upper East Side group from her brief mommy stint in the city and loved cruising through that one, too. It made her laugh now to compare the different tones of the two communities. The Hudson Valley feed was filled with ways to do it yourself, while the Upper East Siders were busy sharing referrals on who best to do it. Recurring themes on the UES group involved noise complaints from downstairs neighbors, nannies playing Candy Crush on their phones while their charges picked up syringes in the sandbox, and which sends the right message to a co-op board—a Kelly bag or a Balenciaga? The suburban ladies were more interested in debating the best age to introduce lacrosse, the scourge of the drop-off line at school, and whether the coveted Williams Sonoma redwood chicken coop delivers the most cluck for their buck.

Raising chickens aside, Olivia was surprised to find herself relating more closely to the Hudson Valley group than to the group based in the city where she had grown up. Having Lily really had her questioning the value of raising a child in Manhattan. If they had stayed, she was sure that Lily would be able to tell the difference between a Monet and a Manet by the time she was five, but she sometimes wondered if the accoutrements of the city were more for the benefit of the parents than for the betterment of the kids. She wondered if she would ever be sure. The feeling that the grass is always greener seemed to be a commonality among mothers everywhere.

But she knew herself too well. Her newfound zeal for the country was more likely due to her natural inclination to make a case for her choices. In the end, there were more similarities between any of these groups than there were differences.

Most groups boast ongoing threads recommending what books to read, which television shows to binge-watch, and which gastronomical treasures are must-haves from the shelves of Trader Joe's. Much time is spent comparing strollers, private and public schools, and imperfect spouses, and all seem to share a great affinity for coconut oil, along with an abundance of suggested and sometimes sinful uses for it.

The groups felt oddly supportive for a sea of strangers. Olivia was more a liker than a poster, benefiting from the group's perspective on a plethora of things from baby names to finding a new doctor to what is this weird rash on my arm. She knew, even right now, if she were to write on either site, "Help! I can't sleep!" sympathy and remedies from A to Zzzzzz would pour in. There was a strength-in-numbers effect that provided real emotional support. She was new to Hudson Valley but had noticed that the women on the Upper East Side were especially game to tackle any problem. Once a woman posted a photo of her daughter's lost lovey, dropped somewhere between the Ninety-Sixth Street playground and their Sixty-Sixth Street home. It felt as if the whole of the Upper East Side banded together; they had it back by bedtime.

She did miss the level of adult interaction she'd had in the city, precipitated by walking everywhere. Getting in and out of your car all day doesn't allow for much communication. Being a part of this group, and a smaller one that she just joined, Valley Girls, helped give her the illusion of local friendships. Parenting did feel lonelier to her here. She opened up the Hudson Valley Ladies' Bulletin Board on her phone to combat it. There seemed to be a big hoopla over whether or not a fourteen-year-old girl should use tampons. People were really giving it to the poor mom who asked the question, except for the one lady who consistently responded to everything with: Follow your mom gut! You're a great mom! It was all quite entertaining. She loved the voyeuristic aspect—the brief peek into other women's lives and concerns.

When there was a fight or a disagreement about ideas, as there was today with the tampon post, it was like watching a car crash on the side of the highway. Everyone slowed down to take a look or to comment. There was no way the majority of these women would say in person what they wrote online. She'd bet the most nail-bitten fingers typed the most venomous comments.

Olivia reminded herself to think twice before posting anything. The tampon post comments were relentless:

Teach your daughter to choose what she does with her own body starting now.

Is it your vagina or your daughter's?

Please tell me you're not worried about penetration. Tampons do not affect virginity. Sex does.

My mother taught me tampons were evil. I still can't look at them. Don't be like my mother.

And then the bohemian comment from a woman who made Olivia chuckle just last week when she asked: "Anyone know where to buy hydroponic, vertically farmed celery?" This time she wrote:

Don't let her plug her delicate organ with bleached-out fibers of oppression.

Olivia laughed out loud, which stirred Spencer.

"Olivia, what are you doing? Turn off your phone."

"I'm sorry. I was just trying to make my eyes tired."

"Well, the phone does the opposite. I have an early meeting with my dad tomorrow to discuss transitioning me to CEO. Come on."

Spencer was always threatening a big meeting with his father to discuss his becoming CEO. In Olivia's opinion, his father's retirement was anything but imminent. But still, out of respect, she knew she should turn off her phone and try to sleep. She scrolled down a little farther.

> **Anonymous:** I just moved here from the city with hopes of starting over after an affair that my husband knows nothing about. The man I was having the affair with followed me here and keeps showing up at my door. Today I pretended I wasn't home. He was banging so hard it scared me. I've told him I want to end things, but he won't have it. I know it's wrong to cheat. That's why I want to break it off and start fresh. Please only comment with constructive advice.

"Wow," Olivia said.

"What are you reading?" He flipped over toward her.

"That local bulletin board where I got the jogging stroller."

"Let me guess. Is it about the KonMari method? Did someone throw out their husband because he wasn't sparking joy?"

Olivia rolled her eyes as he continued what felt like his first foray into dad jokes.

"Did a shipment of cauliflower gnocchi arrive at Trader Joe's? Should I warm up the car?"

He propped himself up on the pillow thinking he was quite funny. Olivia defended her enthusiastic "Wow."

"Actually, it's pretty scandalous stuff."

"I'm sure," he grunted.

"It is! This woman just moved here to get away from a bad affair, and the guy followed her. Page Six has nothing on this town!"

Spencer sat up and flicked on the light.

"Let me see that." He grabbed her phone and read. He seemed to read it three times. Olivia noticed.

"One hundred sixty-one comments. I told you, it's pretty scandalous," she said victoriously.

"Well, now that you woke me, I have to go to the bathroom."
He held his stomach, indicating it may be a while.

"I'm sorry."

"I'm taking your bulletin board for reading material."

"Ha! I told you, I see a *Real Housewives of Hudson Valley*
spin-off!" she yelled out, to no reply. She waited to see if Spencer
was OK, but eventually she fell asleep. In the morning, he was
already gone.

CHAPTER 8

Eliza

Eliza set her alarm for 6:00 a.m. She had much to prepare for the day's guests. She loved a full house, especially when it included the twins' friends. She had missed the comings and goings of their posse since they'd been in college—the cheerful shouting, the stomping around overhead, and the whirlwind left in their wake. In contrast to her own childhood home, Eliza always tried to make hers the house that the kids flocked to. She mostly accomplished this with food.

Eliza's Jewish grandmother was a first-generation American, and though not a particularly religious woman, she was deeply connected to her Judaism through food. The kitchen was her temple. And while Eliza's own mother rebelled against it, Eliza was quite happy to become a member of that congregation.

Eliza's grandma, or Bubbie as she affectionately called her, would spend hours in the kitchen replicating the recipes for stuffed cabbage or kreplach or kugel that had been passed down by her grandmother and her grandmother's grandmother before her. While Eliza's mother had no interest in cooking, Eliza, as her Bubbie would say, took to the kitchen like nobody's business. Together the two of them formed a bond linking generations of Jews, not through the Talmud but through brisket. It bothered Eliza's mother to no end, the way it does when you introduce two of your friends and suddenly they're meeting for coffee without you.

Eliza headed to the kitchen to preheat the oven, then made a beeline for her desk. By the time they were all done catching up the night before, she couldn't keep her eyes open. It was wonderful to have her children home. Being a whole family again made her feel more like a whole person again. The goings-on of the bulletin board seemed trivial in comparison. But this morning, not so much. As she turned on her computer, she crossed her fingers, superstitiously hoping her scandalous post had been a success.

One hundred eighty-five comments—wow! she thought. *That is an epic thread—take that, Valley Girls! We're not going anywhere!* She was even happier to see that the post about tampons was gaining traction as well. It felt as if more people were suddenly spending time on the bulletin board. She did a little cross-referencing of the comment sections on both sites, hers and Valley Girls, to see if any names popped out on both—and they did. The whole thing thrilled her, to the point of embarrassment.

She discarded a request from a mother selling essential oils and another starting the hundredth conversation on the HPV vaccine and posted an announcement sent to her by the local library:

Circle Time for new moms begins this Friday at 11:00.

She had so much to do, but she gave herself a few minutes to read more comments and enjoy the sensation her made-up post had sparked. She imagined other women doing the same—carving out time from their busy lives to scroll. It was gripping stuff. She thought about the old days when the only place to ask anonymous advice was a column in the newspaper. By the time the answer was printed she could only imagine the person asking it had moved on to their next problem. This forum was much more satisfying.

Look internally to why you cheated before moving on. If you don't fix that, it will happen again.

Are we supposed to feel sorry for you? You made your bed, literally!

I don't think monogamy is natural.

Well kindly stay away from my man!

Mine too! LOL!

It's just a matter of time until your husband finds out. I think you should tell him before this crazy guy you got involved with does.

This! Plus marriage counseling.

I agree, too. Assuming you moved here to save your marriage. Tell him now!

Do you have children?

I feel for you. This is very stressful.

You feel for her? Anonymous did this to herself. I feel for the other woman.

You're assuming there is another woman. That's what's wrong with anonymous posts. She can't respond, and we only know half a story.

Yes, her half. Anonymous is clearly selfish. Cheaters always are.

Give her a break. Every life has secrets. Every marriage certainly does. It's just a matter of whether you can live with them or not.

That last comment really struck a chord. As much as she had loved being with her family last night, she had felt like a fraud. Kevin copped to having anxiety about pledging, Kayla about feeling lonely sometimes. Even Luke spoke about missing them more than he'd imagined. Why was she so dead-set on keeping her secret from her family? Maybe it was time to tell Luke, to tell the kids. But even thinking about that conversation was too much for her. As she always did, she buried her feelings and kept scrolling.

The thing that struck her most about the words the women wrote was just that—they were just words. Their tone was up to the reader to determine, and judgment was based on the content alone. No "Never trust a woman in pearls" or "That skinny bitch has no idea what she's talking about." Faceless words.

She further considered how the anonymous posts made it hard to have any back-and-forth. She wondered if she should post a follow-up. She couldn't stop reading the comments and couldn't believe how open the women were being. If company wasn't coming, she would have considered making popcorn and scrolling to her heart's content. She looked at the time. Just five more minutes, she promised herself.

Eliza used to love this time of day—the quiet that only existed in the early morning before the noise of alarms and car pools and phones ringing off the hook. When the twins were home, she would often set her alarm for 6:00 a.m., an hour before she needed to wake them, just to have some time for herself. She hadn't done this in months. Lately she was eager to make her day shorter, sleeping in as long as her perimenopausal clock would allow. But back then, like today, she would relax at her desk with a cup of coffee and alternate between social media, the news, and watching the birds out the window. She would sit there until 6:45, when the neighbor's sprinklers rose from the ground like a maestro's baton, prompting her to rise from her chair. She looked at the clock again—6:45. No whoosh-tic-tic-tic-tic-tic-tic-whoosh of the sprinkler. She guessed the new neighbor had reset it. As she stood up, the next chapter of the drama played out right before her eyes.

Ashley Smith left her house, closing the door behind her. She looked down at her phone before panning the street with her eyes. There, across and to the left behind the Williamses' old oak tree, stood Not-Mr.-Smith. Ashley paused to do a few stretches, signaling with her body for him to run left. He got it and ran that way. Eliza could still see him one house up the street, retying a tied shoe, trying to look natural. Now she was even more convinced that there was some truth to her made-up post. Ashley turned back toward her own house and studied its windows. Eliza assumed that she was double-checking to see if her husband was watching and stepped back from the window. She was well aware that one glance her way could do her in.

Ashley jogged off as if she was acting as opposed to really running. Eliza squinted through the window carefully as they stopped in their tracks. The man showed her his phone. She threw her hands in the air. He shook his head in disbelief. Eliza played out the words in her head.

"Is this about us? I know this is us!"

"I don't even know what this is. You're so paranoid."

She took the phone from him to read it more carefully. She looked confused. She put her hand to her head in worry.

"I swear I didn't write this," Eliza imagined her saying.

He didn't seem to believe her. How could he? It was spot-on. He looked like he wanted to believe her as he wiped what Eliza imagined to be a tear from Ashley's eye. They hugged briefly and ran off.

Eliza sat down at her computer. She was shaking. She wasn't sure if it was due to exhilaration or fear of getting caught. The whole episode filled her with an excitement she hadn't felt since shoplifting in middle school, that thrill of stepping out of the Hudson Valley Mall with a strawberry Bonne Bell Lip Smacker tucked into her training bra. Either way she knew that she had no business messing in people's lives like that. She vowed never to do it again.

CHAPTER 9

Alison Le

Alison Le ducked into Wolf Realty with an extra set of keys to her new home in hand. She had to give a set to someone, and so far, the agent who had rented her the place was the only someone she knew—another reason to shake her head in disbelief over her impulsive move from the city. The key exchange was the last errand on her to-do list. She had no idea what she would do next.

The receptionist seemed to be expecting her.

"Mrs. Wolf asked if you could wait a minute. She wants to see if everything's OK with the new house."

"Sure," Alison replied. She had nothing but time.

"Can I offer you a cup of coffee? And a heavenly muffin from the Café Karma Sutra?"

Alison declined. It sounded like some kind of a cult offering. She berated herself for the hundredth time that day. *What did you do? What did you do?*

If I were to Karma Sutra, she thought, *that could be my man-*

tra. It made her laugh out loud and the receptionist looked at her like she was a bit crazy. Maybe she was right. *Temporary insanity*, Alison hoped.

She sat down and picked up the local newspaper, but after a few pages, her mind began to wander to the circumstances that had led her to uproot her entire life and move to Hudson Valley. The biggest catalyst, her fifteen-week-old baby boy, stirred in his stroller. She ran the back of her hand gently over his forehead and he settled back into his nap. She still couldn't decide if she was a good mother or if she'd just lucked out with a good baby. It was easier to believe the latter.

Alison had spent her entire life acting like a consummate bachelor. She never wore a dress, cursed like a sailor, and never dreamed of marriage with all of its obligations and distractions. She was smart and had worked hard in school, but she didn't spend much time thinking about the racially charged stereotypes about Asian kids that went along with that. She was smart because she was, and she worked hard because she enjoyed it and emulated her single mother, who had worked endless hours to support them.

She attended Wesleyan for undergrad, followed by Harvard Law. After graduation she joined a small firm, intent on being a top criminal defense attorney. At thirty-eight, she was confident she had succeeded. She didn't worry about the age to marry or her ticking biological clock. The only clock that concerned her was the one that tracked her billable hours. Alison was a planner, but the one thing she had never planned on—an unwanted pregnancy—took her by surprise.

Alison Le had been seeing Marc Sugarman, the bureau chief of the Manhattan district attorney's office, on and off for nearly two years. It was an entirely covert affair, as they often tried cases against each other. At first the attraction was ignited by their rivalry, but as time went on, it was really just perfunctory. They each filled a need for the other, figuratively and literally, and they were both on the exact same page when it came to relationships. They both agreed that their careers were their great loves; they even pinky-swore to it on the night of their first tequila-fueled encounter. Neither wanted to be nailed down for longer than the duration of their Wednesday night trysts at the downtown Ritz-Carlton.

On the night that Alison decided to fill Marc in on her pregnancy, she arrived early to get up her nerve. Such a thing would usually be eased by a scotch, but of course that didn't feel right. As if leading a witness, Marc entered and quickly offered her a glass.

"No thanks, I'm not drinking," she said.

"Why?" he responded, half listening, half disrobing.

"Because I'm pregnant," she answered.

He stopped dead in his tracks, mumbling, "Oh. That's unfortunate," followed by a stronger "How could that have happened?"

She ignored him; she wasn't about to school him on the efficacy of birth control. He surprisingly stabbed her impermeable heart again, adding, "You know our deal, Alison, no attachments. I assume you're taking care of it."

She wasn't sure what she'd expected from him but was quite certain this was not it. Her immediate reaction to his words was to build a case against them. She didn't know if it was on account of her natural tendency to argue the other side or the newly acquired mommy hormones, but at that moment her pregnancy went from a problem to a gift. She felt ashamed that it took Marc's heartless apathy to shine that light. She placed her hand on her belly and said, "Yes, I will be taking care of it," taking a beat before adding, "on my own and very well, thank you. I'm going to take a bath, please be gone by the time I get out."

And he was.

Alison hid her pregnancy at work for as long as was physically possible, but when she entered her fifth month, she felt she had to come clean. She stood up at the weekly partners' meeting and disclosed that she was pregnant. The other partners feigned happiness for her, but it was clear they had assumed that ship had sailed and were surprised by the news. Surprised was putting it kindly. They were most likely annoyed, as they'd always thought of her as one of them. She noticed the team's underlying panic and addressed the elephant in the room.

"Gentlemen, don't worry. This firm is my life. Nothing is going to change."

They smiled as if they believed her.

Alison lay awake at night worrying about whether she was maternal enough to raise a child. She was afraid that she didn't have that instinct everyone spoke of. When she saw a child cry, she would often have the urge to laugh: the way they threw themselves on the floor over a lost balloon as if the world were about to end. Then one day, at about thirty-two weeks, she was riding the subway when it came to a jolting stop. She felt the blood rush from her head as her hands slipped down the pole she'd been grasping. A minute later she found herself on the floor of the subway car—her head cradled in the lap of an intimidating-looking man with a string of barbed wire tattooed up his arm beneath the words *Live Free or Die*. The kind stranger, who quite possibly just escaped from jail, escorted her to the street and put her in a taxi to her obstetrician, who informed her that there was nothing wrong.

She said, "When the train jolted, your maternal instinct kicked in and sent all of the blood to your baby."

Alison cried tears of joy. She had a maternal instinct.

A week before she was due, her water broke in a conference room full of partners and associates. She had already seen a difference in how she was being looked at. Creating a puddle on her chair that she later realized she had left for someone else to clean up as she waddled out of the room had to have sealed the deal.

The door to Wolf Realty swung open with a gust of wind and a young mother came in, baby in tow, courtesy of the all-coveted Thule Urban Glide jogging stroller.

"Hi," Olivia York said to the air in general as she moved her hips from side to side in place to keep up her energy. Her baby looked to be around the same age as Zachary.

"Hi. What a cutie. How old is she?" Alison asked, noting the pink baby blanket tucked neatly under the baby's dimpled chin.

Olivia moved the blanket down proudly so that Alison could get a good look.

"She's four months today. Yours?"

"Three and a half. This is Zach," she gushed, realizing it was the first time she had called him that.

"So sweet. This is Lily and I'm Olivia."

Alison laughed at herself for just introducing her baby.

"I'm Alison." She motioned to the baby adding, "She is so beautiful."

"So is yours. I hope I have a little boy next."

"Oh. This is it for me. For sure."

"You can never be sure, right?"

"I can." Alison laughed. "I don't even know how this all happened. One day I was driving on the Taconic, trying to wrap my head around my maternity leave ending, and the next minute I was renting a two-hundred-year-old house on Main Street."

"Ha. It sounds like the plot for a Hallmark movie."

Alison laughed again. "You're right, and my old life sounded like a plot from *Law & Order.*"

"Well, the Hallmark plot seems better, for the baby at least."

"That's what I was thinking when I decided to move."

"Decided" wasn't exactly the correct word. For Alison a decision usually involved hours of research and thoughtful comparisons. This felt more like it happened with no real thought whatsoever.

"Marilyn!" Olivia called out as Mrs. Wolf came out of her office.

"Olivia! How are you? You got the jogging stroller, I see."

"Yes, I was actually jogging by to tell you. Great find. Thanks."

"You have to join, too," Marilyn motioned to Alison. "The Hudson Valley Ladies' Bulletin Board, everything you need to know for living around here. Plus sometimes a good deal on someone's barely used stroller."

Alison noted it in her phone. She needed all the help she could get.

Olivia smiled at them both. "I gotta run. Have to get home in time to nurse. Nice meeting you!" She smiled at Alison before jogging off.

Alison handed the keys to Marilyn. "Here, before I forget. I'm so forgetful lately."

"And impulsive." Marilyn laughed while taking the keys. "Easiest transaction of my life!"

Alison knew that Marilyn wasn't exaggerating. She thought back to the day she took the house. The wonderful nanny she had chosen, from the dozens she'd interviewed, was set to begin the following morning. Alison found herself driving farther and farther away from the city, questioning everything she thought she was sure about. Zachary had started to fuss, so she'd pulled off at the next exit. A right, a left, and a fork right later, she was driving down the main street of a Norman Rockwellian town. By that time the baby was hungry and screaming bloody murder. She pulled into the first spot she saw, sat herself down on the stoop of the house in front of it, and placed the bottle between his clamoring lips. She adjusted herself so that the sun was not causing his tiny eyes to squint and enjoyed the view of the pretty town while he drank his bottle. She had been lost in thought when Marilyn Wolf approached.

"Hello!" she sang. "Are you my eleven o'clock?"

Alison held in a laugh and sang back, "I am not!"

"Too bad for you! This house is a beauty!"

Alison moved her diaper bag out of the woman's way with her foot.

"No worries," Marilyn had said. "Take your time."

The woman popped open the front door of the house, and Alison peered in. She wasn't kidding. It was beautiful. She stood in the doorway, while coaxing Zachary to burp, and took it all in.

The house smelled like a mixture of pine and lavender. She stepped inside to get a better whiff. The entrance foyer led into an oval-shaped parlor with crown molding and parquet floors. The agent caught her peeking.

"Don't be scared, honey. Come on in," she said. "My appointment will be here any minute, but the illusion of competition never hurts. Want to see the upstairs?"

Alison was happy to oblige.

The second floor was even prettier than the first. A cozy living room with a wood-burning stove opened into a large dining room. Out the paned picture window off the kitchen sat a big old oak with the platform of a tree house wedged between its limbs. She pictured sitting up there with five-year-old Zachary reading books and eating homemade oatmeal cookies. She'd never baked cookies in her life, but she was sure that if they lived here, she would.

It was then that Alison knew she wasn't ready to hand Zachary over to the nice nanny she had hired. Images of a black-robed Sandra Day O'Connor spoon-feeding pureed sweet potato to her toddler flashed before her eyes. She had read once that O'Connor took off five years to raise her children before returning to the law. And she became the first woman appointed to the Supreme Court. Alison had given everything to her law firm; certainly, they would understand if she wanted to take a one-year leave of absence.

"I'll take it," she'd said to the agent, rifling around her diaper bag for her checkbook so that the woman knew she meant business.

"You don't even know the details."

She knew enough about real estate to know that subletting her two-bedroom apartment on lower Fifth Avenue would cover the cost of this house and then some—then plenty, actually. It was the perfect plan for her, taking off more time without running through her savings.

As she sat in the office now, she hoped that she hadn't made a huge mistake.

CHAPTER 10

Eliza

The day was long, so long that it felt like the equivalent of two or three combined in Eliza's ordinarily mundane life. At its start she surveyed the spread on her dining room table and filled with pride, pride laced with rebellion. Since food had never been a staple in her house growing up, Eliza always got a little extra satisfaction from filling that same dining room table with a cornucopia of calories. Her mother had maintained her figure by washing down Dexatrim with cans of Tab, while Eliza had sustained herself on boxes of Pop-Tarts and bags of Cheez Doodles she'd kept hidden under her bed next to the Entenmann's donuts. Her mother would regurgitate dieting idioms one after the other like a walking, talking Jenny Craig Pez dispenser:

"Nothing tastes as good as skinny feels!"
"Blessed are those who hunger and thirst, for they are sticking to their diets."
"Brain cells come and go, but fat cells live forever."

And the crowd favorite:

"A moment on your lips, a lifetime on your hips."

Of course, the disparity between her and her mother's relationship with food felt much bigger to Eliza than her mother's pithy slogans had suggested. It's hard to know if Eliza equated her mother not feeding her with her mother not loving her, or the other way around. Either way, one needn't be a shrink to see why Eliza spent her adult life feeding everyone else.

Eliza had been planning today's menu for weeks, scouring online cooking sites and saving new recipes on her computer in a folder marked "Delicious" to mix in with her family's favorites. In the end, the winners were cinnamon roll French toast, morning glory muffins, crustless spinach quiche, scrambled eggs with lox and onions, and her grandmother's noodle kugel. She made everything herself, except for the fruit salad and bagels, and it all turned out so well you might have thought it came from a caterer. Even in her current mental state, she managed to keep up her Martha Stewart ways.

Eliza had arranged for household items and the dry cleaning to be delivered and joined a farm collective and healthy cooking meal club under the pretext of losing weight. Her strict diet gave her a solid excuse regarding eating out, and Luke seemed thrilled to walk in nightly to the delicious smell of a home-cooked meal. He worked hard all week, golfed most fall weekends, and was usually too spent by the day's end to care about going out. Not that their recent routine resembled the second act either of them had imagined.

This fall should have been filled with weekend excursions to the city for Broadway plays and concerts at the Garden, meeting Luke in town for a bite after work, and Eliza finally taking up golf, after threatening to do so for just about ever. Even today's party originated as an excuse—when Luke suggested they do something special and take the kids to see *Hamilton*, she had produced a quick reason not to.

"We can't. They have their hearts set on one of our all-day brunches!"

The kids were psyched that their parents were throwing a party in their honor, but if they had gotten wind of the *Hamilton* plan they may have broken out in song, protesting: "I am not throwing away my shot!" Kayla had played the soundtrack so often her senior year of high school that the whole family knew every word. Of course, Eliza was too far gone at this point to sit in a crowded Broadway theater.

It had been six weeks since Eliza and Luke had brought the twins to his alma mater, the University of Wisconsin, and six weeks since the triggering event from graduation prompted a severe panic attack at the Madison Bed Bath & Beyond. There, another shopper told the manager that a hysterical woman in the bathroom needed help. The two strangers somehow calmed her down enough for her to inconspicuously rejoin her family. It had been six weeks since she had retreated to the safety of her home, and aside from yesterday's excursion, nearly six since she'd left it.

She looked over the dining room table. No amount of crustless spinach quiche could assuage her guilt.

Family friends with younger kids and a few cousins were the first to arrive. Eliza sent the kids out back to toss a football and play on the swing set. Luke had wanted to tear it down years ago when the twins outgrew it, but Eliza had insisted they keep it. At times like this she was glad she did. She watched the children through the kitchen window, flashing back to that time in their lives when the swing set was king. She'd loved those days of being able to watch their every move. She often found herself longing to have them back.

Luke entered the kitchen and wrapped his arms around her from behind. She was so lost in her happy memories that she welcomed his embrace. It may have been the first time since the twins' graduation that she had. It was also the first time he acknowledged their lost connection. He spun her around and kissed her warmly on the lips.

"I've missed you, Eliza."

"I'm sorry—I just haven't felt very . . . sexy lately."

"I wasn't talking about sex. I'm just talking about . . . us."

She of course knew what he was talking about. The space between them that had always been filled with peace and serenity felt suddenly closed off. She knew she was the one who had erected the barrier, but in all fairness, it didn't feel like Luke made much of an attempt to break through. Kevin came into the kitchen, interrupting what could have been the start of a long-overdue conversation. It was fine, as it certainly wasn't the time or place for it.

"Good morning, Momma. I need coffee!" he whined, stretching out the "eeeeee" in "need" to pad his plea. Eliza smiled. She realized that he must be fixing his own coffee at school, but she didn't mind. She loved being needed. From his eyes she could see he was suffering from more than exhaustion.

"Don't tell me, you kids went out last night after Dad and I went to sleep."

"Yup. We went to the Buckboard."

The Buckboard was the local watering hole where the high school kids hung out and drank. Some parents were against them going there—there had even been a huge back-and-forth on the bulletin board about it years ago—but in contrast to her usual m.o. as a helicopter parent, Eliza never cared. She felt that it was safer for her kids to buy a drink or two at a bar in town with their fake IDs than to binge-drink ten in someone's basement. Plus, the advent of Uber had nearly eliminated her concerns about their driving under the influence.

Eliza handed Kevin two cups of coffee.

"Bring one up to your sister and tell her to get down here ASAP."

She was happy to delegate, as waking Kayla was Eliza's least favorite parenting responsibility. Plus, even at nineteen, Kevin was delighted to have permission to annoy his sister, evident in his devilish smile as he left the room.

"I forgot to tell you, I invited the new neighbors," Luke said, nonchalantly.

Eliza turned ashen. He noticed.

"Uh-oh. Did I goof?"

"No, no, it's fine," she lied, realizing for the first time that she hadn't mentioned any of what she had seen or done to Luke. Which made her realize that the whole thing was really not all right. Luke had a true moral compass, and if it was kosher she would have told him for sure.

Luke helped her carry more muffins to the table when the doorbell rang. As if on cue, it was the neighbors. Well, half of them at least. Mr. Smith.

"Hi, I'm Joe Smith, from next door," he declared with an outstretched arm, a bottle of rosé, and an excuse regarding his wife. "I'm afraid Ashley can't make it. When I left, she was in a dark room nursing a migraine."

"I'm sorry to hear that," Luke commiserated. "Eliza has developed migraines too lately. Sometimes she can't leave the house because of them, right, honey?"

It took Eliza a second to remember that, on multiple occasions, she had used a migraine as an excuse to stay home. She looked at her husband's face. It showed genuine concern for her suffering. Eliza felt awful.

"Yes, I have. They're no fun. Hopefully we will meet another time."

She crossed her fingers as she said it. She was relieved Mrs. Smith hadn't come. She was worried that she'd like her and feel even guiltier, or that Ashley Smith would somehow read on her face what she'd done. Eliza brought his neighborly offering to the kitchen just as her old friend Marjorie Tobin arrived and suggested they open it. Eliza looked at the clock, 11:00 a.m. *Too early?* she thought.

Marjorie had a different agenda. "Where's your corkscrew?"

Eliza smiled and handed it to her. It was a party after all.

After Eliza took a sip, Marjorie tested her to see if she'd heard the news.

"So, when's the last time you spoke to Mandy?"

"I don't remember. You?"

"I guess you don't know then?"

"Know what?"

"Come upstairs," Marjorie ordered. Eliza followed her as Marjorie went right to Eliza's desk. Marjorie had gone to high school with Eliza and her across-the-street neighbor, and best friend, Amanda, or Mandy as they had always called her. They all knew their way around her house as if it were their own. The three of them were once very close, though as was often the case with odd numbers, one person felt left out—that person was usually Marjorie. Except on Halloween. On Halloween they would always trick-or-treat as a threesome: the sun, the moon, and the stars; Snap, Crackle, and Pop; Marsha, Jan, and Cindy. One year Eliza's mother suggested they be the Three Musketeers. They put their own spin on it and dressed as three Three Musketeers chocolate bars. It infuriated her mother—which Eliza knew it would. Birdie didn't care for candy, actual or costumed replicas, and would try to bribe Eliza every year to skip trick-or-treating. It never worked. Eliza would stockpile that candy under her bed, giving her sweet sustenance until at least Christmas.

"Google Amanda's husband," Marjorie instructed Eliza. Marjorie was a bit of a gossip—it was probably the reason Eliza never even hinted to her that she was having trouble leaving the house.

She still loved Mandy like a sister, and though she would be the first to admit she'd been jealous of her at times, she always wanted the best for her.

Eliza typed in "Carson Cole," and the page filled up with the morning's news. It all seemed to stem from accusations against Mandy's husband, Carson, in an article in the *Los Angeles Times*:

CARSON COLE'S CASTING COUCH

> Hollywood has been rocked once again by sexual assault allegations, this time against film mogul Carson Cole. The accusations allege that Cole pressured women to perform sexual favors in return for roles in his films. So far, seven women have come forward with similar stories. A representative for Cole denied all charges, saying that these incidents were consensual.

The article went on to detail the accusations, reporting that they had allegedly taken place over the past decade. As far as Eliza could see, there was only a small mention of Amanda and her two daughters—just that he was married to the former actress and the ages of their children.

Marjorie shook her head. "I feel bad. You know we may not live exciting lives like hers, but at least we don't have to worry about our husbands being unfaithful. We don't, right?" She laughed a little.

"I don't think either of us has anything to worry about. But I guess you never know."

As Eliza stood to go back down to her company, she noticed Ashley Smith exercising on her stationary bike. *Migraine my ass*, she thought, before pulling out her phone to message Mandy.

She only needed two words:

Come home.

———————

That night, in bed, Eliza tossed and turned, reliving the day with all of its ups and downs. She would have thought that her discussion with Luke in the kitchen or the awful thing that was going on with Mandy would have been at the forefront of her restlessness, but it wasn't. She'd been obsessing about the lying woman next door. It was so much easier to think about nonsense.

When the Smiths had moved in, Eliza dragged herself out of the house to drop off a welcome note and her signature gift, a Hudson Valley Candle, from a beautiful little store in Cold Spring that makes them. She'd stockpiled a bunch for hostess gifts and whatnot, giving the new neighbors her last precious candle. They never even bothered to thank her; it was another point in the ongoing tally of why Mrs. Smith sucks, mitigating any remorse regarding her salacious post.

Her phone pinged, and she grabbed it, thrilled for the distraction. It was Mandy, responding to her text. It read, See you tomorrow!, followed by an emoji of her head exploding. *Poor Mandy.* More emotions cluttered Eliza's brain.

Curiosity and the need to be distracted got the better of her. She gave up on sleep and snuck quietly out of the bedroom to her hallway office. She knew it was pathetic, but the bulletin board had remained unchecked since that morning and she figured it would clear her head so she could return to bed in peace.

She pulled up Valley Girls first and read the latest explosive post:

"Like" if you put your underwear back on immediately following sex!

Eliza had never thought much about it, but she couldn't get her panties back on soon enough after she and Luke had sex. She would search for them in the covers in the dark like a madwoman until the deed was complete and they were safely in place, closing up shop. Apparently, according to this poll, she was in the minority. If she believed the comments, she may have "internalized labia loathing." She didn't know whether to laugh or cry. She flipped to the bulletin board. The cheating post had sadly lost its steam. She couldn't take it. She needed to do more.

The party and its planning was behind her; her kids would return to school tomorrow and she would be left lying in bed watching the changing patterns of light on her ceiling as the sun peeked in through her bedroom blinds. *Screw that cheating unappreciative Ashley Smith and her fake migraine.* She deserved to be sacrificed for the cause. She typed with a vengeance:

> **Anonymous:** He came back again early this morning on a run. He confronted me about my post; his wife must be on this site, too. If you are reading this, I'm sorry. He says you have not had sex in months, and you have an open marriage. I know men say that. I wish I knew if it were true.

She pressed Post and read it over in situ. The excitement broke through the numbness, and for a fleeting moment she felt alive. Lately she had taken to scraping her thigh with her bathroom razor until it bled to get that effect. This seemed better.

Other insomniacs immediately began commenting, but Eliza felt satisfied and thankfully sleepy. She turned off her computer and headed back to bed.

CHAPTER 11

Amanda Cole

It is commonly said that a woman leaves an abusive relationship an average of seven times before she leaves for good. The first time Amanda tried to leave Carson Cole was just after they were married. It was the first time he had shown his *other* side.

They were having dinner at the famed Beverly Hills eatery La Scala with an actor that he was touting as the next George Clooney, and his girlfriend. The three of them—Amanda, the actor, and his girlfriend—were contemporaries, while Carson was a good deal older, and in the case of the actor, shorter and balder. Both Amanda and the actor had come to LA around the same time. About halfway through their first course, signature La Scala chopped salads, they figured out that they knew each other from an acting class that both had briefly attended. The more they reminisced about the class, the shorter Carson's fuse became. By dessert, when they connected over a band that Carson had never heard of, jealousy all but strangled him. He reached under the table and squeezed Amanda's leg quite painfully. She was meant to somehow keep silent about it but it hurt, and she shrieked. The entire restaurant seemed to stop and stare.

"I'm so sorry, I got a cramp," she lied, as her eyes filled with tears.

That night she packed up a suitcase and escaped to the Beverly Hills Hotel, where she had once waited tables at the Polo Lounge. She still knew the manager there. But, like everyone in Hollywood, Carson knew him better. The next morning, Carson came to get her with a dozen roses and two dozen apologies. He promised her that it was not his way, that his new picture wasn't doing well, and the pressure had gotten to him. He admitted to feeling insecure and overcome with jealousy. He begged her to not to leave him and promised to behave. And he did, for quite some time.

The next time she left, she only got as far as the basement. She stormed out of their bedroom after a fight in which he hurled a barrage of insults at her, including that she was stupid, worthless, and incapable of accomplishing anything on her own. She slammed the front door, but in truth she just retreated to the downstairs screening room. It was late, and she was tired and didn't want to leave the house. She heard him stomping around yelling out loud to himself, "Let's see how far you get with whatever cash is in your pocket."

She cued up a bunch of divorce movies and fell asleep somewhere between *War of the Roses* and *Heartburn*. She may have had the guts to really go then, but she was pregnant with their first daughter, Pippa. She had yet to tell Carson. The next morning, she scheduled an appointment at an abortion clinic out in Calabasas. In the end, she couldn't go through with it and never told Carson what might have been.

The squeeze of her leg wasn't the only time his rage had become physical, but he was never violent enough to give her real ammunition against him. After hurting her, he would taunt her in a condescending voice, saying, *"Oh, I pinched you too hard? Poor Amanda."* It was always just violent enough to belittle her reaction to it. He was way too smart to ever let the words "Carson hit me" come out of her mouth.

Amanda was often the butt of his sexually explicit jokes; his favorites were always the ones that came at her expense.

"We are going home to bed. Anyone want to join us?" he would ask a group of young actresses at a party. Or "Look how well-trained my wife is!" to a group of men in response to her bringing him a drink. He was too full of himself to notice how uncomfortable it made others feel, let alone Amanda, who became instantly mortified. When she spoke out, he would cut her down further, insisting that it was her insecurity talking. He would never accept the blame for her feelings of inadequacy.

As far as other women were concerned, Amanda knew that Carson could get grabby, especially after a couple of drinks, but she had no idea of the extent of it. She often witnessed his hand grazing a woman's buttocks in a way that could be deemed accidental only the first time it happened, not the second or the third or the twentieth. Once, at her birthday dinner with a table of her friends, Carson became so handsy with their young waitress that it decimated the night. When she approached the table to inquire about dessert she stood as far from him as possible. He got up to go to the men's room, pausing at her side to listen to the choices. As he stepped behind the poor girl and began massaging her shoulders, all appetites were lost. It was painful to watch, heartbreaking really, yet no one stopped him. The entire table, Amanda included, just sat silently as the young waitress rattled off the list of desserts like she was calling out casualties of war. By the time she got to the tiramisu, a lone tear formed in her eye and rolled down her cheek. She ran off to the kitchen while a clueless Carson headed to the men's room. One of Amanda's friends' husbands handed the manager a hundred-dollar bill for the waitress with an apology, but no one stood up to Carson. If asked, he would probably say it was absurd, and that the waitress appreciated his kind gesture, that she enjoyed having the great Carson Cole's hands kneading her tired shoulders.

A few days later, Amanda ran off to Disney World with the girls. She surprised them at school with packed bags and promises of breakfast with Cinderella and dinner with Minnie Mouse. Her youngest daughter, Sadie, had insisted on going on the teacup ride three times in a row, and when they were done, she vomited on Amanda's sandals. While she was washing the remnants of regurgitated funnel cake and cotton candy from between her toes, Amanda heard them yell, "Daddy, Daddy!" and they both ran into their father's arms. He had followed the charges on her credit card and found them. He whispered in Amanda's ear, "If you ever pull anything like this again, I'll have you charged with kidnapping, and you won't even be able to get a job here as Dopey."

After that her mind turned from fantasizing about leaving him to fantasizing about his death. She would lie in bed thinking of the phone call from Cedars-Sinai saying, "Your husband had a massive heart attack," or of a policeman at their door, "Your husband's car swerved off Mulholland Drive." Then she could be the lovely widow, and her marriage would not have been a failure, like her parents' marriage was.

The girls both idolized their movie-making father, and the feeling was mutual. How they saw him meant more to Carson than a dozen Oscar nominations. Because of this, he was careful that they only saw "good" Carson. The loving husband that sent their mother flowers weekly and for no apparent reason. The doting dad, who, upon hearing his daughter choose her Wonder

Woman action figure for show-and-tell, arranged for Gal Gadot to show up to class in full costume. The famed producer had such an eye for talent, art, and entertainment that *Variety* dubbed him "Hollywood's Napoleon," his diminutive size and impish looks contrasting greatly with his immense power.

Until the "Time's Up" movement encouraged his previously whispered-about behavior to be shouted from the Hollywood Hills, and thus a window was created through which his wife could orchestrate her escape.

Luckily, when the news broke of Carson's predatory behavior, Amanda was in a really good place to stand on her own two feet. She had begun seeing a therapist a year earlier and, with her help, developed the ability to ignore the disparaging things he said and believe in herself again. She was feeling stronger than she had in years. While there was no leaving the great Carson Cole before— not in one piece, that is—she was confident she could get out on the momentum of the scandal and his public crucifixion. With the world watching, he would have no choice but to behave civilly.

A woman leaves seven times before it sticks. She stopped counting the times and decided that whatever one this was, time was most definitely up. She packed four suitcases: one each for her and her girls and one filled with resale gold—Louis Vuitton and Birkin bags that she'd been collecting for this very occasion. She stuffed her carry-on with gift cards and piles of cash she'd been stockpiling ever since the night she heard him yelling, "Let's see how far you get with whatever cash is in your pocket!"

She reserved three seats on a morning flight out of LAX. By nightfall they would be across the country in Hudson Valley, standing in the safety of her childhood bedroom, her daughters arguing over who would get the top bunk. Eliza's text flashed up,

Come home, and she exhaled in relief, responding, See you tomorrow!

At first she followed it with a smiley-face emoji, but on realizing she no longer had to pretend everything was copacetic, she deleted it and replaced it with an exploding head. The small act of candor spurred a real-life smiley face. Her first in days, for sure.

CHAPTER 12

Alison

When Alison envisioned her life with a baby she didn't take into account the amount of napping it would involve. All the activities she'd pictured herself enjoying while Zach was sleeping—reading for pleasure, binge-watching the water-cooler shows, completing the *New York Times* crossword puzzles—morphed into one thing: the jumping-off point for a nap. She woke up from her morning siesta itching to go out for a walk.

Alison made sure to get out of the house every day, even though she loved her time in her new home. The smell—pine infused with new baby—calmed her as if a yogi had placed a drop of lavender oil on her forehead at the start of a meditation class. Not that she'd ever attended such a class. She laughed at the possibility—the Iron Lady turned yogini—and opened up her computer. It sounded like a perfect question for that ladies' bulletin board. Although asking, "Can anyone recommend a meditation class?" made her feel like she was misrepresenting herself. *Or was she?* She didn't even know who she was anymore.

Once online, she got caught up in the tampon post. There were now eighty comments. Some were tolerant of the question, but most women were responding with such outrage you would have thought that the mom had inquired about female circumcision. At least that was Alison's take. She would have hoped, especially as a single mother, that a woman asking a parenting question would have been treated with more empathy. She typed in a response saying just that, but as she read it over, reminding herself that she was a new person in an old town, she chickened out.

Alison Le, wallflower?

She decided to reach out to the mom privately. She clicked on her name, Jackie Campbell, and messaged her:

> Hi Jackie. I'm new in town. I'm just reaching out to you privately to say I'm sorry you were lambasted for your post on the Hudson Valley Ladies' Bulletin Board. I would have hoped a woman asking a parenting question would have been treated with more respect and understanding. I wanted you to know you have my support.

She pressed Send and went back to scrolling through old posts looking for one on yoga or meditation classes. The tampon uprising intimidated her from asking the question without searching first. She got stuck in the even juicier thread regarding a woman's infidelity.

Her computer dinged as a message from Jackie Campbell appeared.

> WTF! Can you believe these women? I mean, ask a simple question!?!

Ha, Alison thought, *a girl after my own heart.* She responded with a similar vernacular:

It was a real shitshow! They were acting like you were advocating overturning Roe v. Wade.

I know, what a bloody mess, right?

Ha! At least you have a sense of humor about it. What did you end up doing?

I gave her the tampons. After that beating I almost threw in some condoms too.

Was it after you read the comment, "My mother told me not to put anything up there until after I was married, so I rebelled and had a baby at 16"?

You got it!

So funny—to the single mother of an infant at least. I don't envy you having a teenage daughter.

Alison thought back to how hard the teenage years had been for her and her own mother. It was the only time they really butted heads. Bringing up a teenage girl in a totally different world from the one she had grown up in could not have been easy for her mom. Alison knew better than to even ask for tampons. She bought them on her own and kept them out of sight.

Is your baby a boy or girl?

A boy. Zachary Michael. Four months tomorrow. What about you?

It's just my daughter, Jana, and me.

Well, nice to virtually meet you, Jackie.

You too, Alison. Thanks for reaching out. And if there's anything I can help you with, I'm a single parent too and I know it can be hard going it alone.

It's OK. I guess if offered the chance, I would gladly hand him over and go pee or something, but I don't know any differently.

Well, if you ever have any questions, feel free.

Actually, I'm looking to try a yoga or meditation class if you know of any.

I don't, but there is a place in town, Café Karma Sutra. The people in there know all that hippy dippy stuff.

I am so not hippy dippy, but I thought I'd give it a try. Now that I'm on maternity leave, I may be at a place where I can find some kind of inner peace. Before, forget about it. There's no way I could calm my brain down enough.

What do you do?

I'm a criminal defense attorney.

No wonder! Sounds intense.

Do you work outside the home?

Alison had trained herself to ask that question that way when speaking to other women. She was adept at reading people, but you didn't have to be a litigator to see that when you asked most stay-at-home moms what they did, it threw them. Their reactions made Alison laugh now that she was in the position of taking care of a baby 24-7. Most days at the office seemed like a vacation by comparison.

I'm in finance.

In the city?

Yes, but my mom lived with us for 12 years. I don't know if I could have done both, and lived here, without her—not well at least. Do you have family nearby?

She typed and quickly erased:

I don't have any family, anywhere.

She never shared this with anyone; she wasn't about to put it in writing to a stranger.

It all fed right into the fear and doubt that had been brewing in Alison since she found out she was pregnant. She and Zach were very much alone in the world, family-wise, just as she and her own mother had been. Her mother had died two years earlier of leukemia, and Alison often thought about how different things would be if her mom was here right now. Her mother had met her father when he was stationed in Hanoi as a military attaché at the US embassy a few years after the Vietnam War had ended. She had worked there as a translator. Like she and Marc, they didn't have a real relationship, even less of one, really, as they were only to-gether a few times before he was transferred home. Upon discover-ing she was pregnant, and wanting to hide it from her family, she flew to the States to find him and feel out the situation. She waited outside his house only to see him leave with a wife and two small children that she had known nothing about. She walked away and braved it out on her own.

Alison only met her father once, when she was five years old, and quite by accident. They bumped into him on a line to see Santa at Macy's Herald Square. She had only the faintest memory of a very tall man in a long wool coat, but for years later, when a random kid asked about her father, she would say he worked in a top-secret toy factory at the North Pole, and that she can't say anything more about it. It worked every time.

She sometimes thought about what Zachary would say if he asked about his father, and it made her sad. Alison was, of course, aware that she was traveling down the same path as her mother, but she had no idea how to switch directions—or if she even wanted to.

Zachary cried from his bedroom as if giving his opinion, though she wasn't sure what that opinion was. She was aware that she hadn't answered Jackie's question, but went with:

Zach is up. I have to go. Nice chatting with you!

You too. If you go to Karma Sutra, order a rain forest muffin—they're wicked good!

I will!

I guess I'm joining the muffin cult, she thought, as she ran up-stairs to her baby boy.

CHAPTER 13

Olivia

Olivia got Lily to sleep for her afternoon nap with the intention of running a hot bath. She would leave Spencer the monitor so that she wouldn't have to jump from the tub midway through as she had on previous attempts. She was even contemplating lighting a few candles and cracking open a new book. She began stripping piece by piece on the stairs and entered the bathroom to find Spencer oddly skulking in the corner looking at her phone.

"What are you doing with my phone again?" she asked, more confused than annoyed. Spencer answered by tossing it to her quite rudely. She barely caught it.

"What the hell, Spencer?"

"Well, you come in here spying on me!"

"I'm not spying on you. I'm here to take a bath. Look, I'm naked," she said, suddenly feeling it.

Spencer stormed out before Olivia could get to the bottom of his anger. She had such a short bath window that she decided not to care, at least for now. She turned on the water and sat on the edge of the tub, dabbing her feet in and out to adjust to the temperature. She unlocked her phone. *What is with him lately?* she thought. And there it was, in black and white, right on her screen:

> **Anonymous:** He came back again early this morning on a run. He confronted me about my post; his wife must be on this site, too. If you are reading this, I'm sorry. He says you have not had sex in months, and you have an open marriage. I know men say that. I wish I knew if it were true.

Olivia began to shake before she even understood why. *Why was Spencer reading that bulletin board? Why was he so angry about this post?*

She tried to stay calm, but her thoughts were racing. Spencer went for an early run. *Is that where he was at six o'clock this morning?*

Her stomach dropped and her mouth went dry. *Is this woman talking to* me?

She turned off the bath, stepped out of the bathroom, and pulled on a pair of leggings and a T-shirt. She thought that maybe she should wait to calm down before confronting him, but she was too enraged. She didn't know if calming down was even an option. She felt like an animal. There must be an explanation. She *needed* an explanation.

"You're imagining things, Olivia," he'll say. *I will hear his voice*, she thought, *the one he uses to soothe me. I will hear his denial, and everything will be OK.* But she'd never suspected such a betrayal before, and the possibility of it whipped her into a frenzy. She confronted him straight out.

"What the hell is this, Spencer? Are you having an affair?"

"What?" he asked, as if she hadn't said it loud enough, which she definitely had. His non-answer raised her antennae even higher. She repeated the question again, slowly and clearly.

"Are you having an affair?"

"Olivia, are you serious?" He looked adequately shocked. "I would never do that. I love you—and Lily—so much. How could you think that?"

She collapsed onto the couch.

"I'm sorry. This post—it sounded so much like us. You're gone every morning and we haven't had sex in forever."

"I always run in the morning. And you just had a baby. I was being respectful."

He went to hug her and she held out her hand to stop him. It wasn't that she didn't believe him, she just couldn't breathe and a hug felt like further suffocation. But before she could explain that, his expression changed and he turned on her, nearly shouting in her face, "Hey. I read that post, too. I could—no, I should—ask you the same thing!"

The sudden shift and the strength of his animosity was jarring. *This can't be happening*, she thought. Spencer had a tendency to turn things around in a fight, especially when his back was against a wall. But this was insane, even for him. Olivia mocked the absurdity of it.

"Yes, Spencer, your beautiful wife with her leaky udders and stretched-out stomach with this ugly dark line that everyone says will go away, but clearly isn't? Yes, we are all having an affair."

"I'm not joking, Olivia. I'm just a few months away from being named CEO of York Cosmetics. You know any impropriety like that could ruin me—could ruin us."

His logic brought Olivia some relief. Being CEO meant everything to Spencer, and when she really thought it through, she doubted he would do anything to risk it. An uncle of Spencer's had had a very public affair about ten years earlier that had almost destroyed the female-focused cosmetic brand. It was a publicity nightmare and stood as a huge cautionary tale to all the members of the York family. Maybe she was inventing this whole thing in her head? Just as she settled on that, he started up again.

"Did someone come here when I went for my run this morning? Is this why we don't have sex anymore?"

Olivia could not believe what she was hearing. Was he seriously gaslighting her? She caught a look at herself in the mirror. Strange red hives had popped up on her face. She felt the air being squeezed from her lungs again. She gasped for more, but it was as if there wasn't enough in the room to replace it. This whole thing was spinning out of control. She was confused and needed to think it all through clearly, away from him and Lily. She wanted so badly to believe him.

"I have to get out of here," she said. "I need to take a walk. I can't breathe."

She headed to the front door. Spencer chased after her and grabbed her arm.

"Where are you going? To see your boyfriend?"

"Do you hear how ridiculous you sound?" she snapped. "Stop turning this around!"

"Walk out and you'll regret it," he yelled, as if choosing a staple threat from a canned domestic dispute.

At that moment, suffocating was the only credible threat that concerned her, plus if none of this were true then she knew from experience that they both needed to calm down, separately. She slipped on her Uggs by the door and left. No coat, no money, no bra; no bra was the biggest problem. Still, she kept walking. When her breath settled, she sat down on the side of the road and read the post again, calmly. Then she read the first post. Her chest tightened back up. *Could this really be Spencer? Am I being paranoid?* She didn't think she was. Olivia did know one thing for sure: she had never felt this kind of betrayal before. Whether it was real or imagined, she didn't like it.

Her tears flowed, not hysterically, but consistently. Quite out of nowhere she spotted a high-spirited dog trotting down the road. He stopped and looked at Olivia, as if sensing her desperation. She smiled through her tears and reached out to pet him. "Hey, boy, are you lost?"

He perked his ears up, but then bolted away from her until he was invisible among the trees.

A voice called out from the distance, "Here, Truffles, I have a treat. Come on, boy!"

She hoped the dog with the funny name was heading back home. She thought maybe she should do the same, but she needed more time.

She started walking, purposefully breathing in through her nose and out through her mouth. Soon she found herself in town, her mouth dry from gulping down air; she needed a drink. She entered the Café Karma Sutra and went right up to the counter. Her breasts were so full under her T-shirt that she felt as if she were naked. She remembered she didn't have any money. She approached the multipierced barista a bit timidly.

"May I please have a cup of water?"

"Did you bring a receptacle?" he countered.

She was confused by the question. She hadn't brought a receptacle. She wasn't even sure what that meant. *Why did she ever leave Manhattan?* There she would have a million places to run away to, where everyone spoke the same language. Now she was alone and thirsty in a foreign land. She felt the red blotches returning to her face. They were radiating heat. She read the words painted across the wall behind him: "I Am Perfect Because I Exist."

False advertising, she thought. She hated when people pretended to be so Zen but were in fact quite the opposite. It should read, "I'm Perfect If I Exist with a Receptacle." Her eyes teared up and her breathing accelerated. The pierced guy seemed to notice. He took pity on her and filled a glass with water.

"Here," he said in a tone more capitalistic than karmic.

"Oh, a receptacle." She smiled, trying to appear sane.

She turned around and bumped smack into Alison Le and her baby. She recognized her from somewhere, but was too out of her mind to remember where. And she didn't care to find out. She ducked her head, her eye on the door. *Fake left; go right*, she thought. She had no idea that Alison was desperate for adult interaction and that she had no chance of getting away.

"Olivia, right?" Alison smiled. "We met at the real estate office. Alison."

Olivia nodded and shook her hand with one eye still on the door to purposefully signal brevity.

"How are you?" Alison asked naturally. There was nothing natural about her response. Olivia tried to hold back her emotions, which caused them to escape from her mouth in a gust of pain so guttural that she even startled herself. People stared. The "fixer" in Alison took over and she leaped into action.

"I live right down the street. Do you want to get out of here?"

Olivia shook her head yes.

"OK. Wait one second." Alison directed her to a chair and headed to the counter. She thought comfort food might be in order.

"Two rain forest muffins to go, please."

"Did you bring a receptacle?" the pierced barista asked.

"I have no clue what you are asking me," Alison replied.

Olivia laughed, which made her smile. Thank God that she was OK enough to do that.

They walked back to Alison's house, just a few doors away, in silence, each holding a bagless muffin in their hands. Zach had fallen asleep in the stroller, so Alison left him in the foyer of her house and set them up in the living room. Olivia was quiet, somber really. Alison wondered if she should change the subject and talk about the kids or ask her what she was upset about. She unwittingly did both.

"Did you see the post about Circle Time at the library on that local bulletin board?"

Tears exploded from Olivia's eyes. They didn't well up or pour down her face but arrived so fast and furiously that they ricocheted off the side of her nose. Alison had never witnessed anything like it, and she had witnessed a lot.

"I am the woman from the bulletin board. I am the woman," Olivia sobbed. Alison knew exactly what she was talking about.

"Oh my God. You're anonymous?"

"No. It's worse than that." She could barely say it. "I'm the wife."

Now Alison was tearing up. A pit filled *her* stomach and *she* couldn't get enough air. *Motherhood has made me soft*, she thought.

"How awful," she said, hugging her. Olivia melted into her arms sobbing, the two strangers now intimate friends.

As Olivia wept, Alison regained her composure. This situation called for the Iron Lady, not the wussy confection of hormones and baby love that she'd become. Toeing the line between lawyering and mothering, Alison began her line of questioning while brewing a pot of chamomile tea.

"How are you certain it's your husband? Did he admit it?"

"No, he denied it. But I'm sure." Olivia pulled up the first post on her phone and showed it to Alison. She now knew it by heart and read along in her head.

Anonymous: I just moved here from the city with hopes of starting over after an affair that my husband knows nothing about. The man I was

having the affair with followed me here and keeps showing up at my
door . . .

"OK, is this all you've got? Because there is some major circumstantial stuff going on here. I understand that you moved here
recently, but so have many other people. I bet there are other cou-
ples having the same fight right now!"

Olivia wasn't buying it. She scrolled forward to the next post
while explaining Spencer's crazy reactions to reading them, and
how he was gone in the morning at the same time the cheating
woman claimed to be running with her boyfriend. Olivia read the
next post. Alison was skeptical.

"Everyone runs in the morning. Did you confront him?"

"Yes." She began crying again. "He turned it all around, accused me of cheating. It was so frustrating, and . . ." She took a
deep breath to try and calm herself. "And so embarrassing. I
mean, look at me. To accuse me of cheating . . ." Olivia's milk had
come in right on schedule, leaving her with circular stains on her
gray T-shirt over each nipple and a good amount of guilt for having left a now-sure-to-be-hungry Lily at home. She buried her face
in her hands. The teapot whistled. Alison fixed Olivia a cup of tea
and placed it and the muffin in front of her.

"Here, eat something. I'll go up and get you a sports bra and a
clean T-shirt. I'll be right back."

Once upstairs, Alison called her best friend from college, a
detective named Andie Rand, who specialized in domestic dis-
putes after suffering a particularly horrendous one of her own.
Recently engaged, she was finally not rendering anyone with a
penis automatically guilty. Alison came back down, armed with a
change of clothes and some very logical advice. Olivia went to the
bathroom to wash her face and change. She took her time and
came out somewhat renewed.

"I hope it's OK, but I called my friend who owns a detective agency in the city. I didn't give her your name."

Olivia didn't mind. She was desperate for direction. "I'm so thankful I bumped into you," she said.

"Me too. So first off, she understands that you want to hear the truth from your husband, but if he is a cheater, then he's also a liar. She says he will feed you lies, and you'll want to believe them."

So far she was right. Olivia only wanted to hear his explanation, to hear the words "I would never cheat on you" and to believe them and turn the page on this whole episode.

"It's pointless to confront him until we gather as much evidence as possible."

Olivia's eyes filled with tears. Alison assumed it was because she was probably being cheated on, and as the timeline suggested, it was likely going on during her pregnancy. Alison reflected on her own experience of childbirth and shuddered at the thought of it being laced with duplicity. Poor Olivia. How soon before she started questioning months of interactions in her mind? Olivia's awful situation affirmed Alison's decision to go it alone, not that she'd really had much choice.

As it turned out, this trickling of tears was out of gratitude, because Alison had used the word "we."

"Thank you so much for helping me like this. You don't even know me."

That was the best part of it for Olivia. While she was in the bathroom, she had resisted the urge to call her parents, her sister, or her best friend. She knew once she did, she could never take the words back. True or not, the damage would be done, especially if she told her father. She vowed only to confide in this stranger until the whole ordeal was resolved, regardless of the resolution.

"I don't mind at all. I'm happy to be here for you, really."

Olivia shook her head with a mixture of relief and appreciation.

"Did you tell your friend that he accused me back?" she asked hopefully. The more Olivia thought about it, the more she realized that Spencer could have come up with the same conclusions about a cheating spouse from the post that she had. The story did work both ways, and he had made little effort to conceal his behavior.

"I did tell her." Alison paused, as the answer would not be fun to hear. "She said it may be true, but more often than not the guilty party hopes to defuse anger with confusion."

Olivia's face sank.

Alison knew one was innocent until proven guilty, but her career had swayed her to often believe the opposite. She was very familiar with the emotions involved when someone wanted so badly to believe that the person they know is blameless. She felt terrible for this woman.

"She said we can come see her at her office on Monday, if you want."

Again, we. Olivia jumped at the chance. "The sooner the better. I have my sitter on Mondays. She can watch the kids if you want."

"Both of them?"

"Absolutely. She's a retired kindergarten teacher who raised a family of her own. She could probably watch ten babies more easily than we can watch one. I promise." Alison agreed to it.

"The thought of having any control over this . . ." Olivia couldn't finish her thought. Her eyes welled up again.

Alison went into defendant mode. "Don't start. You have to go home and backpedal. Tell him you are not having an affair, and you're sorry you accused him of having one. Then just try and act normal."

Olivia had no idea how she was going to pull that off. Alison read it on her face.

"Remember, Olivia, questioning a cheater only makes things worse. If you signal what you know, he'll cover his tracks, and it will be very hard for us to get at the truth. Plus we have no idea if this is for real. What's that saying about worrying?"

"No use in worrying until you have something to worry about?"

"Yes, something like that."

Olivia knew what she had to do. As she trudged home, she directed her thoughts to uncovering the truth. She swore to control herself and go about everything purposefully and emotionlessly for her and Lily's sake. The only thing worse than being cheated on was being made a fool of, and if that was what was going on, she would take him down. She thought of something that happened last week, something that had touched her. She'd been giggling at a silly cat video when he walked in, caught her, and smiled a huge grin.

"What?" she had asked, and he said, "Nothing, I just love to hear you laugh."

She would think of that nice moment when her mind drifted to hating him and promised to stop before the worst thought took over. The worst thought being that everything, including that moment, was a lie.

CHAPTER 14

Amanda

Amanda had insisted that she and the girls take a car from the airport, but of course her father had completely ignored her. While she appreciated him and had been garnering strength from just the promise of their forthcoming hug, she recognized she would have to draw clear boundaries. Dan Williams could be quite obstinate, especially when it came to his only child, Mandy.

The ride home was particularly uncomfortable. Dan would ask a question, and Amanda would quickly shut it down with her eyes. Finally, she said, "Let's talk when we get home, Dad," as she turned up the radio.

Dan brought their luggage inside. The girls would share Amanda's old room, and Amanda would take the guest room on the first floor so as to give her some privacy, he said. She secretly longed to stay in her childhood bedroom, snuggled up under the primary-colored tulips of her beloved Marimekko comforter. When trying to fall asleep next to Carson, Amanda would sometimes imagine herself in her childhood bed. She would envision the array of stickers that she'd collaged to the underside of the top bunk in middle school—an abundance of Wacky Packs, the bright leopard prints of Lisa Frank, and a mega-sized MTV logo were interspersed with nearly anything with an adhesive back. She doubted anyone else even knew they were there. Sometimes she would lie in her Beverly Hills bed trying to recall every last sticker until she drifted off to sleep.

As Sadie began losing the battle for the top bunk to her older sister, Amanda winked at her and motioned for her to try out the bottom. She did, and upon seeing the '80s time capsule, quickly acquiesced as if she were doing Pippa a favor.

"Fine, I'll take the bottom," she said, with a knowing smile.

The girls thought this visit was about escaping the initial fall-out from their father's indiscretions. "Just until it blows over," Amanda had told them on the plane. But Amanda knew better than to think it would be blowing over anytime soon. She assumed that those first accusations against Carson were only the tip of the iceberg. Her gut told her that her husband would be going down like the *Titanic*, and like on the *Titanic*, all women and children belonged in lifeboats. She helped the girls unpack and excused herself to settle into the guest room.

From her window, Amanda could see that across the street Eliza had company. Her dad had mentioned an invitation in the car, before she'd silenced him. On other visits, Amanda might have run to Eliza's to say hello before even entering her own house, but not today. Until receiving her text, Amanda hadn't heard from her for a few months, and then it had only been to wish her a happy birthday. In the old days, they would have called each other on their birthdays and stayed on the phone for hours catching up. Eliza knew Amanda better than anyone, and would have heard, just from her hello, how unhappy she was. It's much easier to feign happiness over text. She remembered selecting a smiley face in response to Eliza's asking how she was doing. She'd gone with the slightly smiling face as opposed to the big grin to avoid feeling like a complete hypocrite. If she were being honest, she would have sent the exploding head back then as she had yesterday. Texting is both a blessing and a curse.

Eliza's house looked so happy and full. It made Mandy wonder about the life she was so quick to give up. As soon as she was able, she had flown the coop to head to the West Coast in search of something bigger. On the yearly trips back east to see her dad, she could remember her perspective changing. Eventually she would see things through Carson's eyes. The spacious houses in their affluent neighborhood, built in the '70s on a large expanse of undeveloped Hudson Valley farmland, slowly began to shrink as she became accustomed to the mansions of Beverly Hills. The conversations about country clubs, canasta, and composting seemed droll compared to industry talk in LA. Even the bodies were less exciting to look at; everyone seemed to have an extra ten pounds on them yet didn't think twice about ordering a slice of pie for dessert. That part was actually better. In LA, "à la mode" meant with a side of remorse and a promise of three more miles on the treadmill.

She stood there now wondering how she could have become so jaded. How could she have been so foolish as to think this wouldn't be enough for her? But of course, hindsight is everything, and who wouldn't make different choices if they were given a crystal ball? Eliza probably wouldn't, she thought. Good for her. She hoped it were true.

Though Eliza lived in the house she had grown up in, Mandy knew it was now a very different home. Eliza and her mother had been like oil and water for most of their lives, until later, when they were like gasoline and a match. But still, when her mom moved to Florida and offered Eliza and Luke the house, they grabbed it. It was a beautiful Colonial near some of the best schools in the state, plus there was a natural warmth to the place that even Eliza's frosty mother hadn't been able to extinguish. Birdie Reinhart was ice-cold to almost everyone except, oddly, Amanda. Actually, it wasn't that odd. Even a stranger could figure out why Birdie seemed to care more for Amanda than for her own child. In fact, upon meeting Eliza and Amanda in the presence of Birdie, the tactless ones often pointed it right out:

"Oh, how funny that your own daughter (with her frizzy black curls, broken-out skin, and extra pounds) looks nothing like you, and her (fit, tan, blond) best friend (with the wide-set blue eyes and fine features) could be your clone?"

The only thing wrong with that sentence was "how funny."

Eliza was always generous about it to Mandy, making faces and snide comments to defuse the situation.

"Do you want her?" she would ask, referring to her mother. A baited question, since Amanda's own mother had walked out on them when she was seven. Amanda's answer would be no. She didn't want Birdie Reinhart to be her mother, but she did let her spoil her. She was happy to take her hand-me-downs or a gift of coral lipstick when Birdie would buy two because, "It goes perfectly with our coloring."

Eliza always felt like the ugly duckling when the three of them were together, but feigned indifference. She would make self-deprecating jokes and laugh everything off until that one day in high school, when out of nowhere she refused to leave the house. It was as if her entire personality changed overnight and no one, not even Amanda, knew why.

Amanda pulled herself away from the window and opened up

her suitcase. She would visit Eliza tomorrow when her company was gone. It would be too much to walk into her house today. She pictured the Hollywood-style announcement:

Amanda Cole, Hudson Valley's D-list actress, is back for a return engagement with her tail between her legs.

It was not the big comeback she had hoped for.

CHAPTER 15

Jackie & Alison

Jackie made a special trip to the Video Room on Saturday to pick out a movie for him and Jana to watch. He was old-fashioned that way. Perusing the aisles of the last standing DVD store in Hudson Valley gave him a satisfaction he didn't get from streaming at home. The alternative was spending an eternity doing it the Netflix way, and not a happy eternity. Every suggestion by one of them led to the other saying, "Maybe. Let's see what else there is." The delayed start significantly upped the chance of Jackie dozing off halfway through. It had been years since he'd carried Jana upstairs to sleep; lately it was more likely to be the other way around.

He walked in around five o'clock with a bag of groceries, including the newest flavor from Ben & Jerry's, and the DVD of *Drop Dead Fred*. A classic, he told Jana as she came down the stairs to gingerly burst his bubble.

"I'm sorry, Daddy. Lauren Adwar is having people over, and I really want to go."

He made a sad face, but Jana didn't waver. She reminded him that the last time she acquiesced to guilt she missed the party of the year, which fueled a few hundred inside jokes that she was not inside for.

It never seemed to enter her mind that Jackie might also have other things to do. Not that he could even remember having such desires. Jackie's friends used to invite him to join them on Saturday nights, but he would usually turn them down, choosing to spend more time with Jana. Even his mother would push him to put himself out there. He always made excuses. Jackie had no interest in ever being as broken as he was when his wife died. He had his daughter and loving her was enough for him.

"Will her parents be home?" he asked.

"Yup. Call them if you want," she challenged.

"Don't think I won't."

"Oh, believe me, Daddy, I don't think you won't!"

They both laughed. They knew each other too well.

Within an hour of her leaving, loneliness set in. Jackie looked at his DVD choice and bemoaned the fact that he'd had *Die Hard* and *Die Hard 2* in his hands and had put them back. Even the lovely Phoebe Cates couldn't entice him to go this one alone. Jana would be going to college in a few years, and he hadn't bothered to build a personal life for himself. He poured a bowl of cereal, not exactly the dinner of champions, and opened up his computer to throw himself into his work. This was a common defense of his when discontent set in—don't think, just work. He remembered his new mom bulletin board friend and reached out to her instead of delving into a trade index summary report.

Hi! Did you make it to the Karma Sutra? Were there any
meditation classes posted?

She answered pretty quickly, leading Jackie to assume that she
was just as bored as he was. In truth, she was happy for the distraction.

Alison had been lying around all night, obsessing over the
posts about the affair. She was poring through the comments,
looking for clues. She'd hoped it was just in Olivia's head, but the
more she thought about the situation, the more she felt like something wasn't right. The whole thing was making her crazy.

Alison was a good friend to have, both virtually and in the
flesh: the kind of straightforward person who tells it like it is, even
when you may not want to hear it. She had just met Olivia, but still
she couldn't help but feel protective toward her. She had tried
some of the most difficult cases in the state and seen how easy it
was for people to lie. If Olivia's husband was lying, she wanted to
catch this guy and take him down.

Hi! There was a notice for a class called Intersectional
Embodiment. I was too scared to even take the flyer!

HA. That does sound frightening. Did you try the muffin?

Yes. It was wicked good—as promised. You could have warned
me about the receptacle thing though. The guy behind the
counter was pretty harsh.

Ha! I know. I once asked him for a straw for my iced coffee and
he acted like I had murdered a dolphin right before his eyes. I
hate the whole straw thing.

Same. And I hate when people say "clean food." I mean where
did that even come from?

I think it's from *Fight Club*. And sorry for talking about *Fight
Club*!

LOL—too funny.

Jackie was psyched that he had made her LOL. If she didn't
think he was a woman, he would definitely suggest they meet at
the Café Karma Sutra. "I can bring the receptacles," he would say,
probably making her LOL all over again. He took it further:

The bulletin board is kind of like a virtual *Fight Club*, no? Did you
see that cheating post? It pushed me right out of the number one
spot.

Though trained to be the picture of discretion, Alison was
bursting to talk about her day with someone who would get it.

You have no idea what happened to me today.

What?

I can't.

Yes you can, it's like *Fight Club*, remember.

I shouldn't.

As she typed, she knew she was going to. She was usually a
vault, yet here she was gossiping. Soon she would be watching the

Real Housewives franchise, she thought—she had always secretly wanted to.

You can totally trust me.

Jackie forgot for a moment that he was misrepresenting himself.

OK. I'm usually not such a yenta, but I met a woman today who read it too and thinks she's the one being cheated on. She completely lost it in the middle of Karma Sutra.

That's horrible.

I know, right? I feel awful for her, just awful. And to make matters worse, she has an infant!

No way. What a douchebag!

Exactly. If it's true and it really is her husband, then I'd bet it's been going on for a while. The post says he followed her here. If it's him, the timeline suggests he was cheating throughout her pregnancy and childbirth.

Maybe he's one of those serial cheaters. I know some guys like that at work. Total tools. Or maybe she's imagining it.

Maybe. Those new mother hormones can make you think crazy things, remember?

He remembered having all sorts of irrational worries when Jana was born. Checking the batteries in the baby monitor almost

daily; resting his hand on her sleeping back in the middle of the
night to make sure she was still breathing. Though he knew his
struggles weren't estrogen induced, he answered with a warped
sense of honesty.

Yes! It was awful.

It's weird though. From the outside it would look like she had the
perfect life and that I must be struggling on my own. But it's
really quite the opposite.

It may feel good now, to be in control of your own life, but take it
from me, being a single parent can be very lonely.

Well, it doesn't have to be forever. I'm sure I'll have a relationship
again. With better birth control! Lol.

I guess Zach's dad is not in the picture?

Nope. Not at all. Like the song says—It's Saturday night and I
ain't got nobody.

Jackie was happy to hear they were singing the same tune,
though he knew it was selfish of him. He had wondered about
Alison's relationship status. It was left blank on her Facebook profile. He had done his due diligence after the first time she reached
out. She wasn't a big poster on Facebook like some people, but not
as lame as he was. Aside from his profile picture of Jana as a baby,
his page consisted of a few people leaving yearly birthday messages that he never even acknowledged. From her profile he knew
that Alison was thirty-eight, a partner in her law firm, went to
Wesleyan for undergrad and Harvard for law school. Her page

was somewhat political with articles and photos regarding immigration policies and nativism mixed with a spattering of similarly pointed political cartoons from the *New Yorker* and the *Atlantic*. The photos of her were mostly group shots at company outings like baseball games or the occasional benefit or black-tie event. She was very pretty and seemed tall. Jackie loved tall women. He loved being able to look a woman in the eye.

He had mentioned his connection with a woman in the group briefly to Lee and Skip when he filled them in on the thrashing he had taken for the tampon post. They had both laughed at him.

"What I like most in a woman is her unavailability," Lee jokingly imitated Jackie.

Jackie defended himself. "Men meet women online all the time now!"

"Yes, but not men pretending to be women," Lee retorted.

"That's you, Tootsie," Skip added, laughing at both his own joke and Jackie's bent logic.

Truth was, Jackie loved a good roadblock. He had been with a handful of meaningless women over the years since Ann died, but the only other woman he had mentioned crushing on before was a client. It was against company rules to fraternize with clients, and he was a big rule follower, so he never saw it through. This ruse he was involved in now might be the most unconventional thing he'd ever done. He wished he could undo it. Maybe he should just come out right now and tell her that he was a dude, but instead responded with:

That's become my theme song lately. I pathetically brought home dinner, dessert, and a movie tonight without asking Jana first, and she had plans. I think it may be time I get a life as well. I watch so many of those medical shows on TV; I swear I could do a thoracostomy.

Me too! I think I could even do one with a ballpoint pen!

Actually, you may have to clock a few more hours at Seattle
Grace Hospital. I think you're referring to a cricothyrotomy.

Hahaha! What about those fire department shows?

Love them. Fire department! Call out!

Yup! Me too. And I watch all those shows with the initials.

Please, CSI, FBI, SVU, NCIS. I can figure out who the unsub is
before any of them can.

Ha! Who needs a man when you can spend your nights with a
whole cast of them? We should ask for vibrator
recommendations on the bulletin board—then we can really be
all set.

Not quite the relationship goal Jackie was hoping for. He typed
and deleted and typed and deleted. He was at a total loss. On the
receiving end of his radio silence, Alison wrote back in a panic:

Only kidding.

She realized she might have made Jackie uncomfortable. She
reflected on how they met and felt foolish for thinking that a
tampon-fearing woman would enjoy a sex-toy joke. What was she
thinking? She waited for a response, but still nothing.

Are you there?

Sorry, I ran upstairs to my nightstand to look through my bag of tricks.

Alison laughed from her gut. What a relief.

Ha. Do tell!

This time, *I'm* only kidding.

OMG. Maybe we should end this conversation.

Good idea. Have a good night, and good luck with your new friend, and I'm not referring to a dildo.

Haha! And thanks. I'm taking her to the city on Monday to meet with my detective friend. Hopefully, she can help us figure things out.

Hope so. Keep me posted.

CHAPTER 16

Amanda & Eliza

Amanda looked out across her lawn in time to see Luke packing up the car with suitcases. As the twins left the house, she realized that if she didn't run over right away, she wouldn't get to see them. Well, this time at least; she wasn't so sure she wouldn't still be here when they came home for Thanksgiving. She threw on her shoes and ran across the street. Kayla saw her first.

"Aunt Mandy!"

They embraced. Luke and Kevin put down the bags and followed suit.

"Wow! I have to look up at you now!" Mandy said to Kevin.

"Well, it's been a couple of years, I think."

"It has. Too many," she said, hugging both the kids again.

"On Wisconsin!" she added awkwardly with her fist in the air. They both laughed.

"Where's Mom?"

"She's inside." Kayla pointed toward the front door with her chin.

"Go in. She's not coming to the airport," Luke added.

"We have to fly, literally," Kevin chimed in, realizing the time.

Amanda waved goodbye from the driveway, as Eliza did from the living room window. They caught each other's eye and their hearts both swelled. Eliza waved her in. They embraced in the front hall where any bad feelings about who had called who last immediately disintegrated. They had grown up like sisters, and each of them could really use a sister right now.

"Welcome home!" Eliza hugged her again. "How are the girls?"

A hug from Eliza felt like a bacon, egg, and cheese on a roll after a night of excessive drinking—the cure.

"They're hanging in there. Your kids are so big, it's crazy! You didn't want to go to the airport?"

"Nah. It makes me sad."

Amanda looked at her skeptically. Eliza was all about fanfare. The high drama of an airport goodbye was the equivalent of a Broadway show in her books.

Eliza quickly changed the subject. "How long are you planning to stay?"

"I don't know. It's not safe for us there. The paparazzi are relentless and even my so-called friends will be talking behind my back."

"Ugh. It must be good to be home."

"It is. Dorothy was right. There's no place like it."

They looked each other over, standing in Eliza's foyer. They could still see the girls they once were under the fine lines that had developed around their eyes. Amanda was infinitely more kempt, but stress had taken its toll on them both. They both had the same choice to make—open up to the one person they could truly trust or keep up the silly banter that barely scratched the surface. Eliza's face registered concern. Mandy recognized it.

"What? What is it?"

"You're just so thin, I mean, even for you."

"I haven't had much of an appetite."

"That never happens to me. Come on, I'll make you something. I have a ton of leftovers and I want to hear the whole story with Carson."

Even after all of these years, Eliza didn't know very much about Carson Cole. Only the little scraps that Mandy fed her and the occasional mention in *People* magazine. He was a decade older than Amanda and not attractive in a conventional way—or in any way. He was diminutive in size but turned on the charm on a dime. His dime. It was probably why so many women ended up alone with him. That, and of course his ability to make or break them.

Hudson Valley was very far from Hollywood and Amanda was always careful to paint a pretty picture for Eliza and the world to see. It was hard to know where to begin, or if she even had the strength to reveal the truth. She followed Eliza to the kitchen and began with the here and now.

"I'm raw, enraged, humiliated, and just sick about all of it. Obviously, it goes so far beyond infidelity. I think people assume I'm complicit—that I must have known what was going on. And if I say I didn't know, they say, 'How could she not have known?'"

"Well, you didn't know, and you only have to answer to yourself and your girls."

Eliza noticed her wince when she brought up her girls. She couldn't imagine having to explain such things to her own children.

Amanda peeled off her shoes and saddled up to the counter on the same stool she'd been climbing on since she needed a boost. It didn't take long for her armor to come off as well.

"Dealing with the girls is the hardest part. They would *never* have put up with what I did. And I'm the one who taught them to be that way, to speak out, to stand up for themselves."

As usual, thinking about her girls and what this was doing to them sent her mind reeling. She worried about them endlessly. How would they ever trust a man if their own father made them cringe in disgust? She was especially worried about Sadie. At just eleven, Sadie still pretty much worshipped her father, and people were bound to say horrible things about him to her. Even if they didn't, the newspapers, the Internet, and the magazines at the checkout counter would all be waiting to fill her in on the tawdry details. There was no hiding from it. She thought her older daughter, Pippa, seemed to know more than she let on. People talk, and Pippa had always seemed to have eyes in the back of her head. She admonished herself again for not leaving when they were younger. They were probably embarrassed by her as much as they were by Carson. Two girls brought up in the midst of the "Me Too" movement by a mother who remained silent.

She took a deep breath and spoke the painful truth. "I taught them to be brave, while I acted like a coward."

Eliza thought about her own daughter, about her own silence, while responding. "You're being very brave now, and they will learn from that."

Amanda wanted to believe her, but it was hard.

Eliza continued. "I'm so sorry I haven't been there for you. I had no idea."

"It's not your fault. I went to LA to become an actress, right?" She laughed. "I could win an Oscar for my performance as the happy wife."

"I'm your best friend. I should have seen through it."

"How could you have? I wasn't exactly honest with you over the years—or with myself really. I wasn't even completely honest with my therapist because I didn't want to deal with her advice. There were so many times that I almost told you. But once I did I feared there would be no turning back. You would never have let me continue living like that."

Eliza understood that more than Mandy could ever know. They were both members of a different silent generation. As she placed her plate in the microwave, she assured her, "I understand, really I do. But there's no point in bottling it up now, right? You left. You're here. We are here, together."

With that the floodgates opened. The conversation was tough. Painful to hear and painful to speak. But having someone know all she had been through over the years brought Amanda an unimaginable release. She spoke in great detail about everything that had happened and the effects that years of emotional abuse had had on her. It was painful to relive, and by the time she took her first bite of food it was cold again. She struggled to swallow.

"It's cold again," she muttered, sounding more like a child than a woman.

They both laughed as Eliza took her fork and placed her plate back in the microwave. Amanda watched her closely; her right eye twitched and she was all buttoned up to her neck.

What is she hiding?

"Why didn't you go to the airport, Eliza?"

Even though Amanda was sitting in front of her cracked wide open, Eliza fell back into her usual m.o. and went for the joke: "The FOGO—it's back again."

"Fogo?"

"I renamed it, as part of my plan to combat my waning relevancy—fear of going out."

Mandy knew Eliza wanted her to laugh, but she didn't give in. It wasn't funny then, and it certainly wasn't funny now. Eliza saw the concern on Mandy's face and came clean.

"I've hardly been able to leave the house since the twins' graduation."

"Oh, Eliza." Mandy took her nail-bitten hands between her manicured ones. "Do you know what triggered it?"

"I have no idea." She looked away as she said it, and Mandy knew she was lying. It was the same thing she'd said in high school—she didn't believe it then, and she didn't believe it now.

Mandy remembered the day Eliza first retreated to her house like it was yesterday. They were supposed to meet after school by her locker, as they always did, to walk home. Mandy waited and waited, and finally left without her. When she went to Eliza's house, her mom said she wasn't feeling well and had "taken to her room." She remembered her exact words, remembered thinking it was such an old-fashioned way to put it. She went back every day after school for a week, and when Eliza's mother still wouldn't let her in, she climbed through the window. She was all set to ask Eliza what the hell was going on, but one look at her and she thought better of it. She would climb back in every day after school and just lie next to her friend, running her hand through Eliza's hair or gently tickling her arm, if Eliza would allow it. Eventually she asked, "Did something happen to you, Eliza?" Just like today, Eliza insisted that nothing had. On both occasions Mandy knew it was a lie, but she didn't push her. She could tell, even after all of this time, that she still wasn't ready to say more. She loved her so much and didn't want to cause her pain.

"I'm so, so sorry. Is Luke being supportive? The kids?"

"No one knows, Mandy, no one, except now you. All summer I'd get dressed to go wherever we were headed, and half the time I couldn't make it. I made excuses. By the time we brought the twins to college, it had come back in full force."

"Why don't you tell Luke? Eliza, he's your husband. He adores you. He would do anything for you."

"I've tried, but I just can't. I feel like I lied to him to begin with by never telling him that it happened in high school."

She put the plate back down and continued. "Some days are better than others. I've never been a big fan of crowds, or elevators, and he knows that, but to just spill this on him like it's out of the blue, when it's not—it seems so wrong."

"Not telling him is wrong, too."

"I know." Her eyes filled with tears. "He would want so desperately to fix me. The pressure of that—the pressure that would come from him knowing—it's too much."

Amanda rubbed her arm. "I'm so sorry."

"I just have to get through it. Remember how back then it just ended one day? Inexplicably."

From her time in therapy, Mandy knew that this wasn't the best plan, but she decided to wait before pushing her further.

"We'll figure it out. I'm glad I can be here for you. It must be lonely."

Eliza did not want to figure anything out. She joked again, "It is. Thank God for Alexa!"

This time Amanda laughed at her joke, and then laughed harder at her own thoughts.

"What's so funny? Tell me," Eliza begged.

They lived to make each other giggle, and it felt good to slip back into their old roles, especially after all of the serious discussion.

"I just pictured you chatting with Alexa all day: 'Alexa, tell me I make the best three-bean dip in all of Hudson Valley!' 'Alexa, play "Only the Lonely."'"

Eliza playfully swatted her on the arm, laughing with her.

"I've managed to entertain myself in other ways. Come upstairs." As she led Mandy down the hall, she explained her grocery store encounter.

"So I checked it out and Valley Girls was getting way more action than my site. Until last week." She laughed with a slightly villainous tone.

Amanda looked at her suspiciously. She often kept up with the life she was missing back east by scrolling through the Hudson Valley Ladies' Bulletin Board, but she hadn't recently. There was a similar group in Beverly Hills called LA Mommies, but it had a very different vibe—lots of posts complaining about the paparazzi taking up all of the parking spots at the Coldwater Canyon playground, or whether gyrotonics or bumplants (butt implants) are the best way to a Kardashian derriere.

Eliza pulled her by the hand.

"I have to show you what's been going on. We have scandals in the boring suburbs, too!"

CHAPTER 17

Alison & Olivia

Alison and Olivia took the 11:00 a.m. train into the city without their babies in tow. It was a first for both of them.

"I'm nervous. I've never left Lily for the whole day," Olivia said as they boarded the train. Alison suppressed a laugh because Olivia had been the one to convince Alison to leave the babies home with her "overly capable" sitter.

"Two babies are a walk in the park!" Olivia's babysitter, Colleen, had assured Alison in response to her long list of instructions regarding Zach.

In contrast, Alison felt fine as soon as they left. More than fine, actually. She was amazed at how quickly she adapted to the freedom of not being bound to an infant. She was feeling a bit giddy about it, and it was not a very familiar emotion. She controlled herself; after all, this trip was not exactly sold as a fun outing. She correctly assumed that leaving Lily was not at the root of Olivia's anxiety.

As they stepped off the train at Grand Central Station, Alison felt her inner New Yorker come alive. She couldn't keep her focus on one thing; her eyes darted from left to right, taking it all in. Her pace picked up considerably, and she noticed that Olivia was right in step. *This is what I've been missing in the suburbs*, she thought with a sigh. She wondered if Olivia felt the same.

"It feels good to be back, doesn't it?" Alison asked.

Olivia nodded in agreement, followed by an uneasy smile.

She knew that, for Alison, the "country" was a means to an end, that end being a return to the city at some point in her future. But, Olivia thought, she herself had closed that chapter of her life. Just that morning, when she had looked out the window at the ever-changing landscape, she'd been filled with excitement at the thought of their first snowfall in the country. She pictured reading by a roaring fire, the current red-hued panorama dipped in white. She could tell that it didn't mean as much to Alison. As if to prove it, when they stepped out of the station, Alison dramatically breathed in the distinct smells of hosed-down pavement and food cart falafel and sighed, as if they were the smells of heaven.

"Want to walk?" she asked eagerly. "It's just twenty blocks."

"Sure," Olivia agreed. She did love a good walk up Madison Avenue.

As they window-shopped and chatted their way uptown, Alison marveled at how talkative Olivia became. She seemed to have forgotten where they were headed and why, and Alison had no intention of reminding her. The familiarity of every step sparked Olivia's memories of growing up on the Upper East Side.

"We used to eat french fries and gravy in that coffee shop nearly every day after school," she said, "and that's where I got my prom dress!"

Alison had bought her own prom dress at a resale shop on Astoria Boulevard. *Some Manhattan girl, like Olivia, had prob-*

ably worn it to prom the year before, she thought. This little sab-
batical in the suburbs aside, Alison was convinced that she would
be bringing up Zach in the city. She was very interested in hearing
about the schools and lifestyles of city kids. There had been plenty
of Olivia's type at Wesleyan. They had a quiet sophistication
about them, especially the private school kids, who were so me-
ticulously educated that college classes seemed to be a breeze for
them. She had already begun worrying about school admissions
for Zachary.

"I hear the private school admission process is a real nightmare," she said. "I'm not looking forward to it."

Olivia grew quiet.

"What is it? What's wrong?" Alison inquired.

"If this is all true, my whole life will be uprooted. I mean, I
thought I was set for the next twenty years with my modern house,
loyal husband, and two-point-three kids attending one of the top-
ranking schools in the county. But that county is Spencer's. I'm the
city girl. I think Lily and I would be expected to move back to the
city, right? Then I will have to go through all of that school stuff
alone."

"Well, not really. Spencer will always be her father."

Olivia's eyes filled with fear. Alison's expertise in recognizing
the subtle changes in people's emotions was not needed here. Olivia rushed to the corner garbage pail, gripped it with both hands,
and vomited.

As Alison rubbed her hand up and down Olivia's back for comfort, she thanked her lucky stars that Marc Sugarman wanted no
part in Zachary's life. Whether guilty or innocent, Olivia would
be dealing with Spencer York when making every major decision
in Lily's life for as long as they both shall live.

Alison would never describe herself as a warm person, but she
felt surprisingly motherly toward Olivia. Sisterly would probably

be more appropriate, she thought, considering the ten years between them. She pointed to a bench across the street.

"Do you want to take a minute?"

"No. Let's just keep going. I'll never be ready for this; I feel like I'm headed for my execution."

"I know this is awful, but it's the best course of action you can take. Plus, Andie Rand is wonderful, and my closest friend. We're not walking into some seedy office to meet with a man in a trench coat." Olivia shook her head up and down, and Alison took it as a sign to proceed.

Andie was wonderful, as Alison knew she would be. She really got Olivia to relax. She listened to her whole story and took down a complete timeline of the relationship. Alison noticed that she didn't ask pointed questions about Spencer's character or whether he had a history of dishonesty. It struck her as odd, as she definitely would have dug into those tough subjects to get a sense of what they were up against. But Andie's next question explained her approach.

"So, before I give you any advice, I have something to ask you. You need to sit with it and answer with complete honesty." She took a beat while Olivia agreed. "What will you do if we find out that Spencer is cheating?"

Olivia did not need to sit with that question. She had been sitting with that question since it first entered her mind.

"I will divorce him," she said firmly. Andie was not letting her off that easy.

"You say that, but what if in the end he is completely remorseful or offers any number of mitigating circumstances."

"I will divorce him. I am a twenty-eight-year-old feminist woman intent on raising a feminist daughter. We are just starting out on this journey together. There are no circumstances that would make me suck it up."

Alison looked at her new friend with pride. Andie was more skeptical and pressed further.

"So, you're saying that if we proceed and gather evidence against him, and if he reacts by falling to the floor in tears and hysterics and tells you he has made a terrible mistake and will do anything to keep you and your family together, you won't consider it? You'd still want a divorce?"

Olivia paused to think, but the lawyer in Alison believed it was just a tactic to demonstrate to Andie that she was taking her line of questioning seriously.

"There is no doubt in my mind: If he's been cheating, I would want a divorce, especially since Lily is too young to know any differently."

Alison was too curious about Andie's process not to ask. "Why does this make a difference in how we would proceed?"

Every time Alison said "we," Olivia counted her blessings.

Andie explained. "There are many tools that we can use to get to the bottom of this relatively quickly, but most of them involve some kind of surveillance. If you want to divorce, then it doesn't really matter if you read his emails, tap his phone, go through his pockets—so be it. But if you want to stay together and work things out, this will all be a problem. He will hold your spying on him over your head just as you will hold the affair over his. I've seen it time and time again, with disastrous outcomes."

"But you're assuming guilt," Alison countered.

"OK, so let's say we do these things, and we find out he's innocent. Then what? Now you have the secret. *You* have actually betrayed *him*. I've seen that destroy a marriage as well."

They both nodded their heads as she spoke, taking in the complexities of the situation. She made good points. Alison stepped into the protective older sister role that she'd adopted.

"So, what do you suggest she does? This is torture for her."

"I know. But if this is to be done right, there are no shortcuts. Like I said when we first spoke, a cheater is a liar. They go hand in hand. You cannot trust him to tell you the truth; you have to find out the truth on your own, and then present your case. You're actually lucky. You have a first step available to you that doesn't involve surveillance."

Both Alison and Olivia sat forward in their seats to hear Andie's suggestion.

"Contact the moderator of that bulletin board and ask who Anonymous is."

Olivia was skeptical.

"What makes you think she would tell me that?"

"I'm assuming she's not a priest."

"But still. I mean, *I* wouldn't break that trust."

Andie smiled confidently. "Bring your new friend with you. Alison is the best criminal attorney in New York. She can get anyone to talk."

Alison agreed, not on being the best, but on getting the woman to turn. Andie handed Olivia a piece of paper.

"Her name is Eliza Hunt. Here's her address. Start with this and see where it leads us."

Olivia took the sheet of paper. She had seen the street name before. She already felt better with just the little bit of control this plan was affording her.

"Will you come with me?" she asked Alison.

"Of course. I'm all in."

"OK, let me know what you find out," Andie said, standing up to get things moving along. She had happily squeezed them in, but she always tried to keep half an hour between appointments to avoid any waiting room crossover. Most people who sought out her help bordered on paranoid, and often with good reason.

"What do I owe you?" Olivia asked, even though she had no idea how she would pay without Spencer knowing about it.

"All I did was a few searches. No worries," Andie said as she hugged Alison goodbye.

"Do you want one, too?" she asked Olivia, laughing.

"Please," she answered with open arms.

They decided to stop for lunch on the way back to Grand Central. On the way home they ducked into the Campbell Apartment right in Grand Central for a quick bite. It was one of those hidden New York gems that, oddly enough, neither of them had ever been to. After they were done oohing and aahing at the architecture, they settled into a cozy corner table.

They ordered deviled eggs, a cheese board, and Moscow Mules, because why not? Olivia was clearly done discussing her marriage, so Alison offered up her own baby daddy saga. She began with a statement of defense: "I am in no way comparing my drama to yours, but do you want to hear it?"

Olivia was happy for the distraction. She'd been curious about Zach's paternity from the get-go but didn't feel comfortable asking about it. She assumed Alison had used a sperm donor. She never would have pegged her for having an unplanned pregnancy; she seemed like the type that planned everything. Alison went on to tell her about her affair with Marc Sugarman.

"At first it was fun, sneaking around, and I was happy to avoid workplace gossip. I could just imagine it whipping through the courthouses like wildfire. But now, looking back, I think it was his way of making sure we didn't slip into a real relationship. We never even went to each other's apartments—only hotels."

"Do you think there was someone else?"

"No, I really don't. Whenever we crossed paths socially, he was always on his own."

"It sounds like he has commitment issues."

"For sure. In all fairness, he told me that from the beginning. He had no interest in any sort of coupling whatsoever. From the little I put together it seemed like he was the child of a bad divorce and an abusive father."

"And he hasn't been in touch since the baby was born?"

"Nope. Andie tried to convince me to send him a note afterward, but I didn't see the point. What was he going to do, send a copy of *Goodnight Moon*? He was very clear that he wanted nothing to do with us."

"I can't believe it. I mean, imagine not even caring if it's a boy or a girl."

"I'm sure he knows it's a boy. There was a pool at the criminal courthouse. Hopefully they were just taking bets on the sex, weight, and birth date and not on who's the daddy."

"I guess in a way you're lucky. You'll get to raise Zach on your own, and you won't have to deal with anyone else's opinions."

"The funny thing is, Marc has all the traits I would have looked for in a sperm donor. He's exceedingly handsome and electrically smart. Hopefully his douchebag tendencies are nurture, not nature, and I will groom Zach to be a thoughtful, benevolent human."

Alison looked at the time. She needed a few things at the Apple Store, and they had wanted to catch the 5:49.

"We've gotta run."

Olivia raised her hand for the check in response as Alison pulled out her wallet.

"Put that away. This is on me," Olivia insisted.

"Don't be silly," Alison countered in typical "who picks up the check" banter.

"I can't even begin to thank you. I mean, even if, in the end, this is all paranoia on my part, the way you stepped up and helped me to take action and not be a victim of either Spencer or of my own fears is beyond. I think I would be curled up under my covers if not for you."

"I doubt that very much. You're not giving yourself enough credit. Most women make excuses for an eternity before taking any action to get to the truth. I've never been married and have no idea what it's like, but I know that you are being extremely brave. Whatever happens, I know you will be OK."

"Do you ever want to get married?"

"If I ever find a man who's better than no man at all, I'll consider it."

Olivia laughed, both because it was funny and because it gave her hope that in the end, regardless of what happens, everything would turn out fine.

CHAPTER 18

Marc Sugarman

Marc Sugarman pulled out his phone and checked himself in selfie mode before his eleven o'clock. He typically wasn't that vain, but this wasn't a typical meeting. An exploratory committee had been formed to seek the Democratic nomination, and word was, Marc's name was at the top of their list.

It wasn't a surprise to him. He knew he was a natural choice to run for office. Although he hadn't thought a mayoral run would be his first try, he was more than willing to listen to what they had to say. He hoped that they wouldn't mention one of the more ridiculous reasons why people thought he was a viable candidate: his looks.

As he analyzed his reflection in his phone, he acknowledged that he was, in fact, exceedingly handsome. And as if that wasn't enough to tempt the more superficial constituents into thinking he was a contender, he strongly resembled the legendary mayor from the 1960s, John Lindsay. The first time he had heard it was at Yale

Law, where it was pointed out by a very senior professor who had taught them both. His girlfriend at the time looked Lindsay up and it was true; they looked eerily similar. But the resemblance ended with their looks and their shared alma mater. Lindsay was a navy man and a guest host on *Good Morning America*. He was one of those appealing guys with a Kennedyesque charm who rolled up his shirtsleeves and used his personality to overshadow many a flaw. Marc knew that the same could not be said of him. He was more likely to be described as a bit of a prick with an annoying proclivity for sarcasm and arrogance. The perfect amount of arrogance, by the way, to stand his ground on the important issues. The people of New York City would be very lucky to have him on their side. He hoped that everything he had to offer—including his stellar record in court—was enough for a successful run.

In truth, he thought, a better comparison for him would have been Rudy Giuliani. As US attorneys for the Southern District of New York, they had both amassed a record number of convictions. They had even gotten their law degrees from the same university, but at this point even Rudy Giuliani was no Rudy Giuliani. His reputation had nosedived since its peak after 9/11, so drawing parallels with him now wouldn't do Marc any good.

Marc's assistant buzzed to say that the group had arrived. He took one more look at himself before standing to greet them.

"Be charming," he ordered his reflection. He knew he had to convince them he was right for a run. His ego was big enough to believe he could do the job, but history had taught him that he wasn't all that likable. He would have to pull out all the stops to have any chance of leading the city so nice they named it twice.

Two women and a man entered, prepared to be won over. Marc greeted them with a strong handshake and a big smile. They sat on the couch, and he returned to his seat at his desk, where he fidgeted with a plastic straw with the hand they couldn't see, while gesturing demonstratively with the other. It was a trick he used in court to keep his brain from racing ahead of the questions at hand.

As was his usual game plan, Marc began as if the ball were in his court.

"So, what can I do for you?" he asked.

"Well, it's more like what can we do for you," the older of the two women answered. "We are here to discuss a possible mayoral candidacy."

"We think you have a real shot," the man chimed in.

"And why do you think that?" Marc asked in a curt tone, forgetting to lay on the charm just thirty seconds in. They didn't even try to hide their weakest motive.

"For starters, have you seen the Republican front-runner?" the older woman asked as the others laughed along.

The opposition made babies cry when they looked at him. Really. It was a phenomenon that had made him a YouTube sensation. If Marc hadn't disagreed with him on nearly every issue, he might have felt bad for the guy. He knew that his own looks had been advantageous to him, but he thought they had no effect on his success as US attorney. No one gave a crap in court that he was as handsome as Atticus Finch. It annoyed him that these people brought it up first, even in a lighthearted way.

"The vetting process is intense. If you are interested, we would need to schedule another, lengthier meeting, but there are a few nonstarters that we would like to ask about right off the bat," said the older woman, who was clearly in charge.

"All right then, batter up!" he answered with a smile, in an attempt to be endearing.

"Are you current on your state and federal taxes?"

"I am. I have a perfect record on that, audited once but nothing found."

"Great. Any skeletons in your closet, particularly in regard to the 'Me Too' movement?"

"Nothing I can think of."

"That's a good answer, but we'd appreciate it if you really thought deeply on this. People come out of the woodwork," the man added, strategically pressing the point.

"There's no one. I'm sure of it. I have always been very respectful of women."

"Are you currently in a relationship?"

"No, not at this time." He sat back in his chair, feeling confident in his viability. Until a thought entered his brain like a bullet train.

"Wait, there may be one thing you should know. But no one knows about it, so I don't think it's a problem." He paused for a few seconds. It seemed as though he was doing it for effect, but the truth was he had never said it out loud and was bracing himself to hear his truth.

"I fathered a child."

"Really?" and "How long ago?" and "Was it put up for adoption?" they asked unilaterally and with an air of panic.

"He's with the mother. He's a few months old."

"Were you helping out a friend who wanted a child?" the other woman asked, fingers crossed, no doubt. "That's considered admirable," she reassured her cohorts.

"No." *Maybe it could be spun that way*, Marc thought, but he kept that thought to himself. He added matter-of-factly, "A woman I'd been sleeping with on a regular basis got pregnant and had the baby—on her own."

The three of them huddled together in whispered conversation. Marc waited, twisting the straw in his hand until it dropped to the floor and rolled away from his desk. He watched it, wishing he could grab it back. The man spoke.

"Do you have any intention of being a father to this child, and is there a possibility of you getting back together with the mother?"

"We can't get *back* together. We were never really together like that."

"Well, you must have been somewhat together. You made a baby."

"It's no different than if I were a sperm donor."

"I'm pretty sure it is quite different," the older woman countered.

Marc shook his head slowly from left to right with no clear meaning. He was annoyed at himself for not considering this before. It was completely unlike him. The three leaned in again, and then the older woman said, "We are going to have to discuss this with the committee before moving forward."

They all stood. Marc didn't.

"We'll be in touch."

Marc had a real problem. While he wasn't scared of holding what Mayor Lindsay himself coined "the second toughest job in the country," the idea of himself as anybody's father scared the crap out of him. *Still*, he thought, *I can't let this ruin me.*

CHAPTER 19

Jackie

Jackie Campbell sat in his usual seat on the 5:49 and watched as two women bounded on like Butch and Sundance, just as the doors were closing. It made him laugh at first—that mad panic that, as a seasoned commuter and painstakingly punctual person, he never experienced. His smile broadened. Alison's face, paired with the knowledge that she'd be traveling from the city that day, sparked immediate recognition, along with a stirring of excitement he had not felt in quite a while. The train car was unusually packed, and the two women found a spot by the doors to stand. He pulled out his phone to double-check that it was indeed her. He made the mistake of asking Skip, "Hey, doesn't she look like that lady over there?"

Skip took the phone and flipped through Alison's profile pictures.

"Oooh. Nice. She does. Is that the one you've been talking to, Tootsie?"

Jackie took the phone back, shoved it in his pocket, and buried his face in the daily crossword puzzle. Skip was not letting it go. He looked at Lee, who smirked while giving him the thumbs-up. Before Jackie could beg for mercy, Skip was out of his seat.

"Ladies, please, my friend and I are happy to give up our seats for you."

"No, thank you," Alison retorted, as if the offer was insulting and absurd.

"I insist," Skip countered.

"We're good, thanks," Alison insisted back, confident she was putting it to rest.

But Olivia was not good. The Moscow mules had gone to her head while her Ferragamo mules were digging into her feet. Her breasts were engorged like cantaloupes and she kept flashing back to how she had begun the day—vomiting into a trashcan. She needed to sit and she didn't care if it went against Alison's old-school feminist protocol. She shot her friend a look of self-pity and accepted the kind offer.

"Thank you. You are too kind."

Skip brought them over to his seat and Jackie immediately rose to thwart his plan by volunteering to switch. Skip pushed him back down with his right hand while motioning to Lee to get up with his left. It was quite the smooth maneuver, and if Jackie weren't so pissed, he would have been impressed. The two women sat, Olivia next to Jackie and Alison across from him.

One look at her up close and he forgot to be angry with his friends. He watched as she adjusted her long legs and tucked an errant strand of her black silky hair behind her ear just for it to fall back out again a second later. He imagined it was a common occurrence. He pictured himself in her company, tucking it back for her. He blushed and smiled.

Alison was set not to give any of the chivalrous men the time of day, but when the one across from her flashed a sexy, almost nervous smile, she couldn't help but notice his deep brown eyes and angular jaw, and smile back. Both on the tall side, Alison and Jackie adjusted and readjusted their legs to give each other space but at last they gave up, their knees slightly resting against each other's. Alison relished that weird sensation of touching a stranger while Jackie played over his previous online interactions in his head with the woman whose knees were now intimate with his. He looked down at the crossword, reading the same clue over and over again, painfully aware of the opportunity in front of him.

Within minutes Olivia, exhausted from trauma and alcohol, nodded off. A few head drops later, and she unconsciously landed on Jackie's shoulder. Alison held back a laugh as she leaned over Olivia to straighten her head. Within seconds it dropped right back on Jackie's shoulder. Her laugh escaped.

"I'm so sorry. I'll move her."

Jackie, who knew what poor Olivia was going through, stopped her.

"Don't worry about it. I fall asleep on this train all the time, and it looks like she's had a hard day."

"She has. Thanks."

Jackie looked down at the stranger resting on his shoulder, and he and Alison shared another smile. He looked up to see Lee and Skip making foolish motions to him. He shot them a death look. They didn't care. He stared out the window to discourage them from any further shenanigans as the train passed the Columbia University stadium, sped through a tunnel, and emerged in the beauty of the Palisades. He was usually content to gaze out the window watching the changing leaves on the tree-topped cliffs or the occasional sailboat gliding up or down the Hudson depending on the tide. Sometimes his thoughts would wander to the houses cut into the rocky cliffs, wondering who lives there and if they ever stare out at the passing trains in the distance and wonder about him. But not today. Today he was trying to come up with something witty to say to his seatmate. Quite proficient in reading upside down, Alison beat him to it.

"Thirty-two across, Russian peasant is 'muzhik'—M-U-Z-H-I-K."

Jackie smiled. "Thanks!" They bumped knees again and Jackie apologized.

"Sorry, long legs and packed trains don't mix."

"Is this train always this crowded?"

"It can be. But I have it down to a science. I know exactly where to stand so that I match up with the doors to this car no matter which track the train is on," he said with pride, followed quickly by embarrassment upon realizing the nerdiness of his comment. She quickly negated his fears.

"That's brilliant. If I ever decide to commute, I'm going to find you for a tutorial."

That was it. Her interest in efficiency trumped even her black silky hair. Jackie was real-life smitten. He thought about impressing her further with his commuting prowess, letting her know that there are four bridges, two marinas, and two tunnels between here and his stop and that he's timed them all out so that he never has to look at his watch—but decided against it. He went with a question instead.

"What do you do?" he asked, already knowing.

"I'm a criminal attorney in the city, but I'm on extended maternity leave—trying out the suburbs for a bit."

"That's nice. My daughter wants to be an attorney. Well, this week at least. How do you like the suburbs so far?"

"I like it, for now. I love the peace and quiet. And I feel like I'm bonding with my baby without a hundred things pulling me away from him. But I'm pretty sure it's temporary."

Jackie considered asking about her husband, to indicate that he was interested in her. For a successful, good-looking, single guy he was surprisingly inept at picking up women. He knew that's the way it was often done in the movies, but it felt too dishonest since he knew the answer. He was happy when she went for that line of questioning herself.

"Does your wife commute, too?"

"It's just me and my daughter."

Alison became uncomfortable realizing what her question implied. She'd been seriously asking about his marital status to further her fact-finding mission on the efficacy of commuting while single parenting. Her trip to Manhattan, and spending time in Andie's office, had her mind ricocheting to her future. Could she actually do it alone in the suburbs, or was it more prudent to move back? How could she leave Zachary without support close by just in case?

He took her being lost in thought as the end to their conversation and readdressed his crossword. She wished she had brought something to read and gazed out the window, the passing trees hypnotizing her into a trancelike state. She could feel the heat of his leg close to hers. The sliver of space between them felt electrically charged. She snuck a good look at him—he was tall, dark, and handsome, but with just the perfect hint of dorkiness. Picture Idris Elba playing an accountant.

Jackie became suddenly aware that not asking her if she were married in return may imply disinterest. He had already definitively decided the opposite. He couldn't believe the funny woman he had been so comfortable talking to online actually looked like she did. He caught her eye.

"How about you?"

"How about me what?" She laughed.

He laughed, too. "Husband? Kids?"

"Never married. Single mama of a four-month-old baby boy. How old is your daughter?"

"Fifteen years this Christmas."

"That must have been a nice Christmas gift."

That Christmas had been the worst day of Jackie's entire life. He knew it registered on his face, but there was no way he was going down that road. He'd made that mistake before—no buzz-kill worse than telling someone that your wife died in childbirth.

"I'm not big on Christmas."

"Really, why?"

He shared his second reason for disliking the holiday instead.

"Because whenever I did something wrong as a kid my mom would say, 'Santa is watching.' It was like I had to be good three hundred sixty-four days a year just to impress this one fat white dude." Alison laughed. She had a real, from-the-gut laugh, and he liked it.

"You must have been pissed when you found out he wasn't real."

"What? He's not real?"

She laughed again.

Poor Olivia snored, and they laughed even harder. Alison thought there was something so sweet about the way he was letting Olivia sleep on his shoulder. It really touched her.

"What stop is yours?" she asked. "I'll wake her before we get there."

"Hudson Valley."

"Me too! I just moved there."

Her exuberance was twofold. She was definitely crushing on this guy, so it would be fun to possibly run into him again, but also, she was glad there would be a hard stop to their conversation. She had never mastered ending a casual flirtation gracefully; in fact, starting one was not her forte either. Flirting always felt disingenuous. It was one of the reasons her relationship with Marc was so easy for her. It was very wham, bam, thank you, sir.

Jackie looked out the window as they sped through the last tunnel of their ride. Hudson Valley peeked out from the rocks and the river on the other side, indicating that there wasn't much time left. If he didn't make his move, he may not get another shot. He went for it.

"We should exchange numbers in case you have any questions about the town or commuting or whatnot."

"Sure, that would be nice. Thanks."

He handed her his phone for her to type in her number, like the suave person that he wasn't. The train was coming to the station as she pressed Send. He took back his phone as she woke an embarrassed Olivia. He stood up to give them space. When he got into his car, he read her text:

Hope to see you again—Alison.

He wrote back:

Let's make sure of it—Jackie.

He looked at it again before pressing Send and removed the I and the E:

Jack.

CHAPTER 20

Eliza & Amanda

Amanda waited with bated breath for Pippa and Sadie to return home from their first day of school. She was not worried about Sadie, who was totally agreeable, but about Pippa, who was not. She put the odds of her walking through the door happy at about four percent. Amanda's dad saw her pacing and consoled her, "It's OK, Mandy. You did the right thing. We did OK on our own, didn't we?"

It was meant to make her feel better, but it did the opposite. She never wanted her kids to be children of divorce like she was. It was one of the reasons she had stuck it out for so long with Carson. Her initial impetus for running east was to let them take some time off for mental health and to pull them out of the spotlight, but her lawyer decimated that idea before they even got their luggage at the airport. She called Amanda straight away, in response to the email Amanda had sent her from the plane. She didn't even say hello.

"Amanda! What, are you crazy? You're not allowed to run off to New York with your kids. Your domicile is in California. Carson could say you kidnapped them! Come back and file a motion for relocation!"

The luggage on the carousel seemed to be going in one direction, and Amanda's head in the other. She had not slept one minute on that plane. No way was she turning around and going back. She hung up and called her husband at the hotel where he was hiding. She knew from years of experience that she was well within his window of remorse—that short time after an altercation during which she would have the upper hand. She imagined this particular window to be akin to the observation deck atop the Empire State Building, given the circumstances.

"Carson. I thought, considering the paparazzi swarming outside of our house, it was smart to take the kids to my dad's for a bit. I'm sure you agree it's what's best for them."

It was very early in LA, and between that and the fact that she wasn't screaming at him, she found him to be quite docile. He almost sounded beaten. She knew better than to think it would last.

"What about school?" he asked.

She thought on her feet. "I'll sign them up in Hudson Valley for a few weeks."

"You can do that?"

"Sure. Why not?"

"OK, just until this blows over."

The fact that he thought this was something to blow over enraged Amanda. But she kept her eye on the prize, strategically adding, "Can you email me a note for the school? Something like, I give permission for my children Sadie and Pippa Cole to enroll in the Hudson Valley school system?"

"Of course, I'll do it when we hang up."

"Perfect, thank you," she said, ending the call before things could go south.

Kidnapping, my ass, she'd thought. It may have been the most civil conversation they ever had. The front door swung open. The girls were home.

It was Pippa who entered the kitchen first, doing her very best to suppress a smile. She lost the battle: a huge grin covered her face.

"There are auditions for the Shakespeare troupe after school tomorrow. They're putting on *Measure for Measure*. Will we be here long enough?"

Amanda could not believe what she was hearing. Since birth, it was quite obvious that Pippa was a natural actress. They would marvel about how she could turn it on and off in an instant. She was the poster child for Drama Queen in a way that was instinctive, yet totally in her control. But anytime Amanda suggested she take an acting class or audition for something at school, Pippa had shut her down. Amanda was never sure if it was just typical daughter mother defiance or a child not wanting to be in the family business, but Pippa would never even consider it. Amanda knew she should just answer the question, but that motherly need to know won out.

"Sure, we can be. But, I'm curious, why the change of heart about acting?" She wanted to grab the words back as soon as they left her lips, a reaction she was experiencing more and more now that Pippa was a teenager.

"I don't know. It seemed so different from at home." She looked at her grandpa to explain. "Back home everyone wants to be an actress. And even at school, if I tried out for something, I would be trying out as the big producer Carson Cole's daughter. Here I'll just be the new girl."

She looked back at her mom. "It's cool." She placed a piece of paper on the table. "Here's the permission slip and parent volunteer stuff. You can volunteer if you want. I don't mind."

Wow, Amanda thought, on so many levels.

Pippa grabbed a few cookies from the table, freshly baked by Eliza.

"I'm gonna go read the script."

"Do you want me to come up and run lines with you for the audition?" Amanda asked, hopefully.

"Please, no," Pippa replied with her usual disgust.

And she's back, Amanda thought.

Her easy child, Sadie, piped in with a mouth full of cookie. "Mommy, did you make these? They are so delicious, thank you."

Amanda just smiled, not wanting to lie, but not wanting to give up the admiration in her daughter's eyes.

"You want some milk?"

"Yes, please."

They sat together at the same kitchen table where Amanda had sat at Sadie's age, telling tales of her day to her own mother and, later, to her father. He had tried his best to get home early enough to be both a mom and a dad to Amanda. She remembered the pain that she felt when her parents first separated. She looked for it in Sadie. So far, she only saw a spirited resilience.

"Can I go watch TV?" she blurted, little pieces of cookie spraying from her mouth. They both laughed.

"Of course. Go on, honey." Sadie hugged her before she ran off, two more cookies in hand. Amanda picked up the volunteer form and glanced at it.

"I'm going to Eliza's!" she shouted out to her dad, as she had a zillion times before.

Across the street, Eliza was sitting at her desk, trolling her site and eating her "breakfast." Activity on the bulletin board had been growing in leaps and bounds since Eliza's fictional post had stirred things up. In comparison, the Valley Girls posts seemed disingenuous. Eliza spent a lot of her not-so-precious time lately comparing the two, and although she knew she wasn't completely objective, she enjoyed scrolling through her own site much more. Valley Girls seemed to be made up of lots of new mothers asking rookie questions of other new mothers. The greatest example being:

My son just fell and is bleeding profusely. What should I do?

Their responses were even more comedic, as if they believed that nearly every problem could be cured by squirting a little breast milk on it or rubbing on some coconut oil. And some of the anonymous posts felt more like posturing than sincerely engaging with the community:

My husband wants to try breastfeeding. Should I let him?

In contrast, the anonymous posts on the Hudson Valley Ladies' Bulletin Board, which proved to be the key to catapulting the conversation out of the Dark Ages, were smart and often made her laugh out loud.

Does anyone else feel like they have sexual chemistry with Bart, the guy behind the deli counter at the Stop & Shop?

General consensus: Yes!
Favorite comment: "I love when he says, 'I have your pound of meat right here.'"

Do I have to go with my husband for my bitchy mother-in-law's birthday visit every year? He always says "This could be her last!"

General consensus: Mixed.

Favorite comment: "It depends. Are you her health proxy?"

Even some of the regular posts seemed more brazen:

Looking for ways to spice up my sex life. Any suggestions?

Favorite comment: "C-O-C-O-N-U-T."

Followed by an ambiguous: If you know, you know.

According to the whopping 163 comments that followed, no one knew. Finally, the commenter returned to explain that she moves her hips in the direction of the letters during sex and it drives her husband crazy.

There were also posts that reminded her of the reason she started the bulletin board to begin with—to harness the collective power of the women in her community. Last month they organized a meal train for the family of a woman recovering from heart surgery. And today a post about a missing dog named Truffles Goldstein was getting a lot of attention.

Eliza was knee-deep in the dog post when Amanda interrupted her. She had barged into Eliza's house, knocking with one hand while letting herself in with her spare key with the other. She yelled from the foyer, "Eliza! Where are you? Are you alone?"

"I'm upstairs with my lover—a breakfast burrito."

Amanda took the stairs two at a time. Being in her childhood home, and Eliza's, was infusing her with a long-lost and deeply satisfying sense of nostalgia. Quite a miracle really, since she was in the middle of the biggest crisis of her adult life. She found her friend at the computer, her mouth full of tortilla, eggs, and avocado.

"Eliza, it's four o'clock."

"Well, I just got out of bed."

"That's not good—even though your FOGO is as much of a comfort to me as that burrito is to you."

Eliza laughed. "Why, because I'm always here when you need me?"

"Exactly. The cookies were a big hit, by the way. They won't be happy coming home to store-bought anymore."

"Well, not to worry. I send batches up to school for the twins and their friends weekly. I am happy to add in more for your girls."

Amanda held up the volunteer form for Pippa's play.

"Good. Should I sign up for snack volunteer?"

"That would be *me* volunteering, no? Find something that you enjoy. This may be the perfect distraction for you."

Eliza grabbed the sheet and skimmed it. Amanda already had and was cautiously excited about the last bolded request.

"Look here." She pointed to it for Eliza to read.

"You know it's Pippa who will be in the play, not you, right?"

"Yes, I'm very happy for her. Read the last part."

She complied, reading it out loud for effect: "As many of you know, my usual AD is out on maternity leave. We are looking for a parent with theater experience for the assistant director position. Any takers?"

Amanda did her best soft-shoe, followed by jazz hands. "Ta-da!"

Eliza laughed. "It sounds perfect, Mandy. Now let's just hope Pippa gets a part."

That was not a worry for Amanda. She responded confidently, "Pippa will get the lead!"

CHAPTER 21

Alison & Jackie

That night, Alison enjoyed bathing Zachary and getting him to
bed more than usual. As much fun as she had had in the city
with Olivia, she had missed her baby boy. She wondered if she
would get used to missing him when she went back to the office.
All of these feelings were surprising to her. She remembered snapping at a senior partner at her firm when he asked how she would
balance it all after her baby was born.

She'd said, "Did you ask Ken Straub how he would balance it
all when he had a kid?" knowing full well that he hadn't. She loved
not answering a question by deeming it unworthy, when in truth
she didn't know the answer. She still hadn't a clue.

She watched Zach blissfully asleep in his crib for a few minutes
and then went downstairs to the kitchen. The appetizers she and
Olivia had shared at Grand Central left her at that hard-to-satisfy
junction between needing a snack and a meal. She decided to
count it as dinner and went right to dessert. She hunkered down
on the couch with a pint of Halo Top Peanut Butter Cup ice cream,

a spoon, and her laptop. Before long she was immersed in the Hudson Valley Ladies' Bulletin Board, caught up in the story of the missing shepherd/retriever, Truffles Goldstein.

The photo of Truffles's sweet face swaddled in the arms of an equally sweet-faced little boy was enough to gain any and all sympathies. At least that's what Alison imagined. The comments were mixed.

Most people said helpful things, like:

Alert the local shelters, in case someone brings him there.

If you message me Lost Dog signs, I'm happy to print them and put them up!

Me too!

Me three!

Along with some nasty comments, like:

It breaks my heart when people leave their dogs tied up outside a store.

How important is a fancy cup of coffee?

Some people shouldn't own a dog.

Alison messaged Jackie:

Did you read what happened outside of the Café Karma Sutra? Not very Zen! At least they have moved on from Tampongate and are now bashing this poor dog owner!

Jackie was sitting on his couch watching *The Bachelor* with Jana. He had actually taken the advice to do so from a very helpful conversation on the bulletin board on ways to connect with your teenager. It turned out to be quite the resource for a parent trying to be both a mom and a dad. Jana was into it.

When he saw the message from Alison, he was torn. On the ride home from the station, he had decided that his best bet was to only talk to her as Jack from the train. Eventually he could tell her the truth—no harm, no foul. When the commercial break came, and Jana pulled out her phone (the bulletin board advice included instructions about not complaining if your daughter pulled out the phone during commercials), Jackie did the same. Watching all of this dating on TV motivated him. He texted Alison:

> Great meeting you today. Are you free for dinner one night this
> week?

The show came back on, and he put down his phone, pretending to be all in. To be clear, he was at least halfway in. He found the show oddly compelling. A particularly dramatic scene involving two of the participants and a hot tub was playing out, but he was having a hard time concentrating. By the time the deciding rose ceremony was over and there was still no response from Alison, he was feeling an awful lot like the poor girls being sent home on the show. He admonished himself for writing such a forward first text, broke down, and slipped back into his Tootsie role (pun intended). *I will just respond to this one last conversation*, he promised himself.

> Hi, I didn't read the bulletin board today, but I will check it out.
> Sounds scandalous! Speaking of . . . how did it go today with
> your friend?

Great for me and good for my friend, too. She now has a plan of
action, and I think having a plan is helpful for her state of mind.

Bugging out that she wasn't responding to his text, he pressed on:

What was so great for you?

It was fun to be in the city again and to see my college friend.
And . . . I met a cute guy on the train.

Thank the lord!, he thought. He loved this instant messaging
thing. There he was grinning like a fool while typing like he was
cool AF. He joked:

I thought you had sworn off dating.

He knew it was wrong, but he couldn't help it. He promised he
would stop after this.

I know I said that, but you know, a girl has needs.

Damn. Abort. Abort. He had no idea how to respond. He
didn't have to because . . .

Aaaah! I just looked at my phone, he already texted me. He
wants to have dinner. I'm not usually this easily smitten. I think
this baby thing has made me soft.

It can have that effect. I'll let you go.

He can wait, what should I say? Should I go for dinner or ask to
meet him for coffee? I can suggest we meet at Karma Sutra.

I'm going straight to hell, Jackie thought. Yet it didn't stop him from getting what he wanted.

> Go for dinner. You can have a glass of wine; get to know each
> other.

> OK, very true. I'm answering now.

Jackie's phone dinged.

> Sure, that would be great. I'll get a sitter. Do you want to try for
> Thursday night?

Jackie answered the text:

> Perfect! I will make a reservation in town.

She came back to Jackie. He anxiously watched the dots on the screen indicating she was typing.

> I have a date! Thursday night. I'm actually excited! Maybe the
> rejection by Zachary's dad affected me more than I knew, but I
> feel great that someone is interested in me. I may even shave!

Jackie laughed and tried to fall back into Tootsie character by repeating a line he heard from one of the women on *The Bachelor*:

> I always keep my legs shaved and my passport up to date. Even
> though I haven't been out of the country in years!

> That's funny, but I wasn't talking about my legs!

It was then that he realized he had played it too far. He tossed his phone onto the couch and went upstairs to kiss Jana goodnight. While he was thinking of the best next moves for Jack and Jackie, Alison was distracted by another text that stopped her dead in her tracks.

The name "Marc Sugarman" appeared on her phone along with the words:

We need to talk.

CHAPTER 22

Olivia & Alison & Eliza & Amanda

Olivia set out for Alison's Tuesday morning as planned under the guise of two moms out for an exercise walk with their babies. She felt tortured since arriving home the night before but was careful not to show it. She apologized to Spencer again for her suspicions and said she felt much more like herself after spending a fun day in the city with her new friend. He apologized again in return for his counter accusations, saying they were both under a lot of pressure and should forget about the whole thing. She wished that were the case but smiled and agreed as if it were.

She'd planned on initiating sex with him that night, to further prove her stance, but couldn't go through with it. It had now been months since they had been together that way, so he didn't notice or care. She had heard of other new fathers practically begging their wives for sex as early as two weeks after childbirth. At the time she thought, *How lucky am I to have such a selfless husband?* Now it was all coming into question.

She had followed Andie's advice to a T, but in her heart, she still wanted to ask Spencer for explanations. She wanted him to make her feel better, even if his words were lies. She wished she could tell him what she had done that day, how she was sure he was cheating. Then he could respond by telling her he adored her and would never even look at another woman. She could just believe him and that would be that. But that was not who she was.

As she walked to Alison's, the morning mist hung heavy in the trees. It eerily matched her psyche, heavy with burden, her empty stomach so filled with fear that it blocked her breath. She again felt as if she were walking to her execution. She wished she hadn't brought Lily with her and wasn't sure if she could even care for her in her shaky arms, but Alison had insisted. She felt Eliza Hunt would not be able to resist telling the truth to a woman with an infant. What woman could?

Alison was waiting for her, ready to walk, but changed her mind when she saw her. There was a fine line between a sympathetic witness and a pathetic one.

"Come inside for a few minutes."

They had wanted to get to Eliza's early enough that she would hopefully be home, but not too early for it to be rude. Alison had done a bit of online investigating and was confident that Eliza wasn't employed, that her husband was, and that their kids were in college. Arriving between nine and ten seemed like their best shot to find her home alone. Alison looked at the time. They had enough for one cup of tea to calm Olivia's nerves. As they drank, Alison prepped her.

"So, if she's home, I imagine she will come out and talk to us. I'm confident that I can get her that far at least. Once she does, let me do most of the talking."

"Thanks, I would rather that."

"It's fine. I'm going to guide the conversation, I promise, but you have to elicit her sympathy for this to work. You can't appear deranged, not that I think you are deranged—of course I don't—but she has to see herself in you in order to want to help you."

Olivia sipped her tea and nodded her head in agreement. She could see that Alison needed more assurance.

"I got it. I'll be strong. I am strong."

"OK, are you ready?" Alison cheered her on, with two fists in the air.

"I'm ready!" Olivia feigned matching enthusiasm.

For a minute or two, Alison and Olivia stood between Eliza's house and her neighbors', assessing the situation. Actually, Alison was assessing the situation; Olivia was concentrating on breathing in through her nose and out through her mouth.

In for four, hold for seven, out for eight.

In for four, hold for seven, out for eight.

The neighborhood they were standing in was much more of a neighborhood than where either of them lived, with Olivia up in the cliffs and Alison smack in the middle of town. The difference registered in both of their minds.

"It's nice here," Alison said. "More like what I imagined the suburbs to be like."

"I guess," Olivia somewhat agreed. She had not spent much time imagining the suburbs. She was sure she would still be in the city if she hadn't fallen so head over heels in love with her house.

"You good to go?" Alison asked.

Olivia nodded and continued listening to her breath. As they reached the door, she felt a wave of strength come over her. Knowing the truth, whatever that may be, had to be better than living with doubt and uncertainty. She couldn't bear the thought of even one more night of pretending that everything was OK. They had to get an answer.

Alison motioned for Olivia to ring the bell, as if it were symbolic—of what, she wasn't sure. The ring surprised them, it wasn't the normal *ding-dong*, but a repeat of the first four notes of Beethoven's Fifth. They both laughed, causing them to laugh again at the fact that they were laughing. Eliza answered the door. She looked taken aback, but, thankfully, kind.

"Can I help you?" she asked from behind the screen.

"I hope so," Alison answered. "We understand that you're the moderator for the Hudson Valley Ladies' Bulletin Board."

They certainly didn't look dangerous, but Eliza kept a strong hand on the inner door, ready to slam it, if necessary.

"That's correct," she answered cautiously, surprised by the sight of two women with baby strollers standing at her door questioning a forum that had only ever existed online.

Alison smiled warmly, realizing as much.

"I'm Alison Le and this is my friend Olivia York. We both recently moved here."

Olivia smiled, too, and added, "I bought this jogging stroller from someone on the bulletin board. Thank you!"

Eliza relaxed and smiled back now that she felt more confident that this was a friendly visit, odd as it may be. How did these two even know where she lived? She waited for them to get to the point. As she did, she saw Amanda arrive home. She sensed she needed backup.

"Olivia believes her husband may be having an affair with the woman who posted anonymously on your forum. We need to know her name in order to investigate further."

Eliza swayed back and forth a bit with her feet placed firmly in the doorway. *What have I started? Yes, I need backup.* She flicked the outdoor light on and off continuously, an age-old SOS between her and Amanda, but only Alison and Olivia took notice of her strange behavior. She gave up and called out her name, never moving from behind the door.

"Mandy!" she yelled loudly. It obviously surprised them both and Eliza apologized. "Sorry, I was just calling my neighbor over."

Amanda waved, and Eliza waved her over quite intensely, elevating the bizarreness. Amanda approached with an innocent, "Hey, what's up?"

"This is . . ." Eliza had already forgotten their names. They both stepped up, happy to shake hands with someone on the street side of the screen.

"Alison Le."

"Olivia York."

"Nice to meet you, I'm Amanda, Eliza's neighbor and oldest friend." She reached out to shake their hands, adding, "You can call me Mandy, most everyone around here does."

Everyone but Eliza smiled awkwardly. She had collected her thoughts and was eager to dispense with them and move on.

"I'm afraid I can't help you. The anonymous post feature doesn't share names or emails." She looked at Mandy and filled her in.

"These ladies want to know the name of that anonymous poster who's having the affair."

"Oh, hoping for some scarlet letter action?" Mandy asked with a bite in her tone. She was no fan of women who sleep with other women's husbands, but no fan of publicly shaming them either. Two sides to every story, she always thought. It took her a second to remember that this woman was actually created, or at the very least embellished, by Eliza. It was Olivia who set things straight.

"Not at all. I believe it might be my husband who's cheating." She moved Lily's blanket down so they could see her face. "This is my daughter. If it is my husband, then he was cheating on me while I was pregnant, while I was giving birth, and while I've been nursing his baby." The strength in her words and her voice surprised even her. "Do you have children?" she asked. They both nodded yes.

"Then I am you. Do you understand?" She said it again, slowly and nearly begging, "I am you."

It hit home, especially for Amanda. She stepped up.

"Can you excuse us for a minute?" she asked, while making her way around them and into the house. She smiled a forced smile at them and closed the door. They wondered if it would ever open again.

Olivia whispered, "I've been more welcoming to Jehovah's Witnesses."

"It is strange, but don't worry, you did great. Don't say much else. You clearly have the neighbor's sympathy, but it can easily turn."

Inside the house a heated debate was going on. Amanda and Eliza were at odds, with Eliza feeling like she had too much to lose by telling these two strangers the truth. In the end, the hurt of having been recently scorned fueled a passion in Amanda's argument that Eliza couldn't compete with.

"You have to put this poor girl out of her misery," Mandy implored. "Not everyone has a husband as wonderful as Luke. You have no idea of the pain she's in."

Eliza opened the door and asked them in. They sat in the living room where she carefully chose her words, coming up with some version of the truth.

"The anonymous post was fictitious. Someone made it up to drum up controversy on the bulletin board."

They both looked at her confused. She simplified it, "It's fake news! You have nothing to worry about. I'm sorry if this caused you harm, really I am." That part she was sincere about.

Alison was about to question her further, but Olivia let out a cry of relief that pierced all of their hearts. Their eyes teared up as hers overflowed. Eliza doled out tissues, and they even laughed a bit. Olivia never knew such relief existed, just as she had never known such anxiety had existed. She was thrilled to put the whole thing behind her.

As they walked home, Olivia stopped a block from her house to thank Alison and say goodbye. Part of her hoped to never see Alison again. If she didn't, she could go back to her beautiful glass house and ostensibly pretend this entire episode had never happened. But she wasn't that type of girl. She appreciated the way Alison had stuck her neck out for her; she wasn't about to chop it off and keep walking.

"Circle Time at the library on Friday?" she asked.

Alison was relieved; she realized they were at a crossroads, both literally and figuratively, and that their friendship was based on a rather awful and embarrassing experience.

"That would be great. Eleven o'clock, right?"

"Yes."

"Lunch afterward?"

"Perfect." Alison had gotten very close to some of her clients, and when their cases were closed, she often never heard from them again. It wasn't so much that they weren't in each other's daily lives anymore, but that the clients preferred to put the whole thing behind them, without staring into the face of its biggest reminder. She sensed that Olivia might feel similarly.

"It's over now, Olivia. We never have to discuss it again."

Olivia hugged her, grateful that she had read her mind. Alison added, "Plus, I have a date Thursday night with that gorgeous guy whose shoulder you fell asleep on, so we can deconstruct every detail."

Olivia perked right up. "What? Why didn't you say anything?"

"Well, given the circumstances . . . Also guess who texted me last night?"

"The baby daddy?"

"Yes."

"I guess the drama is all in your court now."

"Uh-huh, and it is not the court I'm used to."

CHAPTER 23

Olivia

Olivia went to great lengths that day to get her marriage back on track. Feeling the pain of it possibly ending had been enough to scare her into action. Spencer walked in the door that night to a dinner of homemade osso bucco and mushroom risotto, his two favorites, and a warm chocolate cake for dessert. She knew this couldn't be an everyday occurrence; she had run around all afternoon like a piping plover getting it all together, but hoped the effort would be appreciated. It was.

The night felt like it totally set things straight. They talked about simple, happy things, like what color to paint the den, and whether to go to the Cape or Nantucket for summer vacation. After making love they lay in each other's arms and promised never to doubt each other again. It may have been the deepest love that Olivia had ever felt for Spencer. Lily even cooperated by sleeping through the night, and in the morning, they all woke refreshed and happy. It gave Olivia an idea. After feeding Lily, she poked her head into the closet where Spencer was getting dressed to run.

"If you can wait ten minutes, Lil and I can come with you. I've got a real hold on this jogging stroller thing now!"

"Not today, honey. I have an eight thirty conference call."

"A conference call? While you're running?"

"Yeah. It's a mandatory compliance thing. I mute the phone and just listen."

"Oh well, I guess it's silly then."

"Definitely another time."

He kissed her on the nose in his old sweet way, and any hurt she felt from the rejection of her offer to run with him melted away. Everything felt right with the world.

Until about ten minutes later when, while making the bed, Olivia fanned out their comforter and Spencer's cell phone shot across the room.

"Uh-oh, Daddy forgot his phone," she said out loud to Lily as she looked at the time—8:23.

"I guess he'll be back any minute."

She felt bad for him. He hated to miss a run. She slipped the phone into her robe pocket and continued straightening up while Lily watched her happily from her bouncy seat. As 8:30 came and went, she began to worry that something had happened to him. Soon, she dismissed it and decided that, in typical Spencer fashion, his run came before anything else. He must have put it in front of the call. Lily fell back to sleep, and Olivia quietly stepped out of the room to get a few more things done.

She was in the kitchen unloading the dishwasher when Spencer ran in, sweaty and thirsty. He reached for a glass with one hand, his phone was in the other. Olivia flashed back to the meeting with Andie Rand:

"The worst cheaters have two phones," Andie had said. Olivia remembered it clearly because, at the time, it gave her hope.

"Spencer only has one," she had responded. "I'm sure of it."

He smiled at her. "Last night was great, baby. Thanks again." She just stared, frozen. He was already out of the kitchen and didn't notice.

"I'm taking a shower," he yelled on his way to their bedroom.

She wanted to close her eyes and pretend his second phone was not in her pocket, but she couldn't. Both anger and fear burned inside her. She ran up the stairs, intent on confronting him. As if fate put out its foot, she tripped on the top step and fell forward, knocking the wind out of her. The jolt stopped her in her tracks. She pushed herself up against the wall to get her breath back and regained control. "Stop and think, Olivia," she said to herself.

On one hand she wanted nothing more than to listen to Spencer's explanation, but on the other she questioned what it would do for her. She could picture him making excuses: "I have a second phone for work. I thought we were done with this paranoia."

She longed to hear that, to believe it, and to stick her head back in the sand where she wished it could stay. Andie Rand's words, "cheaters have two phones," ran through her head again. She called Alison and told her what had happened. Apparently, her words were indistinguishable.

"Slow down, Olivia, slow down," Alison begged.

"I can't! Spencer is in the shower. I need to think quickly, but I can't think at all. You need to think for me. I found a second phone caught up in our covers. It's in my pocket. I haven't confronted him yet."

Alison took a beat.

"OK. Leave it in your pocket. See if he looks for it. Do not confront him except to ask what he is looking for. If he lies, then we know there's a problem. If he comes clean, then maybe there isn't. I know what Andie said about second phones, but I used to have two and certainly wasn't cheating on anyone. Maybe it's for work, and you just don't know about it."

The shower stopped, signaling time's up. Olivia took a deep breath.

"I'll call you back."

The only thing worse than being cheated on was not knowing if you were being cheated on. Olivia was sure that she needed to be sure. She straightened herself out and went into the bedroom. Spencer was combing his hair.

"What are you up to today?" he asked, casually.

"The usual nothing much," she responded, impressed by her normal tone. She sat on the bed and pushed herself back against the pillows as she often did to chat with him when he got ready for work. She grabbed her book from the nightstand, pretending to read it. Spencer slid his pants off his valet. He patted the empty shelf above it where his phone usually sat charging. He looked around the bedroom, at first casually then with a bit more urgency. She followed his eyes to the phone he had walked in with. It was identical to the one in her pocket. Their eyes met on it, each of them oddly aware of the other's gaze, albeit for different reasons. He lifted up some papers on his desk.

"Looking for something?" she asked, hopefully.

"No, I'm good, thanks," he responded.

Her chest caught fire—a burning sensation that began in her belly and shot through her heart as if it were in flames. She couldn't breathe. She couldn't keep up the facade for even a second more. In a panic, she reached down to sleeping Lily and pinched her leg, just hard enough to wake her. Lily cried out, instantly filling her with guilt and purpose.

"I have to change the baby," she uttered as she grabbed Lily and left the room. She stood at the changing table apologizing for the awful thing she had done. Lily calmed and cooed. Olivia reveled in her forgiveness until Spencer's phone buzzed in her robe pocket.

CHAPTER 24

Amanda

Amanda was actually waiting outside of school when Pippa came out squealing in delight. "I got the part!!!" It was both amazing and surreal, since Amanda had come out squealing through the same door on more than one occasion decades before. She kept the reminiscence to herself, not wanting either to encroach on Pippa's moment or to see the obligatory eye roll if she did. Mandy was thrilled for Pippa, and more than a little thrilled for herself as well. The first parent volunteer meeting was scheduled for the next day, and Mandy decided to arrive early to pitch "The Bard"—as everyone referred to the teacher who ran the Shakespeare troupe—on why she would make the perfect assistant director. She was over the moon at the thought of being back in a theater.

Stepping into the high school auditorium the next day for the parent meeting was an epic trip down memory lane. Aside from a new curtain and the seats having been reupholstered a strange shade of purple, nothing much had changed. She was flooded with theater club memories of running lines, belting out songs, taking curtain calls, and having her first crush. It wasn't Curly or Jud she was thinking about while singing "I'm just a girl who cain't say no" but the dashing high school drama teacher, Mr. Barr. He arrived just days after Amanda had officially sworn off high school boys, and unlike his hundred-year-old predecessor, he had all the girls swooning. But none more than Amanda, who immediately directed all of her teen angst toward her new unrequited love.

He must be long retired from here, she thought.

At that very same moment, as if she'd conjured him, there he was. Mr. Barr. Making his way across the stage with his familiar stride and surprisingly still thick wavy hair.

Even more surprising was her reaction. Her knees wobbled at the sight of him, just as they had decades before. Her first thought was, *This is crazy*; her second, *I have to get the hell out of here*. As she turned to do so, his baritone voice echoed through the auditorium.

"Hello, hello. Are you here for the volunteer meeting? You're a few minutes early. I'm setting up the chairs if you want to start volunteering now!" He laughed. His laugh was familiar, too. He had that theatrical tone to everything that came out of his mouth. She approached the stage, so she wouldn't need to shout. On the way up, butterflies of excitement danced in her belly. *What the hell?* she thought. *I will just sign up for snacks and be on my way.*

He recognized her immediately, shouting, "Amanda Williams?" while springing off the stage to greet her. He threw his arms wide open for what she thought was a setup for a hug but turned out to be a two-handed shoulder embrace—the kind usually followed by the refrain, "My, my, look how you've grown!" *He still sees me like a kid*, she laughed to herself, and at herself. She gave him the once-over right back.

He was older now, of course, with deep lines shooting out from the corners of his blue eyes and streaks of gray now salting his signature locks. It all worked well—really well. *Men have it so easy in the aging department*, she thought, suddenly self-conscious. He let go of her shoulders, though she wished his hands had lingered there a bit longer.

Sign up for the snacks, Amanda, her brain begged her libido.

"How have you been?" he asked.

"Good, good, and you?"

"Still teaching at Hudson," he answered in a tone that wandered between pride and indignation.

"That's just incredible," Mandy said. "My daughter is Pippa Cole, you cast her as Isabella. Thank you!"

"Oh, wow! I see the resemblance now. She's talented *and* a sweet kid, just like her mom."

Amanda laughed to herself—all that flirting she had done, and he never even noticed. Now on the other end of it, with her daughter under his tutelage, she was happy for his obliviousness.

"I've followed your career over the years."

She was immediately embarrassed, sure he was going to bring up the infamous shampoo commercial that she'd starred in at the very beginning of her time in Hollywood. It had become a cult classic of sorts. For years she would walk into an audition and the casting people would mock her notorious line, "I can't see you tonight, Tommy. I'm washing my hair!" By the time *SNL* did a sketch about it, she was barely castable. If it were now, she would most definitely be a meme. She braced herself for it. He surprised her.

"I loved what you did in *Angelino Heights*. It was the first time I had seen one of my protégées on the big screen."

"Did" was a bit of a reach, she thought. Amanda's first movie was a bit part in a Carson Cole film in which she played a waitress standing outside an LA coffee shop. She had to ask for a light for her

cigarette without using words. She rehearsed what she considered to be an intimate act between strangers—placing your hand on top of theirs as they direct the flame to yours—over and over again.

Mr. Barr may have been the only one who remembered her for that, but she certainly remembered it well. It had been a direct result of meeting Carson. She'd been waiting tables at the Polo Lounge, a storied restaurant for Hollywood types. She'd stepped outside for a smoke, a habit she had only taken up for the break it provided. (At the time it seemed like anyone who didn't smoke didn't get one.) The charismatic Carson Cole came out, asked her for a light, and said, "I just read a script with this exact scene in it. You're not an actress, are you?"

He probably had the scene written in after the fact, but at the time she was obsessed with romantic comedies and thought of it as their fateful, meet-cute moment. He gave her that small part and came to see it filmed. They started dating. During her second film, when Carson noticed the leading man take an interest in her, he made it official. They were married in Vegas that weekend.

Amanda recognized that it was an unbalanced relationship from the beginning. He was a big Hollywood producer and she was a struggling actress with two bit parts to her credit and one television commercial that did more harm than good. But Carson had a funny side to him that made her laugh, and a sweetness that he seemed to share only with her—until he no longer bothered to.

"Do you act anymore?" Mr. Barr asked, hopefully.

She didn't. Carson felt very strongly that two parents in the business wasn't good for the kids. She agreed with the decision. Truth was, she didn't have the backbone for rejection and hated the alternative idea of Carson handing her a career that she didn't deserve. The fallout from the shampoo commercial had really done a number on her.

"No, I haven't acted since Pippa was born," she answered without further explanation. "But I'm thinking about getting back into it," she added, surprising herself.

"I don't know if you read the volunteer form, but I'm looking for an assistant director. Any interest in getting back, behind the scenes?"

Interest is not the problem, she thought. She really wanted to say yes. It was just what she needed, being back in the theater, that is, not fulfilling a high school fantasy with her daughter's teacher.

"If I remember, we collaborated quite well back in the day— things haven't changed much since you played Elizabeth Bennet in *Pride and Prejudice*," he added, encouragingly.

"*Pride and Prejudice: The Musical!*" she corrected him.

"Of course." And with his best attempt at imitating seventeen-year-old Amanda, sang, "Nothing rhymes with Darcy. I wish the British spoke Farsi."

Amanda blushed. "I can't believe you remember that."

"Are you kidding me? You had to know you were one of my favorite students. You were such a good kid."

Since it was obvious that her crush had been one-sided, clearly she could control herself and be his assistant. Other parent volunteers began to trickle in, and he amped up his plea. "It would be great if I can start off the meeting announcing my new assistant director. You can't imagine how many parents falsely think they are qualified for the job. You'd be doing me a big favor."

It would be wrong to say no to a favor, thought her brain and her libido.

"OK. I'm in!"

He smiled. She melted. They exchanged cell phone numbers, and it was the first time in a very long while that she found herself looking forward to something on her own behalf.

CHAPTER 25

Amanda & Eliza

Oh my God! Oh my God! Oh my God!

Eliza read Mandy's text and laughed out loud. She loved having Mandy back home. It was as if they had both regressed twenty years on impact.

What? What? What?

Why didn't you tell me that Mr. Barr was still teaching drama at the high school?

Eliza laughed again.

Really? I kind of assumed you'd moved on.

Never!

Well, now's your chance. I'm pretty sure he's divorced.

Shut up! I'm coming over.

In what felt like seconds, Mandy was at the door. Eliza eyed her skinny frame. "Do you want a protein shake?"

"If by protein you mean tequila, then yes." She followed Eliza to the kitchen while asking, "How do you know that Mr. Barr is divorced?"

"Do you not remember how small a town this is?"

Amanda stared out the kitchen window and focused on the willow tree where they had once stashed their first bottle of alcohol—a Concord grape Manischewitz that Eliza had swiped from her grandma's Passover Seder.

"I do. This whole day is making me feel like I've stepped into a time warp." She shook her head. "And Mr. Barr still looks amazing. I can't believe it."

"Why can't you believe it? *You* still look amazing."

She cozied up to the counter like it was her neighborhood bar-stool to watch the sensation that was Eliza in the kitchen. Always prepared, she pulled limeade and pineapple juice concentrate from her freezer as if tomorrow were Cinco de Mayo and began the show.

"Please, Eliza. When you look at me, you still see an eighteen-year-old."

"What do you see when you look at me?" Eliza asked, not really wanting to hear the answer. She threw an extra shot of te-quila in the blender.

"An eighteen-year-old."

"You do know that I have mirrors in this house, right?"

"Ha, ha. You're beautiful, Eliza."

"It is hard to believe that we're middle-aged."

"We are not middle-aged!" Mandy protested.

"Do the math, honey. I don't know how long you're planning on living, but I am most definitely middle-aged."

Mandy wasn't buying it.

"Age is just a number."

"A statement probably attributable to an underage kid trying to get into a bar."

Mandy chuckled. "I guess it doesn't matter how old Mr. Barr is, then. Not that I have any intention of going down that road."

"Mr. Barr was probably just a few years out of college when he started at Hudson Valley. I bet he's around Carson's age."

"Don't say Carson."

Eliza laughed.

"You really are handling this all so well, Mandy. You hardly even bring it up."

"Please. I'm not handling it at all. I ignore it—though it's hard. Another woman came forward yesterday followed by another denial by Carson. With each one I feel further implicated for my silence. And confused. If you don't come forward, you're weak; if you do, you're doubted."

Eliza understood that. She stood in awe of other women's bravery and felt wrecked when watching them get shot down. The doubt surrounding so many brave women from the mattress girl at Columbia University to Christine Blasey Ford at the Kavanaugh hearings ran though her mind.

Amanda must have been thinking similarly. "And even with all this talk, it feels like nothing ever really changes. Remember how we obsessively watched the Anita Hill testimony during senior year?"

Eliza remembered every second of it. It was during her first bout with agoraphobia. She was glued to the TV. She had no desire to discuss any of this.

"Not really—so long ago," she lied.

"Really? I'm surprised. You cried the whole time. It's all so upsetting. Thank God for Lexapro!"

She looked Eliza in the eyes, knowing she had taken an indirect path toward the topic that had been on her mind since their first heart-to-heart.

"And speaking of antidepressants, Eliza, maybe—"

Eliza turned on the blender, purposefully drowning out the obvious conclusion to Mandy's sentence: "maybe you should see a psychiatrist." She recognized that her problem did not seem to be going away, as it had back in high school. It really was time for professional help, but that would mean telling Luke and probably the kids. She wasn't ready for that. She dipped two glasses in salt, popped in two paper umbrellas for the full effect, and poured each of them a drink.

"Cheers," she said, not meaning it. They toasted and she took a sip for courage.

"I know it's time to tell Luke, but I don't want any of them to see me as broken. I've always been the one my family could depend on. They think I'm perfect, that I do everything perfectly. Look at this margarita, for God's sake. It's like I work at El Pollo Loco, not that I *am el pollo loco*!"

Mandy held it up for inspection. "It is a beautiful margarita." Mandy kept it raised for her toast. "To us two crazy chickens!"

As they clinked glasses, neither knew whether to laugh or cry. Mandy took a big sip of her drink and asked, "You know how much I love you, right?"

"Is that the tequila talking, or are you talking to the tequila?"

Mandy laughed, harder than she had in a long time.

"No one in LA makes me laugh like you do." She reached out her hand and put it on Eliza's. "We'll figure this out, Eliza."

"We'll figure out your stuff, too," Eliza agreed.

"Please, I can't even figure out if I should call the drama teacher Dean or Mr. Barr."

"His name was Dean? That's funny for an academic."

"Of course. Remember Dean and DeLuca?"

Amanda remembered it like it was yesterday, while Eliza never seemed very interested in reminiscing. It often made Mandy wonder if her own tendency to live in the past came from her dissatisfaction with her current life, specifically her marriage to Carson. Was she longing for the glory days, like so many unhappy people seemed to do? Was that why she still felt the remnants of her schoolgirl crush on Dean Barr? Eliza had a more contrived crush on the shop teacher, Roy DeLuca, but she didn't even seem to remember him. The summer before their senior year, the two girls would often take the train into Manhattan and explore different neighborhoods. On one such trip to SoHo, they had wandered into the famous market, Dean & DeLuca, and laughed that it shared a name with the teachers they were infatuated with. They even brought home shopping bags and taped them to their walls next to posters of the Brat Pack and Nirvana. Eliza's mom was extra annoyed because she thought Eliza was now worshipping a food store the way she used to worship Rob Lowe. They loved that no one else knew the bags' hidden meaning.

"I think you feigned interest just to appease me—but I had some significant fantasizing going on."

"Apparently so, since you're still swooning over him."

"You're the one who insisted girls should be able to take shop. Mr. DeLuca was not too happy about that progressive move, if I remember."

Eliza had petitioned to take shop in the fall of their senior year instead of home economics, citing Title IX. Everyone thought she was a feminist trailblazer, but Mandy knew she just wanted to come home and regale her with stories of Mr. DeLuca. As she remembered it, Eliza wasn't really there yet when it came to boys, like she was. It felt like she did it just to keep in step with her best friend.

"I don't know how you remember all of this stuff, Mandy."

"Well, maybe because I'm still swooning over my high school drama teacher, two kids and all these years later."

Eliza raised her glass again. "To your new gig."

Amanda lifted her own and added, "May it be so fulfilling that I will want to stay forever!"

Eliza couldn't help but laugh. "You couldn't get out of here fast enough, and now you want to bring up your kids here?"

"This is the best place I know. I don't know what I was running away from. Plus, my dad is getting older and could use the help."

"Your dad is fine, Mandy. I check in on him all the time. Well, at least I used to. He's doing great." Eliza's tone got more serious, and she looked at her friend—if she could shake Carson Cole by the shoulders, she would. "I hate to think of you giving up on the life you dreamed of because of that jerk husband of yours."

"Believe me, I wasn't living the life I dreamed of. I have to go. Thanks for the 'protein shake.' It hit the spot."

Eliza grabbed her car keys from the foyer shelf.

"Now," she said more brightly, "before you go, can you just pull my car out of the garage and put it in the driveway?"

"I've been drinking," Mandy replied, not wanting to enable Eliza more than she already was.

"It's just ten feet. Please, Mandy. It's been inside all week and Luke knows I hate pulling into the garage. It's suspect."

"Fine." She took the keys and they hugged goodbye—with a little extra squeeze on both sides.

CHAPTER 26

Jackie & Alison

Jackie was more nervous than usual when getting ready for his date, searching for the right words to explain his dual identity while getting dressed. Everything he came up with sounded wrong. Also, he disliked going out during the week. He had to rush home and jump in the shower after work, prepare something for dinner for Jana, and sit with her while she ate. He didn't like breaking that promise for work or for a date. He knew that Jana would have been happy eating her dinner in front of reruns of *The Office*, but she always stuck to the rule that was so important to her dad. Dinner together. Tonight's dinner was unusually interesting because she got to give her dad the third degree on his upcoming date.

"Where did you meet this lady again?"

"On the train," he answered with a wave of nausea. Now he was lying to Jana, too. He couldn't very well tell her that he met his lady friend on account of her lady friend.

"Where are you going?"

"That new Italian place on Main Street. I heard it was great. I'll take you if it is."

"Thanks. What are you going to wear?"

Jackie had already painstakingly dressed for the date in a striped oxford shirt, tan chinos, and loafers.

"This is what I'm wearing."

"Oh."

"Oh, that's nice, or oh, *that's* what you're wearing?"

"Well, I don't know, Daddy. You look so cute in your jeans and that dope T-shirt, you know that one we bought in Soho last month."

"You think? I feel like that's not dressy enough."

"Well, this whole tucked-in look you have going on, I think it's kinda out of style."

She pushed her plate away and brought him upstairs to change. In the end, they agreed on the oxford shirt untucked over a pair of jeans.

"Nice, Dad! You're slaying!"

"That's a good thing, I presume?"

Jana was happy her dad was going out on a date. She'd been worrying about him ever since her grandma died. She was very aware that in a few years she would be going off to college and leaving him alone.

"You gotta go, Daddy."

"OK, I'll come in and check on you when I get home."

He kissed her on the top of her head and was off.

Jackie arrived at Alison's house a few minutes early. He stood at the door staring at his watch, not wanting to interrupt what he imagined was going on inside. He was right. Alison was trying to get the baby down before she left. Jackie waited patiently and rang the bell at exactly eight.

Alison answered the door looking very beautiful, except for a large wad of spit-up perched on her left shoulder. Its presence left Jackie in a bit of a conundrum—to tell or not to tell? He imagined from her glossed lips and pretty outfit that she had gone to some trouble to get ready for their date, so with that in mind, he thought, don't tell. But he knew that, with one look in the mirror, she would wonder why he hadn't chosen to mention that there was a sizable chunk of baby vomit on her shirt and peg him for the deceitful cad that he had recently become. He'd seen other women get angry about such things before, usually in reference to something between their teeth. He decided to say something.

"It looks like Zachary left a little gift on your shoulder," he reported, mirroring its location on himself.

She immediately blushed and looked to the left, her chin grazing the pinnacle of spit-up and transferring some to her face. She had wanted to answer the door as sexy Alison, not mama-bear Alison. It had been so long since she had felt that desire. She even broke out the new lavender-and-vanilla-infused soap that the woman at the local apothecary promised would eradicate the smell of new baby, her unintentional signature scent persistently emanating from her pores. She was sure the gift that Zachary had left on her shoulder would override her efforts. It was not how she pictured this going.

Her embarrassment was slightly tempered by admiration. She couldn't believe Jack remembered Zach's name; she didn't even remember telling it to him. Even dressed as sexy Alison she was still thinking like a mama bear. *Maybe that part of me is dead*, she thought. But when she looked at Jack with his broad shoulders and piercing eyes, she knew that was not the case.

He blushed as well, realizing that she never had—not knowingly at least—told him her son's name. He swore again to stop communicating with her as Jackie from the bulletin board.

"I'm gonna go up and change. I'll be quick," she said, touching him gently on the arm and leading him to the living room to wait. Even with a gesture as small as that, they were both aware of the obvious spark between them.

He looked around, taking it all in—shabby chic meets the baby aisle at Toys R Us—or wherever one would buy such things today. Jackie had no idea. He had forgotten how much paraphernalia came with a baby. He remembered how intent he had been when Jana was small on always having the latest toys and gadgets, trying to make up for the one thing he couldn't give her: her mother. He took a seat on the couch and ran through his "I have something to tell you" plan.

"OK, I'm good to go now." She was back smiling at him in a way that made his heart thump a bit harder. "And thank you for telling me, not everyone would have."

The perfect lead-in, he thought. "I always tell it like it is. But funny enough—"

She cut him right off at the word "but," completely drowning out the rest of his sentence. "I always tell it like it is, too. Maybe it's the lawyer in me, but I have zero patience for dishonesty."

She tucked a loose strand of hair behind her ear as she had done on the train. He again pictured them being close enough to tuck it back for her. If he said something now he may never get that chance. *She barely knows me*, he thought. *I'll wait until after dinner.*

"Let's go," he said, smiling. "We can walk from here."

Both Jack and Jackie really liked this woman. He couldn't risk not even making it out the door on their first date.

On the way to the restaurant, they talked about the weather and the beautiful old Victorian houses along Main Street. It was only after they sat down and had their first glass of wine that the conversation loosened up.

"What do you think is harder, having a baby or a teenager?" Alison asked.

"That's a great question. I thought the in-between time was best. You'll step on a few Legos, which really hurts, by the way, but if you feed them and love them and get them where they need to be relatively on time, you're good. Bringing up babies and teenagers is similarly hard."

"How so?"

"Well, when you have a baby you suffer from sleep deprivation, and it's hard to figure out what the baby wants and needs. And when you have a teenager you have to wait up for them to get home, which is equally exhausting, and you have no idea what it is they want and need."

Alison thought of her online friend and the tampon incident. She almost brought it up, but lucky for Jackie she decided it wasn't good dinner conversation.

"I remember when I was a teenager, I didn't tell my mom anything," Alison said instead.

"Me too, but at least when I did, we could understand each other. My daughter speaks a totally different language. Tonight, she said my outfit slayed. I had no idea if that was good or bad."

"I know that word! It's good!"

"OK, hotshot, how about 'lit'?" he said, matching her quite adorable enthusiasm.

"That's so easy. Cool."

"Hmm. I'm impressed. How about 'boo'?"

"Boyfriend or girlfriend. Give me a hard one."

"Hello?"

"Hi. Give me a hard one."

Jackie laughed. "That was the hard one. If you get a text that says 'Hello' with a question mark, what would you think it means?"

"With a question mark?"

"Yes."

"What?"

"If you get a text that says 'Hello?,' what do you think it means?"

Now Alison was laughing. "This is beginning to sound like the 'Who's on First' routine. It means 'what?'"

"How do you know all of this?"

"I guess from clients. I meet so many different people. I can probably teach you a few to impress your daughter."

He laughed. "We're good. She has SATs coming along soon. I think we should revert back to the Queen's English."

She wondered how old he was to have a teenage daughter. It did seem like he started young. She guessed that he was roughly the same age as she was. He had the slightest hint of gray on the sides of his temples. It was sexy. He was sexy.

Over the main course they ran through all of the typical first-date banter regarding family and school and work and whatnot.

Jackie revealed, without any detail, that he was a widower and Alison confessed that her "sperm donor" wanted nothing to do with their child. They were both surprised by their own candor.

"Would you have been with Zach's dad now, I mean, if he had stepped up? Maybe asked you to marry him?"

She again appreciated how direct he was. "I would like to say that I never thought about that, but I was brought up in the same fairy tale–saturated world as every other girl, so it definitely entered my mind."

Alison couldn't believe how open she was being. She hadn't even admitted that to herself. She added, "It would have been a huge mistake. He doesn't have any of the qualities I want in a partner. He's not my ship, as they say. Know that one?"

Jackie smiled. "I do. I think you would say, 'We're not ship.' But good try, I get what you were going for."

Dessert came, and they lightened things up again, agreeing

first on the best flavors of gelato, and then on more important things: Mets or Yankees. On the walk home, in an effort to assist Alison across a corner puddle, Jackie took her hand. Blocks later, as they approached her house, their fingers were still intertwined. To Jackie especially, it felt natural—very natural actually. It was the first time in years he had felt this type of connection. But that dawning realization was marred by his conscience. He should have told her who he was from the start. What was wrong with him? He'd never done anything like this before, and now he was stuck navigating a lie when all he really wanted to do was kiss her.

"I had a really nice time," she said, as they got close. She stole a glance at him—her belly did a little somersault. When they got to her door, would he kiss her? Or maybe she'd kiss him?

"Me too." He smiled. He took a deep breath and looked into her eyes. He had two choices: *Alison, can I tell you something?* or *Alison, can I kiss you?* He hadn't wanted to kiss someone this badly in ages, but he couldn't kiss her without telling her.

All right, that's it, he would tell her. There's a chance she would understand, but if she slammed the door in his face, then he could go home and get back to his humdrum life as usual. As he struggled with his words he looked up to see a man sitting on her front stoop. He assumed it was a stranger. The house was on Main Street after all, and people sometimes stopped to take a break or wait for someone. Still, he became protective.

"Can we help you?" he asked loudly.

"Hello, Alison," announced the non-stranger.

Alison quickly dropped Jackie's hand. There would be no kissing or telling, Jackie thought, at least not for now.

CHAPTER 27

Alison

Alison could not believe her eyes when she saw Marc sitting on the front stoop of her house. He had now emailed, called, and texted her about getting together to talk. She knew he wasn't one to be ignored, so she shouldn't have been surprised that he had come to see her face-to-face when she hadn't responded. Still, she couldn't get over his timing. She had really enjoyed the night and was even toying with asking Jack in. She was furious that Marc had just shown up as he did, like a cold bucket of water dousing a smoldering fire. She said a polite goodbye to Jack, paid the sitter and sent her home before even letting him inside.

"What the hell, Marc? How did you even find me?"

"I called your office, said I wanted to send you a baby gift."

Alison shook her head, noting that he was empty-handed.

"You were ignoring me. Did you think I would just give up?" She didn't bother answering again as she knew it was a pointless question. Marc Sugarman never gave up. They had that in common. She wasn't sure why she'd ignored him but thought it had something to do with not knowing what she wanted from him. She didn't like being asked questions that she may not have the answers for, a by-product of being an attorney. Never go to court ill prepared. She had just needed a little more time to figure out what would be best for *her* son before having to consider what would be best for *theirs*. Of course, it was much more than semantics.

Marc walked over to the fireplace and looked at the couple of pictures of Zach that she had framed on the mantel. He picked one up and studied it. She wondered what it would be like to look at your son for the first time that way. Did he feel a tug at his heart? Did he see himself in him? She imagined he did because she definitely did. Zach had undeniably inherited Alison's dark silky hair, but his eyes and skin were a clear combination. The shape of his face and the dimple on his left cheek were distinctly Marc's.

"He's a beautiful boy, that's for sure." He cleared his throat in a way that surprised her—as if he was choking up. She put up her guard. He had been such a dick about the whole pregnancy. One compassionate display during an unannounced visit was not going to change that.

"Yes, he is. And sweet, too. What are you doing here, Marc?"

"I just wanted to see my child. Do you have an issue with that?"

"Yes. Of course I have an issue with that. You haven't been here. You wanted nothing to do with me, with *us* really. And you come up here and act like I'm in the wrong because I was waiting to respond to you for a minute."

"It's kind of an absurd thing to play games over, Alison. Don't you think?"

"I wasn't playing games! I didn't want to deal with you." She took the framed picture of Zach out of his hands and placed it back on the mantel. She didn't even want him holding the photograph. "I still don't."

"Well, I'm afraid that's not just up to you."

As he said it, he realized that his approach might be off. He was so used to being adversarial with Alison that he didn't know any other way. Even their sex life had the tone of sparring partners rather than lovers—pleasuring each other was more about who was in control than actual pleasure.

"Of course it's up to me. I'm the parent of record."

Seeing the photo of the baby, his baby, had him imagining things way more consequential than a bid for Gracie Mansion. He recognized that his line of questioning was going poorly and redirected. "OK, withdrawn. I've had a change of heart, and for the sake of our son, I want to discuss how I can be a part of his life."

His saying "our son" threw her. She was not giving in so easily.

"I will agree to discuss this another time, but not unannounced at eleven on a Thursday night."

"I'm on trial, and there was more traffic than expected," he said, adding in a kinder tone, "I'm sorry."

She took a little pity on him. "Well, you came all this way. I imagine you want to come up and see the baby in person?"

A look of panic washed over his face, surprising her. Marc was known for his poker face in court. She was shocked that her offer elicited such an obvious nervous reaction. He answered, counter to his expression, "I would like that. Thanks."

As he followed her up the stairs, she wondered if he hadn't purposefully come so late at night to avoid meeting the baby. *But why?* she thought. *What would be the point?*

As they stood at his crib, she turned on the night-light so that Marc could get a good look at him.

"He's so small," he said.

"Actually, his pediatrician said he's in the ninetieth percentile in weight and height."

She examined Marc's face for another telling reaction. Good

stats of any kind were just the thing that would usually get a rise out of him. He didn't disappoint as he smiled from ear to ear.

"I'm sorry, but I don't want to wake him," she said. There was no way she was dealing with putting him to sleep again after this roller coaster of a night.

"Oh, no, please don't. I figured he would be sleeping."

It was all so confusing. *Who comes to meet their baby when he's sleeping?* She almost asked but thought it best to figure out what *she* wanted before discussing anything further with him. Her gut told her that there was more to this visit than he was letting on.

CHAPTER 28

Alison & Olivia

The Hudson Valley Community Library was the oldest building in town, dating back to 1803. While its churchlike stone facade now contrasted greatly with its updated modern interior, the words inscribed over the front door still rang true: "Medicine for the Soul."

Circle Time at the library had long been the go-to class for the mommy-and-me set. It was well attended by a wide variety of neighborhood moms, and sometimes dads, with infants to entertain. Alison and Olivia had been excited for their first baby class, but today neither of them was really into it. They both needed a bit more "medicine" than was being offered at the library to soothe their worried souls.

Alison arrived first and secured them a spot in the proverbial circle, her mind still reeling from the events of the previous night. One glance at Olivia and she forgot her own troubles. Her friend looked like a shell of herself. The spark of light in her eyes, which had been one of the first things that Alison noticed when she had jogged into the real estate office, was completely extinguished—by tears, no doubt.

Olivia had spent the last two days running the gamut of emotions and had settled on anger. Spencer's rogue phone was burning a hole in her pocket like the smoking gun that it was. She had yet to bring it up or give it up. His obvious frustration about its absence was her only source of satisfaction.

It was almost comical when they placed their babies on the colorful parachute in front of them, both determined to power through "If you're happy and you know it, clap your hands" without contradiction. While the stamp your feet part of the song offered some relief, the big finale, "The Wheels on the Bus," couldn't come soon enough. They both softened a bit during bubble time. Wayward bubbles landed on their babies' noses and eyelashes, prompting scrunched-up expressions of delight that neither of them had witnessed before. But the joy was short-lived. It may have been the first time in Olivia's life that she wasn't in seventh heaven within the walls of a library. They agreed that it wasn't the day to stay for the new-mom mingle and skipped out to Alison's house to strategize.

"You go first," Alison suggested, recognizing that Olivia's issues surpassed her own. Olivia pulled out the phone and placed it on Alison's coffee table. Alison picked it up to inspect it.

"I can't unlock it. I've tried nine passcodes. One more and it'll be frozen."

Alison placed it down, ceremonially. "We can't have that. Should I ask Andie?"

"I think so, if you don't mind."

She texted Andie the question and fixed them a nice lunch of fresh fruit, yogurt, granola, and a locally sourced artisanal honey recommended on the bulletin board while they waited for a response. They sat down at the kitchen table, where neither of them did more than pick at their bowls.

"Remind me to thank Spencer for this awesome 'lose the baby weight' diet that this torture has inspired."

Alison smiled and moved the granola back and forth without taking a bite. Olivia noticed.

"You might as well spill it while we wait."

Alison was happy for the release. "Should I start with the good or the bad?"

"Your choice."

"OK, I will start with the good because I don't want the sperminator to take any more away from me than he already has. My date was so great and so hot. Is it possible that this gorgeous, smart, funny, sweet guy was just waiting for me in the suburbs to spice up my mundane life?"

She realized she might have gone too far, considering what Olivia was currently dealing with. It felt like buying a pair of Manolos, two pairs actually, in front of an unemployed friend. Olivia's face assuaged her concern. She even saw a hint of that old sparkle in her eye.

"Wow! That's amazing, Alison. I'm so happy for you!"

Alison felt embarrassed. Gushing over a guy was so out of character for her. She backpedaled. "It was just a date. Who knows if I'll even see him again?"

"Of course you will. It's good for you to do stuff like this. Circle Time can't be your only weekly thrill," she added sarcastically.

Before Alison could tell her the night didn't exactly end as she hoped, her phone vibrated, signaling that Andie had responded to her text. She read it out loud:

Does it have touch ID?

"I don't know," Olivia responded. "How would we know that?"
Alison dutifully typed:

How would we know that?

You don't until you try it. Sleep hack him.

Olivia looked confused when Alison read it out loud. She explained, "I've heard of people doing this before. When he's sleeping you put his thumb on his phone and if he uses it, voilà—you're in. Is he a heavy sleeper?"

"Only when he wants to be. If he wakes up, I'm totally caught."

"Yes, but I think we are past worrying about that so much, right? If he had come clean about his missing second phone, I would be all Team Happy Marriage. But this behavior is extremely suspect."

Olivia took a beat as Alison's phone vibrated again. She read it out loud:

Once in, she should register her own fingerprint on his phone as well. Then she can slip it back to him and gather more evidence.

"You can do that?" Olivia asked.

"If Andie says so, then absolutely."

Olivia felt overwhelmed. "Let's just take it one step at a time. I will overserve him at dinner and take it from there."

"OK, call me as soon as you know."

"It's going to be in the middle of the night. Are you sure?"

"Yes! I'm up and down all night with the baby anyway."

Olivia promised to do so and went on her way.

At dinner that night, Olivia nursed a glass of Merlot while discreetly pouring Spencer three. Add in the fact that he was up at 6:00 a.m. to "run" and he barely made it through the nightly selection process of their ten o'clock television show. Of course, it didn't stop him from insisting he got his choice. Things that had hardly bothered her about Spencer before were suddenly all-consuming. She wondered if it was a defense mechanism. Maybe the less she liked him at the time of implosion, the less it would hurt? She doubted that was true.

Within minutes of the opening credits he was out cold. She changed the channel to a mindless reality show and noted the time. She had researched when the deepest sleep should occur and decided to proceed in an hour; right after her show was over.

Between exhaustion and anger, there was little room for fear. She took his thumb in her hand and placed it on the phone—presto, just as Andie had said. She went downstairs with it, poured herself the remnants of the bottle of wine from dinner, and got down to business.

The phone's home screen was quite sparse. It had his old AOL account with a bunch of junk mail on it; an app called Map My Run, which does just that; and another called Charity Miles that turns your miles into charitable donations. There was an iTunes account with his running playlist, and even the photos were of nothing more than early-morning sunrises and random shots of bridges and landscapes. So far it looked like it was just a phone for running—odd, yes, but also oddly plausible for Spencer. She wondered why, if that were the case, he hadn't taken it running the day she found it. She assumed it was because of his work call. She finished the glass of wine and braced herself for what she knew would be the final word on guilt or innocence. Her delay in not diving into the text messages right off the bat made her wonder just what she wanted to find. Before she dug in, she clarified her thoughts out loud: "Please let him be innocent."

She breathed in deeply and pressed on the green thought bubble at the bottom of the screen.

All of the texts were to and from one name: Steven Beck.

She collapsed onto the table in complete relief. "Steven Beck! Steven Beck!" she chanted. She had always loved that guy. She called Alison on her own phone. Alison answered right away as if she'd been waiting up for the call. She had.

"All the texts are to or from his college roommate, Steven Beck, who lives up here somewhere, too."

"He's gay?"

"No, what? Wait a second."

Olivia began to look through the chain of texts. They were all about running. She read them to Alison in a tone that rose from giddy to ecstatic.

I'm running 10 minutes late. Sorry.

Hurry up! I'm raring to go.

Feel free to start without me.

I'll have to warm up before you get here.

I only have an hour this morning.

I'm so worn out from yesterday, I don't know if I can do it again.

She felt satisfied. "You get the picture. He is meeting his friend to run."

"You must be relieved," Alison said, in a tone that made Olivia wonder if it were a question.

"I feel like you're not saying something."

Alison paused to collect her thoughts. She was feeling very tired and didn't want to put doubt in Olivia's mind if it no longer existed.

"It's just, why didn't he tell you that?"

"I don't know." Now Olivia paused to think. "Should I ask him?"

"I don't know. Do you care?"

"More out of curiosity. But I would rather stop torturing myself than know his reasoning. I'm going to stash this phone somewhere he will find it and never snoop again!"

"I agree. I'm happy for you. Are you happy?"

"Yes. And excited for a good night's sleep."

Olivia realized that she had been so self-absorbed that she'd forgotten to ask Alison about the bad part of her night. But she hadn't really slept in days and it was nearing midnight. She would ask her tomorrow.

"Thanks again, Alison, for everything."

As they hung up, Alison couldn't help but wonder why Spencer needed a second phone for running. She decided to just follow Olivia's lead and move on.

CHAPTER 29

Jackie & Jack & Alison & Marc

Jackie jumped on board the 5:49 with a little extra spring in his step. It did not go unnoticed.

"So, how was your date?" Lee asked.

"No hello?"

"We say hello every day. How many times do we get to say, 'How was your date?'"

"Fine. It went great."

"You kissed her?" Skip asked.

"I don't kiss and tell."

"That's because you need to kiss to tell, and my gut says you didn't," Skip chided. Lee elbowed Skip and continued in a kinder fashion.

"So you didn't kiss her?"

"No, I didn't kiss her."

Skip chimed back in, "Then it wasn't great. Everyone knows that's the sign of a great first date."

"Are you two still in a fraternity? Do you leave work and go to secret meetings where you haze each other and play beer pong?"

"How long has it been since you've been on a first date? Leave him alone," Lee defended Jackie.

"He doesn't bother me. I know it went great because I just know, and we held hands."

"Oooh, you held hands," Skip mocked. "You better get tested."

"Don't listen to him. I think you should text her over the weekend and ask her out again."

"I already texted her."

"Already! And?"

"And nothing. I haven't heard back."

"When did you send it?"

"This morning on the way in."

Lee was worried. "And you haven't heard back? That can't be good. Ask her how the date went online, as Jackie."

"No way. I'm not talking to her as Jackie ever again."

"Jackie is gonna ghost her?" Skip asked.

"I don't know. You're making me nuts. I'm tired, and word is we have lots of algebra homework this weekend. I'm gonna close my eyes."

Jackie should have known better. As soon as he nodded off, Skip took his phone and went to town.

How was your date?

"He's gonna kill you."

"It's for his own good. What could happen?"

"She could say terrible. Then what?"

"Then he'll know and not make an even bigger fool of himself. It will be a learning experience."

"Who are you?" Lee laughed. Skip laughed, too. But then she answered. And they stopped.

Forget my date! You're not going to believe who was waiting for me when I got home!

"Shit."
"Crap."
"What do I do?"
Lee grabbed the phone. "Give it to me." He typed:

Who?

Zach's "father." I think he wants back in. I just don't know how far in to let him.

They looked at each other.
"Now what?" Lee asked.
"I have no idea."
"We have to write something. How's this?"

No one can tell you what to do with this but you.

"No way. Tell her what to do. Jackie can't compete with the father of her baby."
"We don't know that."
Jackie let out a weird-sounding snore, like a snort confirming their fears. Skip grabbed back the phone, deleted Lee's post, and wrote:

You owe it to yourself to go out with the guy from the train again.

"Don't send that. It's ridiculous."
Lee grabbed back the phone, deleted it, and wrote:

Follow your heart.

Jackie stirred. He added "GTG," pressed Send, and slipped the phone back onto Jackie's lap.
"Yeah. That was a bad idea," Skip admitted.
"No shit."

There were two unanswered texts on Alison's phone. One from Jack:

Last night was fun. Hope we can do it again soon.

And one from Marc:

Sorry to have barged in on you. When is a good time for us to talk?

She thought about Jackie's simple advice, *Follow your heart.* At first it seemed a bit lame, especially since she was always one to follow her head, but maybe not. She followed her heart.

Hi Jack! It was so much fun, thank you again. I'm free this weekend if you are.

She thought it over. It was perhaps a little bold to suggest the weekend, but she sensed that with him there was no need to play games. His quick response affirmed it.

Great! Want to go to the fall fair in town on Saturday?

She had seen the flyers and pictured herself walking around with Zach in his stroller. She'd wondered if it would feel lonely. She didn't usually feel lonely with Zach; mostly she felt solid, like they were a family unit of their own. But she imagined the fair would be teeming with traditional families.

Would it be OK if I bring Zach?

Of course. I figured you would.

She was glad that she didn't have to worry about when was the right time to introduce her son to a guy, for now at least, although introducing him to Marc would be a much bigger deal than to Jack, for sure. Still, she couldn't exactly justify keeping a child from his father. She didn't think Marc would be an every-other-weekend kind of dad. She couldn't imagine him even wanting to be alone with Zach. She called Andie to discuss. An hour later, and with a list of worries like, *What if he gets married and they want to spend more time with Zach?*, she texted Marc back. Suddenly she felt she needed to know what he was thinking.

Anytime works for me. Let me know what's good.

The answer came back quickly.

How about now?

Zach was sleeping. She was awake. Now was as good a time as any. She called his cell.

"Hi."

"Hi."

There was a pause, which she purposefully did not try to fill. He asked to talk; she was not going to be first chair.

"I just want to say again that I'm sorry. I'm really embarrassed about how I behaved and reacted to your pregnancy. I'd like to discuss having some part in Zachary's life, if you would allow it."

Even though his mayoral-vetting committee was directing his every move, there was truth to his words. Seeing his son in person had shifted something in him—something he wasn't all that comfortable with. He'd reached out to the committee after visiting Alison and explained that he was confident he could repair things with the baby's mother, to the benefit of his candidacy. In his heart he knew it was for his own benefit as well.

"How far would you like it to go?" he'd asked.

They knew Marc Sugarman's drawback: He was not a very amiable guy. But the public is fickle. To see an extremely handsome, Ivy League–educated man with a stellar record standing next to his fiancée and baby boy would surely induce visions of Camelot in Gracie Mansion. What was originally thought of as his cross to bear could actually nail down his win. They'd answered, "As far as you are willing to take it."

"Would you consider coming into the city this weekend? We can take the baby to the Central Park Zoo."

She wanted to fully understand what Marc wanted from them, and from experience she knew that he was much easier to read in person. Plus, the zoo did sound nice, and she was free on Sunday.

"How about Sunday? Meet by the seals at eleven o'clock," she suggested.

"That would be great. Thank you for considering my appeal."

She wasn't sure if he meant it to be a joke, but she laughed all the same.

CHAPTER 30

Amanda

Mr. Barr had texted Amanda the night of their first meeting and suggested they get coffee at the Café Karma Sutra over the weekend to come up with a game plan. She knew it was ridiculous, but she was so nervous that she tried on three different outfits, running back and forth across the street for Eliza to give her her opinion. By the third time, her hair was starting to frizz.

"We really need to deal with this," Amanda softly berated her. "You're not going to be able to pull off never leaving the house over Thanksgiving break."

"Oh yeah, watch me," her friend said, smiling confidently. "I thought about it, and last year we spent all of Wednesday cooking, Thursday having Thanksgiving, and most of the weekend eating leftovers and watching football."

"You're not going to see Pippa in the play? That will be suspect, don't you think?"

Eliza became more serious. The thought of sitting in the high school auditorium again caused her hands to visibly shake. "It's not what I *want*, Mandy."

Amanda felt bad for pushing her there. "I know, I'm sorry. Maybe you should consider telling Luke and the kids over the holiday."

"Absolutely not. I can't send them back to school with that worry. If it doesn't go away, I will tell them by Christmas."

Amanda knew she was being tough on her, but coddling her as she had been didn't seem to be doing any good.

"You need to help it go away. Like last time."

"I'm still hopeful that it will just go away on its own. That looks great; wear that."

Amanda wasn't sure if Eliza was being her honest self or just wanted her to go back home and leave her alone. Either way she stuck with the outfit: jeans, a gray cashmere sweater, and low boots—pretty much her go-to.

She met Mr. Barr, *Dean*, at two o'clock in the afternoon. It was a low-traffic time for the bustling coffee shop, making it a great time to sit for an hour without any pressure to relinquish their table. Butterflies again danced in her belly upon seeing him, but the sensation was quickly doused by a particularly delicious muffin and the excitement of once again being part of a theatrical production. They talked about everything from set designs to soliloquies, and the first time that Amanda glanced at her watch she was shocked to see that two hours had gone by. She placed her hand on his arm to announce the time and her need to go and was again reminded of her old feelings for him. Until then she had been too caught up in the play to think about anything else. She was sure of one thing: He wasn't looking at her like a kid anymore, but more like an equal than a conquest. That was fine with Amanda; feeling like someone's equal in the theater satisfied an even greater fantasy.

Rehearsals filled Amanda with an excitement she hadn't felt in

ages. The kids really took to her, and Pippa didn't even mind her
being around. More than that, miracle upon miracle, she sensed
that Pippa was proud of her. It was like a space out of time for
both of them. An escape of sorts where their pain was replaced
with creativity and make-believe.

Amanda loved watching Dean teach the kids—standing on
stage doing his best Laurence Olivier. He had a youthful twinkle
in his eye and a lightning-in-a-bottle type of energy. He was electrifying.

Unbeknownst to Amanda, Dean found her electrifying as well,
though in a different way. Ever since their coffee meeting, he found
he was pushing back feelings for her, internally arguing over the
appropriateness of the inappropriate thoughts running through
his mind: *She's not my student now. She's married, but most definitely separated. She would never look at me that way.* And the
worst of all, *God, she is so beautiful.* All of his thoughts collided
in his brain on a daily basis.

They both intentionally kept a physical distance from each
other, but when they were alone in the close quarters of the costume closet or the wings of the stage, this was difficult to accom-
plish. He could list every time that they had brushed hands or
caught eyes for too long and she could still feel his hand on the
small of her back the one time he placed it there to guide her across
the stage. If it weren't for Pippa losing her phone, that encounter
might have marked their closest intimacy.

Amanda was home cooking dinner when Pippa came down in
a tizzy, looking for something. She had seen this look of panic on
her face before and called her out on it right away.

"Pippa, did you lose your phone again?"

She'd been looking everywhere and was more than happy to
come clean and get help from her mommy. "Yes, I'm sorry. Please
help me, Mommy."

As if on cue, her own cell rang. It was Dean Barr. Pippa had left her phone backstage at rehearsal. Whenever Pippa had left her phone somewhere safe in the past, Amanda had insisted she wait till the next day to retrieve it. It became a lesson to be more careful with one's belongings. But this time she was out the door before Pippa could say "hypocrite." Within seconds of driving away, the sky opened up.

Dean ran out to her car with his jacket propped over his head. He got in and slammed the door behind him.

"I can't believe you went out in this. You're such a good mom."

"It wasn't like this when I left."

It was now teeming—the kind of rain that people pull off the highway to wait out.

"I'm just gonna sit here till it lets up," she decided. Dean looked out the window toward his car.

"I'm gonna do the same, if you don't mind."

"I don't mind."

Amanda was barely aware of the awkwardness of being alone in a car together, she was so charged up about the play.

"You know, I've been thinking about something a little daring," he said, a playful look on his face.

"Pray tell," she said, with a Shakespearean vernacular.

Dean got right on the Bard bandwagon. "Word has cometh to me from the other players that your fair offspring, Pippa, is quite adept at the electric harp."

Amanda laughed. "Methinks that is true, my fine gentleman."

"Well, if it is so, why doth us not set her soliloquy to song?"

"Hark! No finer idea have I ever heard!"

They both laughed. When they stopped, Amanda made a mental note to have Carson ship Pippa's electric guitar. Thinking of that interaction dampened her mood and the change registered on her face. Dean noticed.

"What's wrong?" he asked.

"Nothing." She paused. They had never spoken about much else than the play, but it felt odd not to be truthful with him.

"It's just, as great as this has all been, sometimes my reality creeps back in. And it's not pleasant to think about."

"I'm sorry. It must be awful."

They both sat back and took in the curtain of water enveloping the car. The lull in conversation filled with the sound of the rain pummeling the windows.

"Should we check the weather to see when it's supposed to let up?" he asked.

Amanda looked on her phone.

"It should be stopping in ten minutes."

"Ten minutes," he repeated aimlessly. "It's really coming down."

"It is," she responded.

"I've wanted to kiss you for weeks," he admitted.

"I've wanted to kiss you for years," she admitted back.

It was impossible to tell who made the first move. It was so different from kissing Carson. Even with Dean's strong shoulders and squared jawline, it was somehow gentler, more sensuous. Carson was sloppy in the bedroom and selfish. She could tell if this were ever to go further Dean would be the opposite. She stopped herself from thinking about Carson and relished the sensation of kissing Dean Barr. She laughed inside at the memory of her naive eighteen-year-old self and the laugh surprised her as it exited her mouth. He laughed, too. He had never made out in the parking lot of the high school before.

They started up again and the water pounding down on the car in every direction seemed to encourage the frenzy of their kisses. At some point Amanda climbed on top of him, and while they were both very aware of what was stirring beneath, they stuck to only kissing. She thanked God and Norma Kamali for the jumpsuit she was wearing, its chastity-belt-like qualities keeping her from going too far. In a car. In the parking lot of her daughters' school. Between the outside storm and the inside steam, the windows completely fogged over.

The rain finally stopped, and they took it as a sign that they should stop, too. Amanda climbed off Dean's lap and blushed as she realized that she didn't remember climbing on.

It was the most fun either of them had had in forever.

"I should get this phone home to Pippa," Amanda said, scared to even glance at the time.

He looked at her and smiled before getting out. "Can we do this again?"

"I would like that very much."

The eighteen-year-old girl inside her playfully drew a heart with her finger on the misted window as she watched him drive out of the high school parking lot, while her current self sadly acknowledged that she hadn't felt that way in way too long. The wasted years registered in her brain just as Pippa's phone rang. She grabbed it without much thought.

"Hello?" she said.

"Amanda?" Carson said in return.

Everything in her deflated, as though the sound of his voice were a pin, bursting her utopian bubble.

"Yes, Pippa left her phone at play rehearsal."

"She's in a play?"

"She is, the lead." She said it in an accusatory way, as if Pippa's past apathy toward the theater had been his fault. Which wasn't really true. She reminded herself of her lawyer's advice and changed her tone.

"She's very excited about it. But she needs her electric guitar. Can you send it?"

"Maybe I should buy her a new one. She was vying for that Stratocaster, remember, Mandy?"

His two usual tells for guilty behavior revealed themselves in one sentence. Extravagant spending in exchange for forgiveness and calling her Mandy instead of Amanda. He was always going on about the importance of a strong name. Amanda Cole is a strong name, he would say, *not* Mandy Cole. He had made such a big deal when naming the girls. "My daughters need bold-faced names that will stand out in the press," he'd insisted.

Amanda remembered the first time she had seen his theory in action:

PIPPA AND SADIE COLE SHINE
IN VERSACE ON THE RED CARPET

Now their good names had been dragged through the mud along with his. Her calm intentions left her, and she answered him with rage in her voice. "Just send her guitar, Carson!"

"When is the play?"

"Thanksgiving weekend, but she needs it to practice."

"I was asking so that I could put it on my calendar."

Amanda grabbed the steering wheel to steady herself. *Put it on his calendar?* She wanted to punch something. He responded to her silence.

"Of course I am coming if my child is in a play. How would it look if I didn't?"

She couldn't be sure if he was baiting her or not, but regardless, she took it.

"How would it *look*? You are suddenly concerned with how things *look*? How do you think it *looked* when you humiliated me in public?"

"I have no idea what you are talking about, Mandy."

Again with the "Mandy"—she became enraged. "You degraded me every chance you had, Carson. I can't believe how long I put up with it." The elation she felt from being with Dean had quickly turned to regret—regret for living in limbo for years and years with no regard for her own happiness. She could blame it all on Carson, but she knew that she was also responsible. It was her own life.

"Oh well, I can believe it. You put up with it until I became part of the industry reckoning, and then you conveniently jumped on the bandwagon. What a surprise."

Amanda took another deep breath and got her shit together. "Carson. I'm mortified that it took other women calling you out for me to leave you, but the important thing is, I did. The girls can at least be proud of one of their parents."

She knew it was a low blow. *A kick to the Achilles*, she thought, but she didn't care. A thousand insults wouldn't tip those scales in her favor. He had been demeaning her with words and chipping away at her soul for years. He was silent, and she felt satisfied.

"Send the guitar to my father's address. I will ask Pippa if she wants you to come to her show, and I will let your assistant know the details if she does."

He started to answer her, but she hung up. She was shaking from the call. She could not imagine dealing with him in person, but she knew she would have to find a way. Her guess was that as angry as Pippa was, she would want him there. He was her dad. Amanda vowed not to sway her decision and was already regretting having lost her cool. She promised to herself she'd never let him rile her again. Instead, she'd do and say only that which would advance her cause.

CHAPTER 31

Alison & Jack and Alison & Jackie

N othing brings out the charm of a small town quite like a country fair. The trees seemed to be competing against each other for Best in Show as much as the overall-clad creations that lined Main Street for the annual scarecrow contest. And the creativity on display was astonishing. Alison's favorite scarecrows were the ones dressed as the band KISS, complete with signature painted pumpkin heads. Main Street was closed to traffic and covered in hay for horse-drawn buggy rides. A petting zoo and a prettiest pig competition were set up at one end of the road, and a farmers market selling locally sourced everything stood at the other.

She met Jack at the cider stand, as he had assured her that a hot cup of cider was the best introduction to the Hudson Valley Fair. It was infinitely more charming than meeting someone on the corner of Fifty-Third and Third. He was already holding a cup for her when they arrived. He kissed her on the cheek and said, "Good morning."

As she took it from him she was struck by the ease of their connection—the weirdest combination of familiar and exciting. She flinched at the unfamiliar taste of hot apple cider, but it was even more delicious than promised.

"It's yummy," she said, taking in the warmth in his eyes.

"I knew you would like it." He smiled.

She watched him take a sip. Her mind drifted to the possibility of kissing him. She reeled herself back in.

As they walked through the fair, Alison marveled at every turn, pointing things out to Zach as if he were old enough to understand. She could imagine him one day petting the animals and proudly carrying a little gourd. The longer she stayed in Hudson Valley, the farther away Manhattan felt. In her heart, she knew that she could snap right back into a modified version of her old life, but for now she was happy to sit back and enjoy the smell of wood-smoked air, apple cider, and fallen leaves. She had to admit her seasonal pumpkin spice latte in the city had nothing on the real deal.

And then there was this good-looking guy standing next to her. He seemed to have both appeared out of nowhere and been in her life forever. She couldn't remember ever making such an instantaneous connection with someone. When he reached out his hand to help her onto the horse-and-buggy ride, she actually took it, even though it was completely out of character for her to acquiesce to such old-fashioned chivalry. In fact, she usually made a point to do the opposite of what was offered. But here she was, with a gracious smile and open arms. She chalked it up to a side effect of having a baby, of loving so unconditionally. As the horse trotted through the fair, Jack seemed anxious, his eyes darting left and right like he was watching a match at Wimbledon. It was not the romantic excursion that Alison was expecting. She needed to know why.

"Are you looking for someone?"

He answered sheepishly, "Sorry. I'm looking for my daughter. This is the first year we didn't come together. Well, technically at least. The past few times she 'let' me drive her and her friends. I kind of skulked behind them. They only talked to me when they needed more money or wanted me to win them something at the arcade."

He spotted Jana and hid his face while pointing in her general vicinity.

"There she is. In the pink sweater."

Alison could see a group of young teenage girls and a few guys walking in a pack, laughing and, she imagined, trying to navigate their fleeting youth. She remembered the uneasy feeling of being fourteen. For her it was compounded by being a good foot taller than most of the boys her age. Jackie looked through his fingers and commented, "It seems like there are a few boys with them—I count three."

Alison counted four, but agreed with him, as the truth would make it an even boy-girl ratio and probably stress him out even more. His daughter was lucky to have such a caring dad. Alison knew that not having a father had directed the course of her life in many ways. Her mother had drilled it into her to never depend on a man. "A man is not a financial plan," she would chant. She ended every Cinderella story with her own kicker: "And the moral of the story is—buy your own shoes!"

"I never knew my dad," Alison found herself admitting to Jack, quite uncharacteristically. "Jana is so lucky to have you," she added, turning the attention back to him.

"I never knew mine either," he responded, taking it. "He had a heart attack when I was four. I look just like him though, which makes me feel good. You know, walking through life, trying to do right by him."

Alison thought about the difference between losing a father and having one that didn't want you. She hated to think of Zachary having those thoughts.

The kids got together and posed for a selfie, all pursing their lips or sticking out their tongues, grabbing back Jack's attention.

"Watch this." He texted Jana:

Having fun?

They watched as she looked at her phone and put it back in her pocket.

"Remember how we had selective hearing with our parents? This generation has selective texting. She won't answer me for hours, if at all. And if she does she'll say, 'Sorry, just saw this.' The only way to get her to respond quickly is to just write her name. Jana. It totally freaks her out, as if she has been caught doing something wrong but has no idea what it is. I save that for special occasions, when I really need her to respond."

The whole exchange frightened Alison. She was not looking forward to Zach's teenage years. She patted Jack's hand in sympathy. "Don't worry. They look like nice kids."

It was good to hear someone else's perspective. He rested his hand on hers. "Thanks."

It felt so nice to touch her that he didn't let go for the rest of the ride. He wanted to kiss her, but he knew he had to first tell her the truth. The close quarters of a moving horse-and-buggy ride seemed like the wrong setting to do so.

Alison felt the intimacy as well. Even with her baby on her lap, the scene seemed ripe for a kiss. The feeling of her hand in his left her wanting more. She couldn't remember ever waiting so long for a first kiss. It felt weirdly purposeful and certainly added to her desire.

After exiting the carriage, Alison transferred Zach to his stroller, and as the name suggested, they strolled. They checked out the craft area where Alison bought a funky bird feeder (that's literally what it was called) and Jackie bought a cute change purse for Jana that said "Taco Money" on it.

"It's her favorite food group!" he said, thrilled to have found something she would love.

They sat down for lunch on the porch of a café where they ate Cobb salads and shared an order of truffle fries and a bottle of Sauvignon Blanc. They never stopped talking.

"Do you like it here?" he asked.

"I do. I've never been happier. Though, this may be the first time in my life that I've stopped long enough to consider whether I'm happy or not."

"Then how would you even know?"

"I know. I'm not thinking about my next appointment, or my depo tomorrow, or my trial next week. I'm just here. My mind is here. Maybe I'm thinking about throwing in a load of laundry when the baby naps, but that's it."

"And you're not bored?"

"I'm not. When I was in the city the other day, I definitely enjoyed the whole buzz of it, but I felt good when I got home. I feel more present and contented here."

She talked about being a latchkey kid in Queens, and he about his childhood upstate. They bonded over their strong single mothers and their liberal arts educations, his Hamilton, hers Wesleyan. They both gave so much credit to their moms for their success in life. Jackie spoke with pride of his mother starting a small business to support them after his father passed, and Alison beamed when speaking about her mother's job at the UN. It turned out that both of their moms had passed away within months of each other, and they opened up about the awful and permanent feeling of being motherless.

He, of course, thought of Jana and of his wife, as he often did when such a conversation came up. But to his surprise he found himself talking about it. He revealed the details of Ann's death very matter-of-factly, without taking in the words that were coming out of his mouth.

"Everything was going fine, just as we had learned in Lamaze class. It was crazy and painful and intense and long, but as we expected. Ann was determined and strong, and she pushed Jana out in, maybe, six pushes. She held her for a few seconds and then said she was having trouble breathing, that she felt a tightness in her chest. They handed me the baby. I looked down at Jana's beautiful little face in my arms; looked up at my wife, and she was gone. Just like that. She'd had a pulmonary embolism. A blood clot in her lungs." His tone changed. "It's the number one cause of death in childbirth. They don't mention it in Lamaze. I had no idea."

He paused a second or two for Alison to recover, and let her say, "I'm so sorry for all of you."

He thanked her, and falsely added, "It was a long time ago," as if he still didn't feel like it had happened just yesterday. He changed the subject, asking Alison if she had bought a Halloween costume for the baby (she had, a peapod) and went right into his Halloween-with-a-teenage-daughter fears.

"I watch the neighborhood girls' costumes change as they age. One year they ring my bell dressed as an astronaut or a clown or SpongeBob SquarePants, and the next year, suddenly a slutty clown or a slutty astronaut or SpongeBob NoPants! I'm not looking forward to that fight, but I know it's coming. And don't worry, I know I can't use the word 'slut' in my argument!"

Alison was impressed that although he joked, he was clearly

woke. This roller coaster of emotion coming from this beautiful specimen of a man had her heart thumping around in ways she had never quite felt before. Just as Jack poured out the last smidgen of wine, Zach woke up hungry.

"Can I pick him up while you make his bottle?" Jack asked.

"Please," Alison responded, thinking both: *This guy can't be for real*, and *This must be what it's like to have an extra set of hands.* She took Zach back to feed him while Jack paid the bill and stopped to use the restroom. By the time he returned she had burped Zach, placed him back in the stroller in an upright position, and put a little hat on his head to block the sun. As they walked away, she thought about how hard she tried to do everything correctly. She looked down at her baby and suddenly revealed the thing that worried her most.

"Sometimes, when I look at him, I just wonder how badly I'm going to fuck him up."

Jack laughed. "I felt the same thing when Jana was a baby. My mom told me something very cheesy, but it stuck with me, and it helped." He hesitated but Alison coaxed him on. "She said a baby is like an apple seed. That tiny seed already contains everything needed to make an entire tree. The strong trunk, a host of branches, even the apples, it's all predetermined in the DNA of that little seed. Most of the job is done. You just have to tend to it. Just like a baby."

"I love that," Alison responded. "Your mom sounds like she was a very smart woman."

"She was. I miss her," he said, and the melancholy in his eyes matched his words.

"I miss mine, too," she said, with uncharacteristic vulnerability.

He wrapped his arms around her, slowly and purposefully, enveloping her in a sensation of both tenderness and strength. She sunk into his chest, giving of herself in a way that she never had before.

She couldn't take it any longer. She placed her hands against the cut of his jaw, looked into his eyes, and kissed him. He responded with a desire he hadn't felt in years, and all thoughts of needing to come clean before being intimate with her escaped his head. While they were both aware that they were standing in a public place, they continued kissing until they literally needed to break for air. There was a tender hunger between them that Alison was not used to. She considered asking him if he wanted to come back to her house. Though achingly aware that she had made the first move with their kiss, things were stirring so strongly in her she couldn't bear not to satisfy them.

Jackie felt similarly and it stopped him in his tracks. He knew he had to tell her, and he knew it had to be done immediately. As he struggled to find the words, Jana bounded up, interrupting them.

"Hi, Daddy!" she exclaimed with a little extra sweetness in her words. She was clearly there to check out his date. He felt flustered—all worry of telling Alison the truth replaced with concern that Jana may have seen them making out like two teenagers in the middle of town. He rallied and introduced them.

"Hi, baby," and then, "Alison, this is my daughter. Jana, this is Alison and her baby, Zach."

"He is so cute," Jana squealed. "If you ever need a babysitter!"

Alison allowed herself to envision this sweet girl caring for her baby. Maybe she would invite them both over for dinner next week.

"Did you eat?" Jackie asked, like the good parent that he was.

"I had pizza."

"She gave half of it to a stray dog," the boy next to her said, with a weird look of admiration in his eyes.

Jackie thought of the dog from the bulletin board, but he still had his head on enough not to blow his cover. That is until the boy put his hand casually on Jana's back and rubbed it in a way that rendered him not just any boy. As if Jackie's own horrifying thoughts weren't enough, the voice of God came back, reminding him, *Tampons lead to sex.*

The boy(friend?) removed his hand from his daughter's back and reached it out in introduction. "It's nice to meet you, Mr. Campbell. I'm Conor. Conor Heslin."

It was only then that Alison realized she hadn't known Jack's last name. Or had she? She was confused. It did sound familiar. The kid continued, "I'm a year ahead of Jana at Hudson."

An older boyfriend, Jackie thought, while temporarily forgetting every other aspect of his life. All of the balls he'd been juggling dropped to the floor as he reached out his own hand and offered, "You can call me Jackie. All of Jana's *friends* do."

It only took a second for Jackie to comprehend what had happened, but of course it was too late. He felt the heat rush to his face in the way it does when you realize you've said the wrong thing and can't take it back. He witnessed Alison snap to attention. Her revelation was evident in the change in her expression, from joyful to pained.

Jackie Campbell, the same name as her friend from the bulletin board. The one with the fourteen-year-old daughter. The hair on the back of her neck stood on end as she searched her brain for a logical explanation.

"Conor and I are gonna head over to the Karma Sutra for matchachinos," Jana said.

Jackie switched back into parenting mode. He wanted to say, "If you have caffeine now you'll have trouble sleeping tonight," but he refrained. His head was running in ten different directions. He went with, "Get a rain forest muffin. They're wicked good," and hammered the last nail in his coffin.

They smiled and went off. Jackie took a deep, cleansing breath to prepare his thoughts. Alison just stood there, waiting.

"I was just about to tell you."

"Really? You expect me to believe that?"

She felt foolish for the feelings she'd had just a few seconds before, foolish for subscribing to the fairy-tale scenario that she had been eternally warned to reject. She even felt a little bit frightened and exposed—especially having exposed her baby to him. She adjusted Zach's stroller and quickly walked away. He chased after her, careful not to make a scene but desperate to fix the situation.

"Alison, you have to believe me. I was just about to tell you the truth when they walked up!"

"I *have* to believe *you*?"

She was furious, and hurt. Oddly hurt, actually. She thought she'd found a prince and he was really a troll. She picked up her pace while she vowed to never go down this quixotic road again. He followed. She stopped in her tracks and asked, "Is this a thing you do regularly? Catfish women online?"

"Cat-what?" He looked horrified. "No, let me explain! I didn't know what to do when Jana got her first period. I was really lost, and my buddies from the train—you met them—they suggested I post on that ladies' bulletin board. I really go by Jackie. I didn't mean for this to happen."

Alison kept her face free of expression—a technique she used in court to get people on the stand to further incriminate themselves—and continued toward home. He kept in pace with her.

"I would have told you right away, but it was never the right time. I'm not used to lying."

"Well, you seem to have gotten the hang of it pretty quickly."

"Come on, Alison, I stopped talking to you as Jackie as soon as we went out for dinner."

She stopped again and thought. *Did he?*

And then she remembered his *follow your heart* advice and her fury rebounded.

"Seems like you can't even keep your lies straight." Alison the attorney's shoulders squared.

Jackie was confused, and he should have countered, but he was more concerned with making things right.

"I should have told you on the train—or maybe when we were messaging. I don't even know how I got in this deep. I'm so sorry. It's just, I liked talking to you and then we met, and I really liked you and I was worried I'd blow it, that you would be angry and not want to see me again."

Alison ran through what else she remembered of her Jackie conversations in her mind. She was instantly embarrassed and doubly pissed. She stopped and looked at him, and the corners of her mouth turned up into the smile that her opponents in court knew meant their defeat.

"Well, Mr. Campbell, you got two things right."

He hadn't known her long, but he could already see she'd closed herself off.

"I'm angry, and I never want to see you again."

CHAPTER 32

Olivia & Spencer

t had been a week or so since Olivia had solved the mystery of the second phone. It was back in Spencer's possession and everything had been seemingly fine. If anything, she thought that Spencer must think her a bit crazy, with her frequent fluctuations: She loves me, she loves me not. Right now, she loved him.

It was Saturday night and they actually had dinner plans with Steven Beck and his wife, Lauren. As she applied the finishing touches to her makeup, she wondered whether Spencer and Steven would talk about running together. She hated the thought of having to pretend she didn't know about their morning ritual if it came up in conversation. She had since attributed Spencer's secrecy about it to not wanting to hurt her feelings—his desire to run with his faster, stronger friend as opposed to his slower and out-of-shape wife. She thought about coming clean regarding the phone, but remembered what Andie Rand had said about snooping being a betrayal as well. She decided to keep her mouth shut.

Things were finally normal between Olivia and Spencer and that feeling of contentment was trickling down to encompass her whole being. She had been devouring a book on the landscape painters of the Hudson River School and even had a selection of watercolors and brushes in her Amazon cart, just waiting for her to push the button so she could set up her old easel on their back deck. She hadn't painted in years, and though just a hobby, it relaxed her like nothing else.

What good would telling him do? she thought again, while dabbing one last coat of powder on her cheeks.

Spencer liked to take his Porsche out on the weekends instead of the family car. It was red and a bit showy for Olivia's taste. And he definitely drove it too fast, but tonight she didn't mind as much. When they stopped at a red light, Spencer rested his hand on Olivia's bare knee. "You really look beautiful tonight."

A couple of good nights' sleep and the utter relief she'd been feeling had Olivia glowing with new energy. She even fit back into her favorite dress, a little black number by Max Hammer that she'd only had the chance to wear once before becoming pregnant. She ignored the fact that her weight loss had been stress and worry induced. When she looked in the mirror, she really did feel beautiful.

Her happiness soon soured to guilt, and by the time they got to the restaurant, Olivia couldn't hold it in any longer. The thought of sitting with Steven Beck and listening to them talk about their runs without saying anything felt like she would be outright lying. Spencer reached to open the car door.

"Wait, Spence, I have to tell you something."

She looked quite serious. He gave her his attention.

"I have to admit something to you, and I know it's awful, and I'm really sorry."

"You're scaring me, Olivia. What is it?"

"I know about the second phone."

Spencer's face remained blank. He didn't say anything, no explanation, no denial, nothing. His mind raced in every direction for the right words, but it was actually his silence that saved him. Olivia took it as anger and tried to talk *her* way out of it.

"You left it home the other day, and I'm sorry, but with all that went on with the bulletin board misunderstanding, I was still feeling doubtful, and I looked at it."

Still nothing. Silence. He had no intention of incriminating himself, so he just shut up, his brain racing to recall what was on that phone that could ruin his marriage and ultimately his promotion. York Cosmetics' latest campaign—a Family Company with Family Values—ran through his mind. The picture of him, Olivia, and Lily front and center. He had set everything up so perfectly. Even Ashley was convinced that they could have their cake and eat it, too.

Not knowing how else to break the silence, Olivia continued. "I know it's just for running. I felt like such an idiot when I saw the pictures and the texts from Steven. I'm sorry, Spencer."

He sighed a huge sigh of relief that Olivia interpreted as frustration and went for the spin.

"Wait, you had my phone the whole time I was looking for it?"

"Yes, I'm sorry."

"This is crazy Olivia, I thought we were past this crap. Spying on me, really? Where is the trust?"

Olivia started to cry.

"I'm so sorry, Spencer. Please, please forgive me."

He took a minute, for effect.

"Are we good now? Can we move on with our lives without you questioning everything I do?"

She wanted to say, I don't question everything you do, but thought that, since he seemed to be forgiving her, she should just cut her losses.

"Yes. I'm so sorry. I'm done. Nothing like this will ever happen again."

Spencer saw the Becks pull into the lot.

"They're here. Wipe your eyes, please. I don't want them to see that you were crying. They'll of course assume I'm to blame."

Olivia pulled down the visor mirror to fix her face while Spencer got out of the car. He walked right up to Steven and gave him a big frat-bro hug. During which he whispered in his ear, "We go running nearly every morning together, OK?"

He recognized the angry look on Steven's face. Spencer had not been faithful to Olivia since the day they met, and Steven had bore witness to a lot of it. In fact, he'd been sitting right next to him on that fateful train to Florence when Olivia put down her book and stood with her coltlike legs and Julia Roberts smile, catching Spencer's attention. Spencer had pointed at her and said, "She's the one!" Spencer was not a romantic. Steven knew that if he were to have completed that sentence it would have been, "she's the one who will meet with my parents' approval." Everyone knew that Spencer's parents' ways were not to be challenged if he was to succeed at his ultimate goal: to become CEO of York Cosmetics and ride the York family gravy train for life. That trajectory included being paired up with a girl with pedigreed DNA by graduation. Everyone knew, that is, except for Olivia.

The last time that Spencer asked Steven to cover for him, Steven had told him outright, "I am no longer your alibi." He had always cared for Olivia and they were not frat boys anymore. Spencer knew Steven well enough to understand exactly what he was thinking. He added, "This is the last time, man, I swear."

Beautiful Olivia walked up to greet them; a warm smile crossed her face. He nodded yes to Spencer, but more for her than him.

They had just had a baby; he couldn't take part in breaking her heart right now.

Once inside, Olivia knew enough not to bring up running or anything that would remind Spencer of her sneaky behavior. She was thankful that she'd told him, relieved to be liberated from her lie. He seemed to have forgiven her, for now at least, but she knew it would be the first thing he would bring up in a fight. He never fought fair.

Before dessert Spencer pulled Steven away to check the score of the baseball game at the bar. That was fine with Olivia. She liked Steven's wife, Lauren, very much. She, too, had originally been a city girl. Though they'd moved out a year earlier than Spencer and Olivia, Lauren was still delighted to go through the city versus suburb laundry list of pros and cons with her. As they were rattling off the pros, from barbecues to closet space, Olivia innocently added, "And the guys get to run together again. That's a plus!"

"Well, not since Steven started his new job. He has to be in the city by eight, poor guy, and he hates running at night."

The men came back to the table in time for dessert: four spoons, one piece of cheesecake, and one giant lie about to be exposed.

"How do you like your new job?" Olivia asked Steven, assuming he had started that week.

"It's not exactly new, almost three months now. But no complaints."

Three months. Olivia smiled falsely as the feeling of betrayal, and all that came with it, returned. Her heart tightened in her chest, but still she smiled. Lauren politely asked Spencer about his work, and thankfully all eyes turned to him. She was glad that she had put her thumbprint in his phone. As soon as he fell asleep she was going to find it again, open up his Map My Run app, and see exactly where he'd been running to every morning.

On the ride home from dinner Olivia was silent. She knew Spencer would notice, knew he would ask what the matter was, but she couldn't bear to make small talk. "Cat got your tongue?" he asked.

He thought he was being cute, but he had no idea how telling his little idiom was. Olivia pinched herself. College was not so long ago. Her sophomore class at Wellesley on the history of idioms had been one of her favorites. The phrase "cat got your tongue" was derived from ancient Egypt, where liars' tongues were cut out and fed to the cats. She looked over at him and saw who he really was—a liar. He was a cheat and a fraud who had now made her life fraudulent as well.

It took every ounce of self-control to keep her mouth shut. She thought about her confession earlier, and how he had made her feel like she was crazy. It had felt awful to question her own sanity like that. To feel like some kind of lunatic wife who had come undone.

She stopped herself from rehashing everything that had transpired that night and focused on the possibility of creating an authentic life without Spencer, centered on caring for herself and her beautiful baby girl. She thought about the watercolors in her Amazon cart and diving back into graphic design again. An old client had left her a message just the other day about updating his logo. Thinking about things in her control calmed her. She breathed in and out purposefully and let her mind go to what needed to be done in order to achieve her goals—finding that second phone again and using it to bury the stranger sitting next to her.

"I'm just sitting here thinking how lucky I am that you forgave me for snooping," she responded.

"You're not yourself, honey. I understand. It's the hormones."

He put his hand on her leg as he had on the way there. Now she recoiled from it.

At home she purposefully spent an extra few minutes in the bathroom getting ready for bed. He was out cold when she returned.

She said his name quietly. "Spencer?" Nothing.

And a little louder. "Spencer!" Still nothing.

She threw in a few choice words before heading to his closet to search for the other phone. By the time she reached the point of frustration, Lily cried her hungry cry from the crib, saving her from looking further. As she nursed, she pondered what could be so bad about it being just her and Lily. Alison was doing it alone and seemed so happy. But she gulped away tears as that desire faded; she was and had always been a Disney princess kind of girl whose happily-ever-after had always included a prince—a loyal prince, that is. This scenario—with Snow White busily keeping house while Prince Charming jogs by Cinderella's every morning for a quickie—was not her dream.

She fell asleep in the chair; a blessing really, as she knew there was nothing lonelier than sleeping next to someone you despise. In the morning, Spencer came into Lily's room and kissed her on the top of her head. She felt a pang of love: a moment in which she'd forgotten what was really going on.

"Come back to bed, baby, and get some rest," he said.

"I'm OK." She smiled, still vacillating between sleep and hell. She woke up and thought it through. It was Sunday, Spencer would not be running, and she would have little chance of finding that phone. She changed her mind.

"Actually. Would you mind taking care of Lily? I'm not feeling great and could use some more sleep."

She stayed in bed until noon, a personal postcollege record. She only had to make it ten more hours without bludgeoning him.

CHAPTER 33

Alison & Marc

When Alison left for the city the next morning there were already three messages from Jack or Jackie. It didn't matter what she called him now because she vowed never to call him again. Brought up by a woman deceived, she loathed any kind of deception. Still, she was feeling horrible and confused as to why she was feeling *so* horrible and confused about a man she barely knew.

When she'd returned home the night before, she went through their entire online correspondence. Her anger increased exponentially with each duplicitous post. Especially his last—*Follow your heart.* She was done with that; she was back to following her head again as she always had. Her mother had been right all along.

She was looking forward to seeing Marc—anxious to hear what he had to say and eager to make the right choices for her and Zachary without a romantic component. It was bizarre to admit, but she felt the sting of Jack's betrayal on a much more personal level than she did Marc's rejection of her pregnancy.

Her first thought upon hearing that Marc wanted to talk was, *I will not lose control of my child*, though she knew she couldn't assume a court would side with her if she denied Marc's paternal rights. She spent the night tossing and turning, but that was not what kept her awake. Her thoughts turned to Zach's future and how important it was for him to have family in it. She realized that, in the time between her mother's passing and Zachary's birth, she had felt unanchored. She never wanted him to feel that way.

Had she known what it would take to pack up a baby for a whole day and drive into the city, she might have walked around handing trophies to new mothers who did so. As she pulled into the parking garage on East Sixty-Eighth Street, she had never felt more accomplished.

She met Marc at the Central Park Zoo as planned. He was practically dressed for a deposition in a sports jacket and khakis. It made her laugh to think that this was his casual Sunday look. She realized he wouldn't be the kind of dad that would play ball with Zach, if she were to welcome him that way. But that would be OK. She had a pretty good arm for throwing a baseball. Maybe Marc could teach him how to play chess and squash. She had no idea if he played either, but if she were to guess . . .

He greeted her with a kiss on the cheek and Zach with an awkward pat on his head. They walked around the whole zoo as if they had a curious toddler with them, not a clueless baby.

"I'm embarrassed to say this," Marc admitted, "but I haven't been here since I was a kid. I've hardly visited any of the city's tourist spots in years. I'm always working."

"One good thing about having a kid: You get to see things anew through their eyes."

"That's true. I remember loving the top of the Empire State Building when I was young. Maybe I can take Zach there when he's old enough."

Alison was happy to hear, for Zachary's sake, that Marc was thinking past today. She was glad that his words elicited a positive reaction in her, as opposed to more panic over losing control. Though it all felt simple while they were walking around the zoo, she knew it could easily become quite complicated. She wasn't committing to anything.

They returned to the seals for feeding time, along with just about every person at the zoo that day. She imagined that since Gus, the famous neurotic polar bear, had passed away, the seals and the penguins had been duking it out for top billing. She was clearly right.

Alison pulled out her phone and took a selfie of her, Zach, and Marc with a seal perched up on the side of the glass enclosure photobombing them. It was a great shot of a seemingly happy family. If today was all there was of the story of Zachary Le and Marc Sugarman, then at least she could give him this picture one day. *This is your father. He just didn't have it in him. It is not a reflection on you.*

"Can you send me that?" Marc asked. As she forwarded him the picture, she thought back on all of the time they had been together. There had never been any need for photographic evidence or a desire for some memento of their relationship. It's funny how a baby changes everything.

By the time they reached the petting zoo, which neither had any interest in, it was time for Zach's bottle. They walked uptown a few blocks and settled in under the shade of an oak tree overlooking the Seventy-Second Street playground. Alison handed the baby to Marc while she mixed the bottle. He held him so awkwardly that it made her think about how she had felt when Jack took him in his arms. She shook herself mentally. Why was she hung up on this guy she'd been on two dates with? So what if he didn't turn out to be who she thought he was? It's not like that hadn't happened before. She looked at Marc, who was holding Zach with the ease of a vegan holding a piece of raw chicken, and laughed.

"Let me show you how it's done."

"Please."

When she finally got the baby situated, she asked Marc if he wanted to feed Zach the bottle.

"I'll try," he responded nervously. Zach was extra hungry and really sucked the bottle down, which made it easy in some ways, but harder in others. She sat back so as not to hover over them. She was being careful to appear to be a good mother. She wondered why, wondered if it was the lawyer in her building her case—"the defendant is an excellent mother, even the plaintiff would testify to that." They were having a surprisingly nice day, but she was suddenly eager to hear the bottom line. What did he want?

When it was time to burp him, Alison took over, in more ways than one.

"You did good," she said kindly. Zach let out a power burp, and Marc beamed.

"Wow! That was some burp!"

A feeling of pride came over him that until then had only been reserved for court or a winning squash set. It surprised him.

Alison knew his facial expressions well enough to notice something was up. She couldn't wait any longer.

"Marc? What's going on?"

He paused. "We've always been honest with each other, right?"

She nodded her head. "Absolutely."

After the Jackie fiasco it seemed even more important.

"I came to see you the other day because I've been approached to run for mayor. The candidate they were exploring before me was Reed Coakly, so needless to say he's out."

Like the rest of the free world, Alison knew that Reed Coakly had just been exposed in a sexting scandal similar to Anthony Weiner's. "Exposed" being the key word. Marc continued, "They put a lot into him, both time and money, and they can't risk another mistake. It turns out that fathering a baby who I have nothing to do with is considered a mistake."

She shouldn't have been surprised that this whole reunion of sorts was so calculated; everything Marc Sugarman did was calculated. But she was. Both surprised and hurt. It showed on her face, and he immediately addressed it.

"I'm sorry I didn't mention this on Thursday night, but when I got to your house my underlying motives suddenly felt irrelevant."

She didn't seem to be budging.

He continued. "You know I'm not a very sensitive guy. When people say 'all the feels,' I have no idea what they're talking about. But when I picked up the picture of Zach, just the picture, I felt more than I'd ever felt in my life."

His candor was touching. Alison was most definitely touched.

"So, my real reason for coming suddenly felt idiotic, and I was scared you would slam the door in my face if I presented myself as the selfish prick that I usually am."

Alison smiled at his honesty, albeit delayed. At least he owned up to it, unlike someone she knew—or didn't know, as it turned out. She was curious and, as she usually was with him, direct.

"OK. Tell me more about what you need from me."

"The committee to elect is hoping you would be on board, in some fashion, for the campaign."

"Meaning?"

"Anything from not hurting my candidacy by revealing what a complete jerk I was about the pregnancy and the baby . . . to marrying me."

He laughed. So did she. It was funny.

What she didn't realize is that he would seriously consider

marrying her. In fact he had already done a pro-and-con spreadsheet. When he sat down and thought about it, thought about her, he realized he'd never been more attracted to anyone than he was to Alison. And it wasn't just a sexual attraction; he was equally enticed by her brilliant mind and her one-of-the-guys attitude. The only cons were his disdain for emotional intimacy and the interruption of his alone time, both overridden by an increasingly burning desire to become the next mayor of New York.

But she laughed when he said marriage, causing him to backpedal.

"I told them there is no way you would enter into a fake marriage." He paused for her to confirm or deny his statement.

"That is correct. I don't even know if I would enter into a real one." She laughed again.

No one understood her point more than Marc Sugarman. Bearing witness to his parents' toxic marriage and wicked divorce poisoned him against the institution long ago. Still, he knew that nothing could humanize him more than a woman like Alison and their son standing by his side. He came right out and said it.

"I really need you, Alison."

"I get it. I believe in you, Marc. I want to be there for you on this."

He smiled with relief. It made her smile, too. Mostly because of the irony of him needing her when she had managed to not need him whatsoever.

"The best alternatives are: You stand by my side without much explanation to the press, or I call you my fiancée until sometime after the election."

His team was very hopeful that they would land on the fiancée agreement. After Alison's response to the M word, he was not.

Alison sat back against the tree, her mind running in many directions. She had very high hopes for Zachary, and being the mayor's son wouldn't hurt his future. She couldn't help but consider the leg up that would give him in life. Gracie Mansion was quite the leap from the one-bedroom in Queens that had housed her own inauspicious beginnings. Not that she hadn't done fine, and she relished that self-made success.

There was another factor that she needed to consider, one that Marc guessed would weigh heavily on her when he brought all of this nonsense up. She very much believed that Marc would be an excellent mayor. Despite his lack of easygoing charm, Marc cared about the city, a lot. And would be just the right amount of asshole to get things done. *And* she despised his opponent. His proposed policies would have horrible repercussions on the city's undocumented immigrants, and Alison saw her mother's young face in every one of them.

She couldn't deny how exciting it would be to be a part of the good fight. Maybe a "for appearances" relationship would give them time to discover if anything more between them was possible? Maybe this was a chance for her and Zach to have a family of sorts—the pragmatic, anti–fairy tale that was more her speed. She asked the hard question: "We first need to discuss what part you really want in Zach's life—not just for the cameras."

"Of course. I'm sorry for not bringing that up first. I can tell you that I very much want to be in Zach's life in some capacity, regardless of what you decide. I know it's up to you. I can see that you're a great mother and I trust you to do what's best for him."

And then the oddest thing happened: His eyes began to well with tears as he ran his hand through Zach's sparse hair. He choked up.

"Thank you for giving me a son, for seeing his life as a gift. I feel ashamed for not having seen it that way myself. Very ashamed."

His tears begat hers. They both laughed and wiped their eyes.

"I will stand beside you, Marc. But I don't think the press will stand for your no-explanation idea. How about when asked we say we are engaged to be engaged but want to concentrate right now on the election."

Of course she came up with a better plan than his team of experts, he thought.

"Thank you, Alison. That sounds perfect."

"You will be a great mayor, Marc, and, I bet, a good dad as well."

"Well, at least we know he'll be proud of me on snow days!"

They both laughed, the way one does when it's really needed. It was a tough thing to figure out and they both felt satisfied with the resolution.

They sat back quietly and stared at the kids playing in the playground. Within minutes Alison found herself wondering what Zachary would be like at their age. Marc found himself wondering if a promise to upgrade the city's playgrounds would secure the mommy and daddy vote. If they had expressed their thoughts out loud, they might have realized how far apart they truly were.

CHAPTER 34

Olivia

On Monday morning when Spencer left for his run, Olivia set up Lily's baby monitor in their bedroom for his return. She was leaving nothing to chance. She watched from the kitchen as Spencer walked into the room and immediately slipped the phone under the mattress. *Got you*, she thought.

She was still seething when he kissed her goodbye, a Stepford smile plastered on her face.

"It should be a light day today. I'll be home for dinner for sure."

"Great!" she responded without breaking.

When he left, she felt a weird sense of strength come over her.

The running app was quite simple to figure out. *I'm as resourceful as Macaulay Culkin in* Home Alone, she thought with a laugh. Not a big laugh, but enough to pinch the anger a bit.

What she discovered threw her for a loop—that loop being a direct line from her house to Eliza Hunt's.

As Olivia waited outside Alison's house, she looked in the mirror. Her eyes were unrecognizable—as if something inside of her had come unhinged. She needed to wrangle in the anger a bit. At least she had the presence of mind to call her sitter after hanging up with Alison. Lily did not need to be anywhere near her right now. She did her four-seven-eight breathing while Alison strapped Zach into Lily's car seat.

"Do you want me to drive?" she asked.

Olivia could picture herself ramming her car through Eliza Hunt's garage door, so she unsnapped her seatbelt and relinquished the wheel.

On the way there, Alison logically lectured her on how unlikely it was that her very young husband was having an affair with the middle-aged moderator of the Hudson Valley Ladies' Bulletin Board, but Olivia wasn't having it.

She got out of the car at the Hunts' house and rang the doorbell incessantly.

"I think she heard you."

Alison may have only known Olivia a short time, but one thing was clear to her: Olivia had lost it.

She looked Olivia in the eyes, trying to ground her. "Maybe she's not home. Let's go."

Olivia ignored her and rang the bell some more with the added bonus of looking through the living room window and yelling, "I'm never going away!"

Even Alison was happy when Amanda showed up to help.

"What's going on here, ladies?" she asked.

Olivia was convinced that Amanda's presence was indicative of Eliza being at home. She continued her doorbell campaign. *How much ringing could one woman endure?* she wondered. Negotiations between Alison and Amanda began. Amanda assured Alison that there was no way Eliza was having an affair. Alison informed Amanda that there was no way Olivia was leaving without speaking to Eliza in person. Amanda made a phone call and then confronted Olivia.

"She will let us in if you promise to remain calm."

"I promise," Olivia mumbled.

Alison didn't believe her. She pulled her aside.

"Olivia. If for some godforsaken reason your husband is having an affair with this woman—who I'd like to add is about twenty years older than you—doing something crazy to her will make you the villain here. Do you get that?"

"Yes," she snapped.

The door opened. They all went inside. Olivia took one look at Eliza and realized she was being ridiculous. But why was Spencer coming to her house every day? She calmly, yet maniacally, asked for an explanation.

"Why is my husband coming here every morning?"

Amanda looked at Eliza and pleaded with her eyes for her to tell the truth. Eliza acquiesced.

"Can I see a picture of him?" Eliza asked.

Olivia pulled out her phone. Eliza studied it. She could tell it was him. Then Olivia pulled up the Map My Run evidence and showed it to them both. There was nothing left to do but tell her the truth.

"I'm sorry, but I think your husband is having an affair with my new neighbor. A man who looks like him visits her every morning after her husband leaves for work."

"Which side?" she asked, ready to rumble. Alison stopped her.

"What are you going to do, go next door and beat her up? She probably won't even answer the door for you, and then again you won't have proof. He can just say he runs with her and thought you wouldn't be cool with it."

"She's right," Amanda said. "It's not enough."

"I just want to look at her. I want to see her face."

Mandy whispered to Eliza, who reluctantly agreed. "We can sometimes see her from my upstairs window, if she's home. She doesn't sit around all day," she said, as if doing so was pathetic. When she heard her own words, they stung.

As they climbed the stairs and set up a stakeout of sorts at Eliza's desk, Olivia suddenly felt overwhelmingly awkward about their intrusion. She had no idea that Eliza spent most days alone and was actually thankful for the company.

"I'm sorry to put you in the middle of all this," Olivia said. Eliza was filled with guilt; she knew that *she* had put herself in the middle of all of this.

"I'm sorry I didn't tell you more when you came last time. I was honest when I said that someone made up the post. But I didn't mention that that someone was me."

"I don't understand. Why would you do that?"

Olivia looked so betrayed when she asked the question. It made Eliza feel awful. She did her best to justify her behavior, though she doubted her company would understand.

"I heard about this younger and hipper group called Valley Girls. I was trying to keep up with them—be more relevant—give the people what they want. I'm so sorry. This all spun out of control."

Alison chimed in, with the intention of taking Eliza out of the hot seat. She was unsure about the stability of the witness and wanted to keep her from being on the defensive.

"I went on the Valley Girls site once. Besides the fact that I didn't find it helpful in any way, I couldn't relate at all. The women seemed like a bunch of phonies. I know I'm not married, but I can't believe these exercise-obsessed women with their perfect one-point-eight kids are having that much sex. I'm not buying it."

"I thought the average was two-point-three children?" Olivia moaned. "I wanted to have three. Now I will probably just have the one."

"That's not true," Mandy piped up. "You have your whole life ahead of you."

Alison redirected the conversation. "I understand why you got competitive, Eliza. I don't blame you. But what happened next?"

"I saw her husband visiting Ashley Smith and I dreamed up the affair in my head."

Olivia looked like someone had punched her in the gut. Her heart sank to her stomach and the room began to shift.

"Did you say Ashley Smith? Ashley and Jim or John or something-with-a-J Smith?"

"Joe, yes. Why?"

They all held their breath.

Shock, betrayal, grief, and pain fired at her from all directions.

"Where's the bathroom?" It was clear she was going to vomit. She made it just in time, locking the door behind her. The three women stood outside the door trading sympathetic looks. Little Zachary cooed and kicked his legs in the BabyBjörn that Alison had thrown him in so as to have her hands free, or possibly her fists.

"How are you doing in there, honey?" Eliza asked, to no reply.

They heard some stirring inside and the sound of running water stopped. Alison took a shot: "Come on out, Olivia."

She came out and slid down the wall to the floor while the three of them looked on. She explained in a tired, heartbroken voice, "Around eight months ago Spencer and I were out for dinner in the city. A couple that he knew passed by our table. Well, he knew her, but I can't even remember if he said where from. He asked them to join us. She said no, but he insisted, and the husband eagerly gave in to the idea. She seemed nervous the whole time, really uncomfortable, while her husband seemed really friendly and nice. I remember feeling bad for her, trying to ask her questions to warm her up. It seemed to make things more awkward. And then, in the end, the baby was doing crazy flips. You know, the kind that makes one whole side of your stomach rise and fall like an alien. Spencer noticed me holding my belly, feeling her move around. He turned to Ashley and said, 'Do you want to feel my baby?' I remember thinking that it was such a weird way to put it, 'my baby,' and even weirder that he was pimping out my stomach for this woman to feel."

At this point in the story, the three women were glued to Olivia's every word. None of them could believe that she unknowingly broke bread with the other woman. They all hated Spencer now, really hated him. They were holding their breath praying that the woman didn't touch her belly. When she reported that the woman said, "No, thank you," they breathed a collective sigh of relief. Olivia noted it and actually felt relieved that this was all as horrible as she thought it was.

She continued. "But he insisted on it. He took her hand and placed it on my belly. I remember we even got into an argument about it later that night." Olivia went on. "She had the strangest look on her face. At the time I thought, I bet this poor woman is having trouble conceiving or something like that. Her expression was so pained. I even told Spencer my theory. I was worried about *her*!"

The other women sunk to the floor as well and consoled Olivia. They grieved with her, bonding over their shared humanity as women, both vulnerable and strong.

She had yet to utter a word of any of this to her parents or her sister or to any of her old friends. When she did, she knew there would be no turning back. For now she felt seen and heard and known by these three women, even though she hadn't known them for longer than the hot minute it took for her life to unravel before her eyes, before their eyes. At that moment they were quite miraculously enough.

CHAPTER 35

Amanda & Eliza

A manda stayed on after the Saturday rehearsal to help Dean organize the costume closet. It was a completely overwhelming task as the place was a disorganized mess.

"I wouldn't be surprised if we come across my old Ado Annie costume in here. It looks like this place hasn't been touched in fifty years."

"I bet it would still fit you."

"No way."

"Absolutely," he said, placing his hands on her narrow waist and pulling her toward him. "Let's take a break."

"Did you make up this project just to get me alone in here?"

"Possibly."

He kissed her again, as he had done nearly every chance that he'd gotten since their rainy-day interlude. He apparently didn't shave on the weekends, his silvery scruff making him even more handsome but prickly to the touch. Fifteen minutes in and she had to stop, citing beard burn. It was both true, and an excuse. As the shock was wearing off about all that had happened over the past weeks, the magnitude of what Carson had done, and her impending divorce, felt omnipresent. It cast a cloud over their dalliance, along with every other sunny thing in her life. She left, saying she had to get back for her kids.

Before stepping out of the car at home, she checked herself in the mirror. Between her smudged makeup and chafed cheeks, she looked like she had indeed spent the day making out in the costume closet. As she wiped the stray mascara from beneath her eyes, she caught a glimpse of a limousine idling on the street, an odd sight in Hudson Valley for sure. She got out of the car and knocked on the driver's window.

"Can I help you?" she asked.

"No, I'm just waiting out here for Carson Cole."

She took a beat before entering her house, promising herself that she would not lose her cool, no matter which Carson, combative or contrite, she found inside. She entered, armed with the confidence of being on her home turf.

"Hello, Mandy," he said, clearly on purpose, again, to soften her. Everything with Carson was a manipulation. It was why he was so successful in Hollywood: He always had an agenda, and he twisted and turned everyone around until he got his way. But she had an agenda as well.

"What are you doing here?"

"I brought Pippa's guitar."

"It's not a puppy; you didn't need to hand deliver it."

"Well, I missed my family, so I did. Is that OK with you?" His tone was biting. He didn't seem to be going for the repentant approach after all. She countered, suddenly not caring about her lawyer's advice to stay civil.

"If you had any respect for me, you would not have shown up at my father's house unannounced." She held the front door open. "You can leave, and come back when you're invited."

He closed it.

"Pippa invited me."

"So you've seen them."

"Yes, all afternoon. Where have you been?"

The question threw her, but she collected herself and ignored it. "How long are you in town?"

"I'm staying through Thanksgiving. I'll text you to make arrangements for the girls to come to the city to see me. I'm at the Plaza, and Sadie is excited to stay where Eloise stayed."

She remembered him reading *Eloise* to the girls when they were little. He even once brought home Eloise dolls from a business trip to New York. *More bribery*, she thought. Although, if she were being honest with herself, she would have to admit that the girls missed him. Pippa may have been a little too young still to understand the nuances of consent and power dynamics, but if nothing else, she was angry that her father cheated on her mother. Even so, she loved him and was concerned for him. Amanda had certainly felt that way when her own mother walked out. The really deep and permeable anger came later.

In that moment, she wished he had been an awful, negligent father and that she could have nothing further to do with him, but having been a child on the receiving end of that kind of rejection made her sensitive to its repercussions. She was happy for them that he cared enough to come east for a while. She admonished herself for feeling something positive about Carson when, as if on cue, he admitted his real reason for staying.

"I need to hide, and I can't run away to Europe right now."

Any shred of compassion was wiped away.

"Do you realize the damage you've done?" Amanda asked, her voice rising. "Not just to our family, but to the women, the women you abused?"

"Do you think I need to hear this from you, Amanda?"

She laughed at him. "You've got to be kidding. You don't think I have a right to be angry? Your infidelity is the least of it. You don't see that I have been abused all these years, too?"

"Me too! Me too!" he shouted, mocking her.

"I'm married to you, Carson. It wasn't supposed to be 'me too'; it was supposed to be just me."

"You knew who you were marrying. It's not like I'm Bill Cosby or Harvey Weinstein. It was all consensual! I'm the victim! I got caught up in this witch hunt."

"You know better than to say it was consensual, and it's not a witch hunt! The witches were innocent, and you didn't get caught up, you just got caught, period."

"Powerful men have been facing these allegations for years, but all of a sudden it's a life sentence?"

She could barely wrap her head around everything that was wrong with what he was saying, but standing in the foyer of the house she had grown up in, having moved her kids across the country, she felt brave. She felt responsible to show this man, her husband, who had hurt so many women under her nose, the pain he had inflicted. She collected herself and gave it to him.

"You are not owed a second chance. That is the same sense of entitlement that led you to believe that you could treat women as you did, treat people as you did, treat your wife, who loved you and gave you two beautiful children, as you did. You will never change until you understand what your words and your actions do to people."

There was something so strange about having the upper hand, having the truth and the public on her side. She opened the door again and said, "You are a disgrace. Please leave my house, and don't come back unless you are invited—by me."

He left. Amanda wanted to think with his tail between his legs, but the truth was, he hardly even heard her. She ran across the street to tell Eliza, just as Luke was getting home from his office. They entered the kitchen at the same time, both equally agitated. Amanda took the back seat to Luke; she had never seen him worked up before.

"Eliza, is there something you want to tell me?"

She shot Amanda a look of panic before turning back to her husband and shaking her head no.

"A new patient named Shari Livingston came in today. She said she got my name from the bulletin board."

That's nice, Eliza and Amanda both thought, wondering what the problem was.

"Have you heard of her?"

"No, but our membership has nearly doubled this year, I can't know everyone," she said proudly.

"What about her husband, Hank Livingston?"

"No. What's going on, Luke?"

"When I looked in this poor woman's mouth and commented how perfect her teeth were, she burst into tears. She said she had just moved from the city, just had her teeth cleaned, but she was worried that her husband was cheating on her and heard that my wife might know if it were true. Do you know if Shari Livingston's husband is cheating on her, and if he is—how the hell do you know that?"

"Oh boy," Eliza said and sat down at the kitchen table. How many suspicious wives was she torturing right now? She felt like an even bigger snake than she had before.

"Maybe I should go?" Amanda piped in, feeling that painful awkwardness of witnessing another couple come to blows.

Luke's tone was unusually indignant. "Maybe you should sit down, too. I have a feeling you know all about this."

They both flashed back to being sat down together in the same kitchen by Eliza's mom—she may have even used those same words. Eliza recalled a chocolate stain on the couch; Amanda, a couple of cigarettes missing from Birdie's pack of Virginia Slims. Suddenly, as it had been then, it was hard not to laugh.

Eliza straightened herself out and owned up to some of it. "Our neighbor, Ashley Smith, is having an affair with our new friend Olivia's husband, and it all came to light on the bulletin board. That's what she must be referring to."

She opened up her phone and pulled up the last post. "Here—read this."

He did. "Wow, does Mr. Smith know?"

"We don't think so."

"Well, that's unfortunate. He seems like such a nice guy."

"You want to tell him?" Amanda asked, thinking it could help Olivia.

"Very funny," he said, turning to his wife. "I'm just glad it has nothing to do with you." The recent distance between them was causing him to question things he never would have before.

More deceit, she thought, suddenly feeling ill. Luke noticed the subtle change in her and apologized.

"I'm sorry, baby." He stood to give her a hug. She acquiesced, happy to have avoided further confrontation. She felt an unexpected wave of comfort come over her—it was quickly washed away by guilt.

CHAPTER 36

Olivia

Aside from avoiding Spencer by feigning "the worst period in the history of periods," Olivia spent the next few days trying her best to unravel all of the lies that had come before. To try and put a timeline together of just when the affair had started.

Olivia had conferred with Andie Rand again. Even though this affair was now a sure thing, physical evidence was needed if she wanted to overturn their prenup. The best form of proof would be a picture of the two of them together. It would be a tough thing to get because a photo of them running together would be just that, a photo of them running together. If she really wanted proof, the photo needed to be intimate.

A plan to catch him in the act had been hatched over margaritas at Eliza's and was to be executed over Thanksgiving weekend. Olivia told Spencer that she had to go to Miami with her parents to visit her grandmother, with the excuse that her grandmother wasn't doing well and she wanted her to spend time with Lily. She knew it would go uncontested, as there was no missing a York Thanksgiving for Spencer. She also knew that Spencer would jump at the chance to copulate with his mistress in every room in their house. It was exactly what he had told Olivia when they first looked through the blueprints: "Six thousand square feet of places to fuck!" he had proclaimed. He rarely spoke that way around her, since he knew she hated it. She hated the word "fuck," vastly preferred "making love" or even the British slang "shagging." She wasn't a prude, but she just wasn't turned on by vulgarity. She wondered if Ashley was, if she yelled out dirty words when they were having sex. Did Ashley Smith fill a need of Spencer's that she didn't? When she shared those self-deprecating thoughts with her new crew, their responses blew her away.

"It has nothing to do with you," and "I hate to tell you this, but I doubt this is the first time he's cheated."

It had never entered her mind that this wasn't his only affair, that it was possible he had been unfaithful before. It was so hard to believe, until suddenly it wasn't.

Olivia thought back to an incident that happened before they were married, a drunken night with his frat brothers when they talked rather disgustingly of passing around a girl they referred to as "Motel Michele" during their last year of college.

"Spencer checked in first," one of them joked. "And last," another chimed in.

She saw Spencer shoot the guy a look, "a shut the hell up" kind of look. She asked him about it later. He insisted, "I shot him a look because it wasn't true. I would never cheat on you, baby."

She chose not to question him further. The invitations for their wedding were already in the mail. She reprimanded herself for it now and swore never to stick her head in the sand again. She was so angry about this ruse of a life. She thought about the fool she was, and all of those friends of his, knowing what a shit he was on one hand while toasting their wedding vows with the other. Their girlfriends probably knew as well; the Becks did for sure. She'd counted them as her friends, too.

Lily reached up to her with her dimpled little hands, batting her lilac eyes. Olivia was so in love with this baby girl. She hoped it would dissipate the bitterness. *You have your beautiful baby. You have your integrity. You have your whole life ahead of you.* She begged herself to think better, not bitter. It was all so brutal.

Olivia began her investigation of Spencer's affair by checking her past Open Table reservations to see when they had had their forced double date at the little Greek restaurant on Madison Avenue. She would forever think of that place as an integral scene in her Greek tragedy, as opposed to how she'd thought of it before— the place with the yummy lamb meatballs and spicy grilled octopus. Open Table had the reservation listed at one month before her due date; but clearly, at that point, Spencer and Ashley were quite familiar with each other. She jumped forward in her mind to the day that Lily was born, the night really, as she came into the world a little before three o'clock in the morning. *Was there any sign that it was going on then?*

She desperately wanted to think not, as she ran the evening over in her head. Spencer was present and focused throughout the entire birth experience, from what she could recall. She wasn't exactly focusing on him.

Then she remembered: She remembered the one odd thing that occurred at the hospital, and as she did, tears stung her eyes.

She had drifted to sleep soon after they arrived in her room, and Spencer had kissed her atop her head and said, "Get some sleep. I'm going to get some air, pick us up some bagels and good coffee."

About an hour or so later the nurse wheeled Lily's little bassinet into the room. They had teased her thick patch of jet-black hair into a mock pompadour. Olivia laughed thinking about the fun the nurses must've had with Lily's unusually abundant newborn locks. She had gingerly propped herself up to greet her baby.

"She looks like Elvis!" Olivia had exclaimed.

The nurse laughed as she placed Lily in Olivia's arms. "That's exactly what your sister-in-law said!"

"My sister-in-law is on a business trip in China," Olivia replied, not thinking much about it.

"I must be confused," the nurse answered, adding, "I haven't slept much."

In retrospect, thought Olivia, the nurse wasn't confused. Spencer had brought that woman to see her baby and passed her off as his sister. In fact, she had seen her baby before her own family did. He couldn't be that cruel, could he? But then she remembered that he had bought a house and moved them out of the city to be near his mistress.

She took a break from thinking, crawled back into her bed, and cried. The rain crashing against the windows could barely drown out her sobs. *I can't do this for a second more*, she thought. *I'll manage without the money.*

She logged on to the Hudson Valley Ladies' Bulletin Board and wrote a post. She didn't think about it, didn't weigh one word over another; she just wrote. She closed her laptop, crawled back under the covers, and went back to sleep.

CHAPTER 37

Eliza & Olivia & Alison & Amanda

Eliza woke up with what felt like a hangover, except that she didn't drink. She wanted to go out to her desk and spy for Olivia, wanted to turn on her computer and approve posts for the bulletin board, but today the thought of getting out from under the covers made her anxious. *I'm getting worse*, she thought. It frightened her. The longer she stayed inside, the scarier the outside world became. She was dressed in layers upon layers of clothing, a pair of underwear and a sports bra under her flannel pajamas. On top of it a long cardigan sweater covered the dried-up blood that she hadn't bothered to wash off of her arm where she had deliberately cut it the night before. The weather report quoted unusually high temperatures for this time of year. Even the rain didn't cool it down.

Luke was beginning to notice that her behavior was, at the very least, strange. The previous night, upon seeing her layers, he'd asked her, "Are you feeling OK, honey?"

"I'm fine," she'd answered blankly.

He reached over and put the back of his hand on her forehead to see if it felt warm. She jumped a good foot in the air.

"I'm sorry, you startled me," she said. Poor Luke, the most loving man she'd ever known, couldn't even touch his wife's forehead. *It might be the time to tell him that I can't leave the house,* she thought, but they were both so tired, and she knew that he had to perform an early root canal the next morning. *How can I bring it up now?* It never felt like the right time.

What she didn't know was that he wanted to delve deeper, to ask his wife what was going on. There had been hardly any intimacy between them all summer. He thought she was depressed because the kids had left. He felt it, too. He thought he should just give her time, not make her feel worse by throwing his needs into the mix, but it seemed like more than that. She literally jumped at the touch of his hand. And it hadn't been the first time. Last week when he reached behind her and rubbed her shoulders, an act that usually caused her to lean in, she recoiled.

Eliza shut her eyes in an effort to go back to sleep, to cut her long, lonely day by an hour or two. She drifted off, but soon found herself in the middle of a nightmare. She opened her eyes wide, hoping to expel the awful images of her dream from her head. The pain that was once encapsulated in her memory felt as if it had metastasized and was now spreading throughout every cell in her body. She got out of bed with the feeling that no place was safe, went down to the kitchen, and put a pod of Kona coffee in the Keurig. She was thankful again for the bulletin board, thankful for the distraction.

Sitting at her desk, sipping her coffee, she looked out across the lawn to her neighbors' house. It looked like no one was home; their cars were not in the driveway. She turned her attention toward the bulletin board. Truffles Goldstein, the shepherd/retriever mix, was still missing. She wondered if he were to run by her window right then, if she would have the courage to go after him. She doubted it. Just yesterday she noticed a woman in a blue sedan idling outside her house. From where Eliza stood it looked like she was crying. Her gut told her it was another situation like the distressed patient at Luke's office. How many women had she spooked? She wanted to go outside and say "Can I help you?"; she even put on her sneakers, but she couldn't do it.

At least, according to the comments on the board Truffles was thankfully alive and well.

> I believe I saw the missing dog at the playground in Memorial Park.
> I called out his name, but he took off.

> Truffles spotted at the parking lot behind the dry cleaners this morning.
> No luck catching him.

And today from the Goldsteins themselves, still desperate to get Truffles back:

> Remember if you see Truffles, yell "Treat!" And don't look Truffles in the
> eye. He's very skittish. Thank you for helping to bring our boy home!

Eliza reattached the picture of Truffles, hoping to keep him fresh in people's minds. She was a bit behind in approving new members and posts. She began with the posts. The first one she saw made her feel completely out of touch with this generation of mothers. As she read it, she didn't know whether to laugh or cry.

> My two-year-old is showing innate musicality. He is constantly banging
> things and I notice a distinct beat. Can anyone recommend the best
> drum set for preschoolers?

She wanted to suggest two wooden spoons and some pots but refrained. Last week a mother of a three-year-old was looking for a math tutor. She couldn't wait for the comments. In her head she imagined a barrage of "What, are you crazy? Let a kid be a kid! Math for a three-year-old?" But, to her surprise, people responded with names of tutors and computer programs. She thought back to the torture of flash cards and times tables with the twins, and that was in elementary school. *These poor babies*, she thought. Maybe she was a dinosaur. Maybe those Valley Girls were right.

She was ready to give up and crawl back into bed, this time in front of a movie or a reality show, when the next post demanded her attention:

Dear Anonymous Adulteress,

I know who you are. We met when I was pregnant. What kind of woman sleeps with a pregnant woman's husband? I'm coming to get you!

Anonymous Wife

"Oh my God," Eliza said out loud. She wondered if she should call Alison or Olivia herself. She decided on Alison. Within a half hour, her doorbell rang. *These women don't believe in the phone*, she thought as she looked in the mirror to see if she was in any way presentable. She looked like a hot mess.

"One second!" she yelled, whipping off her sweater and pajama top and throwing on a somewhat cleaner Wisco sweatshirt. A little better, she hoped. She answered the door with a smile and her best attempt at self-deprecating humor, "Would you believe I woke up like this?"

Olivia looked worse than she did, even with all of her youth and beauty. *This poor girl*, she thought. Both she and Alison had their babies with them; they were carrying them in their car seats as if they were baskets of fruit. Both had fallen asleep on the drive over. Eliza looked down at the sleeping infants and thought of her own babies at that age. Right there at arm's reach, able to control everything and everyone they interacted with. She longed for those days.

"Do you want some coffee?" she asked, with a motherly smile.

They both nodded and followed her into the kitchen. Eliza pulled some homemade mini blueberry muffins out of the freezer and threw them in the microwave. She reached out to Mandy and before long they were all sitting around the kitchen table commiserating with Olivia.

"Is Ashley Smith even on the bulletin board?" Amanda asked Eliza, after hearing what was going on.

"Yes. She joined the morning after my first post. She probably checks the comments all the time—I would, if I were her."

They all nodded in agreement.

"What are you hoping to achieve with this post?" Amanda came right out and asked Olivia, adding, "From the two minutes I've known you, I know you're not going to really *get* her."

"Maybe I am," Olivia said, unconvincingly. They could all see she was barely able to eat her muffin, let alone go next door and pummel Ashley Smith.

"Alison could defend me. Temporary insanity."

"One can only hope it's temporary," Eliza added, thinking more about herself than Olivia.

"I know you all want me to be strategic and wait this out, but I'm done. Every day I feel more damaged. I can't take care of Lily like this. I feel like she senses it." She looked around Eliza's suburban kitchen and continued. "I thought I was going to have all of this." She pulled a family photo from a high school lacrosse game off the fridge. "I came here for this storyline."

It threw Eliza. This pretty young girl wanted to be her. She wanted to have her seemingly perfect life. She felt like a fraud.

"It's not all rainbows and butterflies, Olivia."

"I know that—I was prepared for storms and termites, but not this. This is too much."

Alison steered the conversation away from sentiment and toward reality. "Just let me call Andie Rand to see where you stand with the proof you have right now. Please?"

"Fine. But it doesn't mean I'll listen. I can't lie next to this man anymore. I need to confront him."

Alison called Andie, who, she reported, was in a meeting.

"Let's wait for her to call back. You've waited this long."

Olivia stood so dramatically that it almost made them laugh.

"I'm done with this! Eliza, please post my post!"

Eliza looked to Alison for direction. Alison threw out, "Let's at least make sure Ashley is home."

"She's not. I saw her drive off about an hour ago."

"Why does that even matter?" Olivia protested.

"Because maybe this post will smoke them out. Put yourself in her shoes. What would you do if you were home and read it?"

"I'd get the hell out," Mandy interjected.

Eliza agreed, but added, "Me too, but I would probably call Spencer first."

Olivia began to get her mojo back. "And Spencer will probably call me to suss out what's going on."

"Exactly! So, if that happens, you won't answer your phone, and then, hopefully he will come here to save Ashley or to calm Ashley."

"Or to fuck Ashley." As the words rolled off Olivia's tongue, they left a bitter taste.

"On the bright side, that would make for the best photograph!" Eliza pointed out, adding, "Let's sit by the window in the living room and wait for her to come home. Then I will post it." She realized that it was best for Olivia to be in control. "Does that sound smart to you?"

"OK. I've waited this long," she agreed. Olivia popped a muffin in her mouth, and the women smiled at her newfound strength.

They fed and burped the babies, a wonderful distraction, with Eliza and Mandy begging to take a turn, and Alison and Olivia happily relinquishing control. Sitting among this newly formed friend group felt inspiring to Eliza: The beauty of women who didn't know each other very well having one another's backs simply because of the sisterhood. On one side of her sat Mandy, whose personal life was front-page news, and on the other, Olivia, who may as well have been standing there naked, she had exposed herself to them so fully. It made Eliza feel like a sham. She wanted to come clean and finally release the secret that had been tucked away in the depths of her soul for so long. In the end, she was too afraid, and only admitted to her agoraphobia without divulging its hideous cause.

"I have crippling anxiety. I don't leave the house," she blurted out.

Her admission was met by two stares and an encouraging pat on the back from Mandy. She continued. "Since the twins' graduation, I've been consumed with fear whenever I try to go out. I've gained weight and I hardly bother showering. I barely recognize myself." It wasn't entirely true. She did recognize herself: She was the same girl from those four awful months of high school.

They all looked at her sympathetically. Mandy with tears in her eyes.

"Did something trigger it?" Alison asked. She was very familiar with agoraphobia; she had used it as a defense in a murder case. Eliza panicked. She should have realized that these women would want to get to the bottom of her problems. Luckily for her, Ashley Smith provided a diversion.

"Ashley is home!" Mandy shouted.

They took off to Eliza's desk, babies in tow. Olivia sat on the floor with the babies while the others gathered by the window.

Everyone but Olivia watched as Ashley Smith entered her house, walked into the kitchen, and poured herself a cup of coffee. Eliza bent down in front of Olivia.

"Are you sure you want me to post it? We can still wait for Alison's detective friend to call back."

Olivia got up, grabbed the binoculars from the shelf, and took a good look at the enemy.

"It's definitely her. Post it. I think our new plan is good."

Eliza nodded in agreement and got down to business.

"Done!" she said. "Now we wait."

They could easily see with their naked eyes what was going on. Ashley climbed the stairs and appeared again in her bedroom window. Alison watched through the binoculars for more detail. They were all ready to duck out of sight if she shot a glance their way. The comments on the post were already pouring in.

Paint an A on her lawn, scarlet letter style!

Call her husband. Let him "get" her.

Really? Are you really promoting domestic violence? Forget him, go beat her up yourself!

WHY ARE YOU BLAMING HER? WHAT ABOUT THE HUSBAND? HE'S THE ONE WHO DESERVES THE BEATING!

Eliza didn't read the comments out loud. They would only have been entertaining if the victim of this whole mess hadn't been sitting on the floor dangling a rattle in front of her baby girl. But

Olivia stood again and checked them out herself, addressing the last one.

"I know I should be concentrating on Spencer and that this woman has no loyalty to me, but I can't help but feel betrayed by her as well."

They understood—at this point they all hated her, too. No one needed binoculars to see what happened next. Ashley sat on her bed, took off her shoes, and pushed herself back. She grabbed her phone and began to read.

"She's on her phone," Alison reported to Olivia. "It looks like she's listening to a message." Alison looked through the binoculars.

Olivia began to purposefully breathe in and out. The others unknowingly followed suit. Ashley Smith dropped her phone on her bed and covered her face with her hands.

"She read it!" Alison shouted. The three women stood, grasping hands, as Alison reported her every move.

"She's making a call. She's talking on the phone. She hung up. She's putting on her shoes!"

Alison looked down at the four women's feet. Everyone was wearing shoes but Eliza. Ashley sat down on the edge of her bed. She held her phone in her hands as if it were the Holy Grail. Olivia's phone rang. They all screamed, "Don't answer it!"

"I'm not," Olivia said, and somehow laughed. They all joined in. She looked down at the name. It was Spencer. He left a message. She played it on speaker. He sounded weird.

"Ummm. Hi. Um, where are you? I have a question. Call me back. Umm, OK, love you."

Olivia picked up Lily and stood. They all watched as Ashley answered her phone, shook her head, grabbed her purse, and hightailed it out of her bedroom.

"We have to follow her!" Alison shrieked. Olivia started to go, but Alison grabbed Mandy. "You! You come with me. You two stay here with the babies."

Eliza took Zach. There was no time to think or waste. Olivia agreed, and within seconds Mandy and Alison were following Ashley Smith's car down the road.

"This is insane!" Mandy said.

"Should I stop?"

"Absolutely not. Let's get this bastard!"

Olivia called Alison's cell, and she connected the Bluetooth.

"What's going on?" she asked.

"We're right behind her, on River Road."

"I'm staying on the phone. Be careful."

"Don't worry. She's not speeding, she's just driving—somewhere," Mandy added, which made Olivia feel a bit better about not risking their lives.

Olivia read more comments popping up on Eliza's computer. She actually made a joke: "She's lucky the whole town isn't chasing her with burning stakes."

"She's getting on the highway."

"Which direction?"

"North."

"Spencer's office is at exit twenty-two. I bet she's meeting him up there. Why else would she be going that way?"

Andie Rand cut in. Alison was more than eager to confer with her and tell her what was going on. Andie was adamant that they still needed a photo.

"I'm telling you. I reviewed her prenup. Visual evidence that can be exposed to the press is her only way to get what she deserves. I see this all the time. In the heat of the moment women just want out, but she's only been married a short time. I'm concerned that she'll be very much on her own without physical proof."

Her words gave Mandy and Alison a renewed sense of purpose.

"Wait, she's pulling into a truck stop."

"OK, pull in, too, but a few spots away from her. Feed Zach, as if that's why you pulled over," Andie instructed.

"Do you think I brought Zach on a high-speed chase?" Alison interjected.

"Oh. That's a bummer. Babies are great props."

Alison turned to Mandy. "Remind me never to let her babysit."

Eliza called Mandy's phone. "What's happening?"

Mandy put her on speaker, too, as Spencer showed up in his stupid flashy car. He pulled in right next to Ashley. Mandy reported it loud and clear.

"Does Spencer have a red Porsche?"

Olivia confirmed it, more embarrassed than ever to be married to him. She managed another joke. "Yes, and a small penis." She blushed as she said it. All the women laughed, except for Andie Rand, who was all business.

She made her feelings evident. "OK, no more jokes. We have one shot. This is what has to happen. Spencer will get into her car. You are to wait for them to go at it."

Alison was suspect. "How do you know they will?"

"I've been doing this a long time. Trust me, they will. Don't jump right out; give it about thirty seconds, then one of you has to approach the car. Who's going to do it? Decide now."

"I'll do it," Mandy said. She felt good about it, like she was doing it for the women who came out against Carson. "I got this."

Alison shot her a look of confidence.

"OK. Open the camera on your phone and switch it to video. Do you have enough battery?"

"Yes, I'm at sixty percent."

"Great. Make sure it's on record before you get out of the car. Walk directly there with the phone facing forward. Record them until they notice you; as they do, keep it on record but motion for them to pull down the window. Look right at your phone, like you are reading an address, and ask them directions. Got it?"

Alison interrupted. "Look, they're already on top of each other. Sorry, Olivia."

Mandy jumped into action as Alison reported her every move. She held the phone steady in front of her, alternating between looking at the car and watching the seconds rise on the counter. She stood at the window and recorded them. They were all over each other. She could see that Ashley's blouse was open and that she looked like she'd been crying. She couldn't believe they didn't notice her. It felt like minutes, but when she looked down at the timer, she saw that only thirty-four seconds had passed. She waited a few more, then knocked on the window. She watched as Spencer flipped around toward her. As he rolled down the window, Ashley straightened herself out.

"Can I help you?!" he barked.

Mandy looked down at her phone as if reading from it. She saw that she was still recording. She knew it was priceless, albeit the footage was a little shaky from her nerves.

"I'm sorry. I'm having car trouble. I'm looking for Wally's Garage."

Spencer was furious. As if being caught on tape with another woman wasn't enough, he was quite rude. "I don't know, lady. Look at your GPS and get the hell away from our car!"

Mandy murmured an apology, but couldn't help the grin bursting from her lips. His glare turned to confusion.

You'll figure it out soon enough, she thought, as she hurried back to the car.

CHAPTER 38

Alison

Being a part of the big sting wiped out any lingering doubt in Alison regarding whether she was a fairy-tale girl or not. Until then thoughts of Jack—and Jackie—kept running through her mind. She had wondered how it was possible to miss someone she barely knew, or more accurately, didn't know at all. After witnessing what she had with Olivia and Spencer, she was more sure than ever that there was no room for dishonesty in a relationship. She junked his last email attempt at an apology without even reading it and wrote one to Marc, asking him to come up to see the baby.

She fussed around the house a bit, straightening up before Marc got there. With rush-hour traffic and the rain, she was sure that it would be close to eight o'clock when he arrived. Eliza, who was now her second-best friend in town after Olivia, suggested making a lasagna and saving the last ten minutes of baking time for his arrival. She wasn't sure why she was acting like the happy homemaker, or why she was so quick to forgive Marc for being such a colossal prick regarding her pregnancy. For a second she wondered if she was creating a charade to distract herself from the one she'd unknowingly gotten caught up in.

The doorbell rang at ten past eight. She looked in the mirror, straightened her hair, and waved a coat of pink gloss over her lips. "Who are you?" she said out loud to her image, as she wiped the gloss off on the back of her hand.

Clumsiness always crept in when she was casually conversing with Marc Sugarman, and having delivered his offspring hadn't made it any easier. In fact, his lack of emotional intimacy became more obvious in the emotionally intimate state of parenthood. His recent mushy revelations aside, he was not a people person and certainly not a baby person. On the plus side, he *was* refreshingly self-aware about it all.

"I think I'll be better with Zachary when he's more sturdy," he said hopefully, looking down into the baby's crib.

"You're fine, Marc. Don't worry about it."

"Wait, I brought him something," he whispered, opening his briefcase and pulling out a pile of books. Not just any books, but a very thoughtful collection of childhood classics. Alison knew that Marc could not have selected the books on his own; in fact, he may not have even gone to the bookstore himself, but when she flipped through *Ferdinand*, *Where the Wild Things Are*, and *Caps for Sale*, and landed on *Guess How Much I Love You*, she was touched. As they left Zach's room and passed her open bedroom door, something stirred in her. *I never mind a crispy lasagna*, she thought as she led Marc into her bedroom.

Sex between Alison and Marc Sugarman had been molded to perfection over the years—each of them getting great pleasure from pleasuring the other. Alison knew that it was more about ego than anything else. They had established a rhythm, much like two Olympic figure skaters going for the gold. She could almost imagine the judges calling out their perfect scores for technical merit, required elements, presentation, and grade of execution. If emotional connection were part of the criteria they would have fallen flat. No triple axels in that category, for sure.

Alison was aware that people, especially women, often thought about many things during sex. She did not. Occasionally her mind wandered to the brief she had to prepare the next day, but in general, she focused on what she was feeling and where she was feeling it. She did not think of Brad Pitt or her old boyfriend from high school or the cute exterminator who popped his head into her office on the first Monday of every month and asked, "May I enter?" She didn't even like to listen to music during sex. She preferred that her mind and body be one.

But today, as Marc's hands were hungrily roaming her body, her mind started to wander to Jack Campbell. She thwarted it by purposefully opening her eyes and looking at Marc, watching his hands ride up the side of her torso; his lips trace her navel and come up between her breasts. But when she closed her eyes again, she pictured Jack's lips and Jack's touch. She remembered the C-O-C-O-N-U-T advice from the bulletin board and tried it out. The distraction was only temporary, within minutes she was back to picturing Jack, and with his image her desire grew exponentially. It felt too good not to continue, and so, for the first time that she could remember, Alison combined sex with fantasy. It was only when she realized it had never felt that good before that it concerned her.

As they lay spent next to each other, Marc noticed that she wasn't all there.

"Was that good for you?" he asked.

"Very," she responded, hiding her concern.

Over lasagna, the awkwardness between them that was never found in the bedroom or in the courtroom crept back in. Alison wondered whether they were trying to fit a round peg into a square hole. As if reading her mind, Marc came right out and addressed it.

"Look, Alison, I know what I'm proposing is not some great romantic love story, but I think I know you pretty well, and I think you're just as pragmatic as I am."

She hoped that he was still right. It really bothered her that she had been thinking about Jack during sex. It was as if having a baby had weakened her constitution, cracked it, like the Leonard Cohen lyrics, allowing the light in.

"Let's just take it one day at a time."

"How about two days at a time? Can you join me with the baby at my press conference announcing my candidacy?"

"Of course," she said, adding with real honesty, "I'm looking forward to it."

CHAPTER 39

Amanda

M andy dragged Pippa with her to the Stop & Shop with a huge list from Eliza for Thanksgiving. She'd given Eliza a bit of a hard time about it, as she felt like she was getting worse and she wasn't doing anything to help herself. The list of local therapists that Mandy had put together had remained uncalled; the self-help books she had taken out of the library for her, untouched. She was happy to help, but hated enabling her, even if this was a lot easier for her than baking a pie.

As she contemplated the difference between yams and sweet potatoes (Eliza had asked for the latter), she spotted Dean Barr out of the corner of her eye. There was something about seeing him in this conventional environment that broke the spell. She laughed at herself for thinking about him in those adolescent terms, like he was still her teacher and ate all his meals in the school cafeteria. Every risqué encounter thus far had been in the high school or the parking lot.

It was an odd thing; obviously as two adults they could "get a room." She imagined that Dean had a room or two of his own to spare. She knew this cat and mouse game they were playing would either fizzle out or lead that way. She wasn't sure which direction she wanted it to go.

Pippa flew by her like a whirling dervish, bringing her back to the Stop & Shop.

"Look, it's Mr. Barr!"

She wanted to stop Pippa in her tracks and avoid having what was sure to be an awkward encounter in front of her daughter, but how would she explain her reaction? She followed Pippa to the butcher's counter just in time to hear Mr. Barr's heartbreaking order.

"Hello, what's the smallest size turkey you have? It's just me, but I'm good with leftovers."

Pippa looked up at her mother as if a puppy was about to be put down.

"It's not our place to invite more people to Aunt Eliza's," she whispered. Pippa gave her the death stare. Amanda gave in.

"Hi, Mr. Barr."

He blushed. She wasn't sure if the source of his embarrassment was his turkey-for-one request, or a reaction to seeing Amanda with her daughter in public.

"Hi, I, um, usually go out of town to my sister's for the holiday, but with the play this weekend . . ."

It was the turkey.

Pippa doubled down on her stare. Amanda reacted.

"We are spending the holiday at our neighbors'. She loves a big crowd, if you would like to come."

"That's so nice, but I couldn't impose."

Amanda breathed a sigh of relief. It was short-lived.

"You have to come!" Pippa insisted, and added, as if starring in a Frank Capra film, "No one should be alone on Thanksgiving."

Mr. Barr smiled as the butcher made a suggestion. "How about a Cornish game hen?" he asked. His name tag read "Bart." Mandy remembered the discussion on the bulletin board about him and tried not to get caught checking him out. She was beginning to feel like a real floozy. She smiled. He smiled back.

"Do you know him?" Dean asked.

She blushed. "No, no. Why?"

"I swear since I've been standing here four women have come over and checked him out." Mandy hid her laughter.

Bart returned, holding up a small chicken like a product on the Home Shopping Network.

"I won't be needing it after all. Thanks." Mr. Barr smiled shyly.

Amanda took that as a yes and graciously gave him the details. They finished up their shopping. She stopped at home to drop off Pippa and a few bags before bringing the rest to Eliza's. Her dad came out to the car to help.

"Pippa invited Dean Barr over to Eliza's for Thanksgiving," she whined.

"He's a dean now?"

"No, that's his first name," she said with a laugh.

"That is funny. You know, you used to have a giant crush on him in high school."

"You knew that?"

"Please, Mandy, it was pretty obvious."

"Ugh. Dad, don't embarrass me in front of him please."

"I'm the least of your troubles. Your youngest just invited your husband to Thanksgiving."

"What? She can't just do that!"

"Well, she just did, and I will leave it to you to tell her otherwise."

She knew the thought of their father eating dinner alone at the hotel bar on Thanksgiving would break their hearts. More manipulation on his part. She thought about calling her lawyer, but she knew that she would encourage her not to keep him from his children. Spending four hundred dollars to hear that would only make it worse.

"This is nuts. I'm taking the rest of the stuff to Eliza's. She's going to kill me."

"No, she won't. You know she'll say the more the merrier."

He was right, but she wanted to go there anyway and complain about the insanity of Thanksgiving dinner with Carson and Dean Barr. Neither guest was appetizing to Eliza, but, in her typical fashion, she went for the joke.

"Don't worry, there's room at the table. My mother just informed me that their flight arrives *after* dinner. She claimed my father wanted to save on airfare, but you know she would do anything to avoid communal eating."

"That's insane, but more sweet potato pie for us!" Mandy proclaimed proudly, pulling a yam from the grocery bags.

Eliza weighed whether or not to send Mandy back to the store. She seemed so proud. She remembered an old recipe she had for candied yams and passed. She imagined they would all need a little sugar to counter the presence of Carson Cole.

She would act hospitable for Mandy's girls. If Mandy and her father could tolerate him for their sake, then she could, too.

As if Mandy sensed what Eliza was thinking, she added, "I'm sorry, Eliza, to be such an imposition."

Eliza took Mandy's hands between hers. "Don't worry. It will be good to provide some normalcy for the girls."

Neither of them could predict just how far off that statement would prove to be.

CHAPTER 40

Alison

Alison arrived at Grand Army Plaza to stand by Marc's side as he announced his bid for mayor. His team had picked a Brooklyn location, as opposed to one in Manhattan, so as to paint Marc as an ordinary man of the people rather than a highbrow attorney who had enjoyed a privileged childhood. Alison was well aware that she and Zachary were an integral part of his new image.

Press, news cameras, faces she recognized from court, and bigwigs of the Democratic Party were all in attendance. It was invigorating for sure, but mostly she wanted to find a quiet corner where she could feed Zachary. She weaved her way through the dense crowd armed with "SUGARMAN IS THE MAN" signs and found her predesignated spot. Once there, a young woman, whose name tag read "Abby Holtz," approached.

"I'm your handler," Abby announced.

"Do you know how to handle a baby?" Alison joked.

"I'm afraid not," Abby replied, looking as if Alison had asked her to charm a snake.

Abby led her behind the podium to a curtained-off area. Marc was there and introduced her to his campaign manager and a few others whose names went in one ear and out the other. She had a very small window between Zach's next bottle and standing by Marc's side for the announcement with a quiet baby who was through spitting up. One of those guys, whose name escaped her, came along while she fed Zach.

"We would rather you not take any questions afterward, as you haven't been thoroughly prepped. Is that OK?"

"That sounds perfect, thanks."

It was a relief. She was becoming increasingly unsure about how to honestly answer questions about the future of their relationship. With each moment she spent with Marc, her original concept of them being engaged to be engaged felt further and further from the truth. The nameless guy continued explaining the logistics.

"The lieutenant governor will do a brief intro for Marc and then call him up. You will stand to his right with the baby. His campaign manager and some members of his team, plus a few celebrities, will stand with you as well."

Alison scanned the small group behind the curtain: an interesting mix including the district attorney, the lieutenant governor, a point guard for the New York Knicks, and a famous Broadway diva. The nameless guy went on. "At the end of his speech, when he actually announces his candidacy and the crowd cheers, he will reach for your hand. Together you will lift your clasped hands in the air to signify Marc's status as a family man. No words will be necessary after that. A photo-op moment is all we need from you today."

"Got it," she agreed, while burping Zachary. He looked so cute in his fancy outfit. It was the first time he was wearing it—and the last, she figured from the way she was barely able to snap it closed. She took out her phone to take a picture of him, or more accurately, the tenth picture of him that day. She scrolled around on her phone afterward, checking her emails and deleting spam. She saw Jackie's last email in her junk folder and opened it. It only said four words:

My aim is true.

If it were her heart he was aiming for, it worked—she actually felt it sink. *She* wasn't sure if other people would connect the words to the lyrics from the Elvis Costello song that she shared a name with, but anyone with the name "Alison" certainly would. She sang the eerily accurate verse in her head:

I'm not going to get too sentimental like those other sticky valentines,
Cause I don't know if you've been loving somebody.
I only know it isn't mine.
Alison, I know this world is killing you.
Oh, Alison, my aim is true.

And somehow she believed him. She believed that he got caught up in something that went against his usual integrity—a single dad doing the best that he could in the face of such loss. She believed that his aim was true. She wasn't running to give him another chance, but she understood that he was most likely one of the good guys. Marc came over to them and gently placed the back of his hand on Zach's cheek. He smiled at Alison, said, "Thanks for bringing him," and headed to his spot next to the stage to await his introduction. She knew, right then, that there was nothing of substance besides Zach between them. Suddenly the whole charade felt wrong.

The lieutenant governor approached the stage and quieted the crowd. He went into great detail about Marc's education, Supreme Court clerkship, and trajectory at the US attorney's office, with zero mention of his personal life. It was quite evident that it was up to her and Zach to complete that picture. He concluded with, "It is now more important than ever to have a solid citizen of our great city in Gracie Mansion—and who better than the man who has prosecuted more crime and corruption than any other prosecutor in our history? Ladies and gentlemen, I give you New York City's next mayor, Marc Sugarman!"

The crowd began exuberantly shouting, "Sugarman, Sugarman," with an unusually strong emphasis on the third syllable. His posse, Alison included, took their places around him. Marc waited a few moments to quiet the crowd as he stood, taking it all in from the podium. He certainly had the telegenic appeal of a charming politician. The crowd finally calmed at his request, and he flashed them his JFK smile.

"First of all, thank you. Thank you to the lieutenant governor for that wonderful introduction, and thank you all for being here today. Like millions of New Yorkers, my life is deeply intertwined with those around me in our beautiful melting pot of a city. I love this city deeply and have been honored to represent its eight-point-four million constituents as the US attorney for the Southern District of New York. But there is a great deal more to achieve beyond the parameters of that office."

He went on to brilliantly explain his platform, touching on everything from the city's failing infrastructure to education and prison reform to fair immigration laws. It was a very strong speech from a very strong candidate, and it left Alison thinking that the smart people of New York City would choose him, or not, regardless of her and Zach.

The crowd cheered as he wrapped it up. "I know what it is like to fight tooth and nail for justice for all New Yorkers. Everyone deserves a seat at the table and a fair portion of all that is served. I am Marc Sugarman, and I stand before you today to announce my candidacy for mayor of the great City of New York!"

The crowd went wild. Wild! Their candidate was young and handsome and experienced with ideas that people were longing to hear. He had dedicated his life thus far to public service, and it was quite evident, and truthful, that that was where his passions lay.

The moment came: Marc reached down to take Alison's hand, and as he would later say, she balked. She took the same hand that was supposed to be grasped in his in unity and laid out an open palm in his direction. Her "Let's hear it for this guy" movement signaled support, but clearly not unity. He shot her a look, more annoyed than hurt, and reached one fist in the air to signal strength. He knew better than to think it was a mistake. Alison Le didn't make mistakes.

A s Jackie boarded the 5:49 train and sat in his usual spot, he was quick to notice that something was up. Lee and Skip were glued to their phones, and both quickly shoved them away upon his arrival.

"What?" Jackie asked.

"Nothing," Lee responded.

"That seems a little ridiculous, Lee," Skip scoffed. "He's gonna see it just like we did."

Skip handed Jackie his phone. Jackie watched the press conference very carefully, his face dropping within seconds, clearly focusing on what they had seen: Alison Le by the candidate's side, holding their baby. From the video it was quite clear that they were back together. Quite clear that Jackie had irrevocably blown it, and that she was not responding to him because she had moved forward—or in this case, backward. Skip and Lee flashed each other sad emoji faces until an odd smile sprang from Jackie's down-turned lips. He watched the end of the clip again and smiled some more, before showing them what he perceived to be evidence in his favor.

"Look. Look right here." He paused the video and held it up for them both to see. "See, he goes to reach for her hand, and she pulls it away."

They look. They disagree.

"I'm not sure I see that, man. She's standing right next to him, with their kid."

"But if she loved him, she would have taken his hand. There is still hope!"

Lee had had enough. "How is there still hope? Have you heard back from her yet? At all?"

"No."

Skip put his hand to his forehead in frustration. "Dude. She's not into you. She thinks you're a big fraud. And she's a big fraud, too, because she's with this mayor guy. Find another girl, an available one."

Lee had known his friend long enough to see he wasn't listening.

"OK, promise me you will run this *whole* thing by my very smart, very female wife at Thanksgiving tomorrow, and see what she has to say about it before doing anything else."

"OK, fine. I can do that."

Jackie took out his own phone, watched the video again. He smiled his smile of relief. Skip and Lee both shook their heads at what they deemed a lost cause and went back to wasting time on their own devices.

CHAPTER 41

Olivia

Olivia pulled a tape measure along the floor of what was formerly Spencer's side of their walk-in closet, measuring out space for a standing desk and wall unit. She was excited to have a designated space to do her design work. Eliza had already hired her to create a new logo for the bulletin board.

She had just put two homemade apple pies in the oven, her first-ever attempt. She and Alison had gone on a little field trip to the local cider mill the day before. Apparently apples were a local industry that neither city girl knew much about. They returned home with cider and donuts and a bushel each of apples, way too many for two women with toothless babies. Alison decided to make sauce, and Olivia, pie, to bring to Eliza's for Thanksgiving. One thing was for sure: She knew she was thankful for her kick-ass new friends.

When Mandy and Alison had returned with the video of Spencer in the car on that awful day, Olivia watched it in silence. They all stared at her, waiting for her to implode, but she didn't say a word. She didn't even cry. It felt as if fear were gripping her throat as she sat back on Eliza's couch, watching the different paths of her uncertain future roll out in front of her eyes.

How would she survive this? She would have to tell her parents, have to tell her friends. The thought of their faces when she did mortified her. She was so ashamed. Why was this embarrassment hers? She'd done nothing wrong. Spencer was the one that should be embarrassed and pitied, not her, but she knew that wasn't the way it worked.

She'd been overcome by a feeling of loss. What would happen to her and Lily? Where would they go? Her parents would tell her to come home, and a big part of her wanted to do just that. She could move herself and Lily into her childhood bedroom and take comfort in sentimental things like the mac and cheese her mother used to make when Olivia wasn't feeling well. This was surely a mac-and-cheese-worthy situation.

She went through it all in her head: The doormen she'd grown up with smiling at her when they opened the door but shooting each other "poor Olivia" looks behind her back. She pictured walking into the local coffee place and bumping into Heidi Siegel, pushing her baby, too. "You're back in the city? I knew the suburbs weren't for you! Let's have dinner with the guys!" followed by Olivia's dramatic explanation, followed by that pathetic look again, the one that rightfully belonged to Spencer.

The thought of going back to the city a failure made her physically ill. She hadn't even had the chance to set up her old easel and break out her new watercolors. She could tell that at any moment the leaves would drop off the trees, and she wanted to capture how, when the morning sun hit just right, it was hard to tell where the rocks ended and their reflection began. Now she felt that way about the truth and the lies.

It was Eliza who had broken the silence.

"What are you thinking, honey? What do you want to do?" she said in her most motherly tone.

Olivia just shook her head. Mandy stood in front of her and took her face in her hands; she looked right into her eyes. "I watch you, and I wonder, what would my life have been like if I had confronted my fears at your age? You have so much ahead of you. There is plenty of time for a do-over."

Olivia appreciated Mandy's words. They gave her hope, and at a time like this, hope was the best thing she had to cling to.

As usual, Alison wasn't wasting time with emotions. "Can I send the video to Andie and let her take care of it?"

"She could do that?"

"Absolutely. I'll talk to her after she watches it and see what she thinks is best."

Olivia nodded in agreement, and Alison took Mandy's phone from her to proceed.

Olivia thought of the pictures on her own phone. The slideshow of sunsets captured from her deck, each one a close tie to the beauty of Lily's smiles. Oranges and reds and yellows and pinks painting the sky, the river, and the bridge in the distance, before fading to black. She did not want her life here to fade to black. To see the sunset in Manhattan, you needed to climb on the roof or stand on the exact cross streets for the slivers of light to funnel through the buildings and grace you with their presence. A lump formed in her throat that felt too big to swallow. She held on to Alison's arm.

"I know we all just met, but I don't want to leave. I like it here. Maybe it sounds crazy because my life here has been a lie, but in some ways, I feel like this is where Lily and I belong. I spent so much time thinking about bringing up my family in that house, my house. I don't want to leave it. I don't want to give up the entire dream."

"Then don't!" Eliza roared. "Why do you need to be the one to leave?"

"For one thing, Spencer's parents are the ones who bought us that big house."

"I have no doubt that Spencer's parents will be receiving the video very shortly. I'm pretty sure you have a window now to get nearly anything you want," Alison stated reassuringly.

It hadn't entered Olivia's mind that she could stay. It was only then, only when she figured out a happy path for her and Lily's future that the fear that was gripping her throat subsided. She took a deep breath, her body calmed, and she said with confidence, "I'm staying. I want to stay."

It all worked just as Alison thought it would. Andie sent the video directly to Spencer's parents and left it to them to show it to Spencer. The scene that followed was even better than they could have imagined.

After both calming down and arousing Ashley, Spencer sauntered back into the York offices feeling all right. He stopped at his assistant's desk to ask for his messages. He had only one: "Your father wants to see you immediately."

Her tone set up the mood, and on his way to his dad's office, Spencer played out all of the different reasons for being summoned. Most involved missed deadlines and poor sales reports. None involved his father turning around his computer screen and presenting Spencer with video footage of the next CEO of York Cosmetics cheating on his wife and baby.

"Where did you get this?" Spencer asked.

"A private eye just sent it to me."

Spencer was shocked and furious, but not at all remorseful.

This infuriated his father even more. When his mother walked into the office, having already had the privilege of viewing the footage, she got right in his face.

"How could you let this happen?"

"Mom, I'm sorry. I can't believe Olivia did this! I know she was having doubts, but to go behind my back and hire a private eye?"

Evie York wasn't having it. "No woman wants to buy lipstick from a man who cheats on his pregnant wife, Spencer, not in today's environment, that's for sure!"

She was sick and tired of working her ass off to build a cosmetics empire just to have some horny man in her family threaten to take it down. It had almost happened with her brother, and now, it seemed, her son was cut from the same shabby cloth. This time she faulted herself; she had always known he was a liar. He had been since he was a child. She should have known better than to let him have a public position in the company.

"Besides being a liar and a cheat, you are a complete moron. Our sales force is a fleet of women, for God's sake! I just got off the phone with our attorneys. They are going to offer Olivia whatever she wants to make this all go away."

Spencer thought it through, picturing Olivia moving back to the city and he and Ashley screwing in every room in his house. And there could be other women, too, he realized. This whole thing really wasn't his fault. He wasn't cut out for monogamy. It was forced on him. He shook off the moron comment and smiled.

"That sounds like an excellent plan, Mother. We can put this behind us and go through with the announcement as scheduled."

"Not quite, son. Your mother and I had our reservations about you before, but as our oldest, we thought it wouldn't be right to skip over you and make your sister CEO. Now, after this, we have no choice. You have terrible judgment and no self-control."

———

When the York family lawyer called Olivia that day, she referred him to Alison. She knew that matrimonial law was not Alison's thing, but the faith she had in her outweighed her credentials. Olivia wanted the house, money for its upkeep, and fair child support. All were granted, plus a million dollars in exchange for her signing a nondisclosure agreement.

"Things could be worse," Alison told her, laughing at the ridiculous simplicity of the transaction.

Olivia took the money and ran, or rather, she took the money and stayed put.

She boxed up Spencer's stuff and left it in the garage for him to pick up, which was arranged through the lawyers as well. She knew she would have to deal with him eventually—he was the father of her child—but for now it was all through emails, with Alison as the intermediary. Not to say it was easy; it was actually the hardest thing she had ever been through. The healing process was arduous. The grief, combined with the fact that she was caring for an infant on her own, often left her feeling exhausted and drained.

As the sweet smell of apple pie traveled up the stairs and into her bedroom, she thought back to Amanda's words of wisdom. She had warned her of the difference between anger and bitterness.

"Anger can be expelled, but bitterness is internalized," she said. "That's why it leaves a nasty taste in your mouth."

She promised that she would not become bitter and was committed to keeping that promise. Besides, there was a lot to be said for not having to share a closet.

CHAPTER 42

Eliza

Everything is perfect, Eliza thought, while placing the last decorative gourd on her Thanksgiving table. She took a step back and thought it again: *Perfect.*

For holidays as big as this, Eliza did things very methodically. She had a typed-out schedule taped to the fridge specifying when each dish needed to go into the oven and when each was due to come out. She attached Post-its to all of her serving platters and bowls advertising their future contents and lit candles infused with dried apples and cinnamon an hour before the company was due to arrive. They were the ideal accompaniment to the smell of the turkey roasting in the oven. She'd made two kinds of stuffing, sausage and oyster; candied yams; orange-zest cranberry sauce; potatoes au gratin; skillet green beans; and buttermilk biscuits.

She chilled the white wine and opened up a few bottles of red to decant. In his typical over-the-top manner, Carson had sent her a case of each the day before. She was disgusted with him, of course, and she knew that disgust would not sit well with him. If it weren't such good wine, she might have ceremoniously dumped it.

Carson had a soft spot for Eliza, who chalked it up to ugly duckling bonding, or the fact that she made him feel welcome when Mandy's father did quite the opposite. At the time they thought he was just being overprotective, but in hindsight, father knows best. Either way, on the rare occasions when Carson would come east with Amanda, he would always stop by Eliza's to say hello. He seemed to love her sarcastic sense of humor and she enjoyed playing to his audience.

"You're the most interesting thing in this mind-numbing town," he would say, while popping some fresh-baked morsel into his mouth.

It was one of those compliments wrapped in an insult that was hard to digest. But he was like that, always keeping you guessing about what he really thought. There would be no guessing involved this time, for either of them. When he looked at Eliza he would see revulsion in return, and she knew it would pain him. At the very least, it felt good to have that kind of power against a man like Carson.

As she attached the last place card to its ceramic turkey holder, she said a little prayer that her seating chart would allow for everyone to have a good time, or at least not kill one another.

The first guests, Alison and Olivia and their babies, arrived. Eliza was excited to have two babies in the mix. Luke and the twins were quick to get on the floor and make a contest out of who would roll over first. By the time the other guests arrived, they were taking bets. Of course, Mr. Barr and Carson came at the exact same time. *What are the odds of that?* Eliza thought, as Luke sent Mandy to answer the door just to mess with her.

"Thanks a lot!" she teased him afterward.

"You made that bed," he said with a laugh.

She laughed, too. *That Eliza confides in him*, she thought.

Pippa and Sadie were all over their dad, which was good for all involved, and Mr. Barr was happy to talk to everyone. He knew Kayla, who had been in two of his shows in high school, and although not a huge football fan, he enthusiastically joined Luke, Kevin, and Mandy's dad to watch the college games.

There were so many helpers in the kitchen that Eliza made everyone but Kayla and Mandy leave, and the three of them got everything set on the table and buffet. At five o'clock, Eliza announced that dinner was served. Everyone began to load up their plates in that artful way one does on Thanksgiving. The colors alone were enough to make their mouths water. Soon the phrases "This is delicious," "Yum," and "Pass the gravy" could be heard from every direction.

The conversation was light. No politics, and everyone knew to steer away from hot-button topics. Between Olivia's recent drama and the ominous presence of Carson Cole, it was best to keep things upbeat. And that's how it went.

"Are you excited for the play?"

"Have you two decided what you are going to major in?"

"How do you like living on Main Street?"

"Is your baby always this good?"

Until very innocently, and quite out of nowhere, Mr. Barr said, "Kevin, I never knew that Kayla had a twin. I guess you weren't much of a theater kid."

"No, not at all. I spent most of my time on the lacrosse field or in shop class."

Mandy's dad cut in: "Is that fellow Mr. DeLuca still the shop teacher? He was on my bowling team for a season or two. Single guy, used to flirt with all the ladies."

Hearing his name spoken at her table felt like a quick punch to her gut.

"No," Kevin said, "I had Mr. Delgais. Mr. DeLuca was a legend, though. Everybody said he was the greatest teacher—he died recently. They dedicated the auditorium to him at graduation."

"Oh, that's a nice honor."

Eliza had a hard time getting air.

Mr. Barr put down his fork. "I was completely against that. In fact, it infuriated me."

Mandy's father made a joke. "Why? You wanted them to save it for you?"

"Let's just say there were rumors about him being inappropriate with some of the students. Too many for it not to be somewhat true."

Carson rolled his eyes. "Here we go," he said under his breath.

Amanda looked right at him and shut him down with one word: "Don't."

He listened and filled his mouth with turkey. As he did, Eliza said quietly, but loud enough for everyone to hear, "I was raped by Mr. DeLuca when I was seventeen."

She looked back down at her plate and moved her food around a bit. Her daughter, Kayla, let out a gasp, followed by a teary "Mom." Luke, who was sitting at the head of the table, dropped his wineglass, and it shattered on his plate. Red wine splattered everywhere, yet literally no one moved to clean it up. Tears trickled down Kevin's face. And then, as they all watched, Eliza picked up her plate, still full of food, and stood up. She looked at Mandy.

"Should we clear the dishes?" she asked, in a stupor.

Amanda led her away from the table. "I think people are still eating. Why don't we go upstairs?"

She let Amanda lead her away. Luke instructed everyone to stay put and followed them up. Sadie and Pippa were soon in tears, too; Sadie's were quite uncontrollable. It was obvious that Carson was feeling both guilty and overwhelmed. Alison and Olivia took the girls away, offering up the babies as a good distraction. Dean

Barr was ashen, completely destroyed by what his comment had ignited. Mandy's dad tried his best to make him feel better.

By the time Mandy came down, everyone had dispersed from the table. Kayla, clearly her mother's daughter, was bagging up the leftovers into Tupperware and Ziploc bags to send everyone home with food for when, if ever, their appetites came back. Dean approached Mandy.

"I'm going to go. I feel awful."

"It's OK. I'll walk you out."

As Amanda stepped out of the house she remembered lying on the front lawn when she was a little girl, staring at the clouds, wondering if that moment was real or just a dream. It felt a bit like that right now. Unreal.

The streetlights came on, flooding her with more memories: the hours she had spent with Eliza running around with the neighborhood kids playing Capture the Flag or Red Light, Green Light, until those same lights signaled it was time to go home for dinner. She had thought theirs was the most innocent of childhoods, until tonight.

She pictured their teenage years, dousing themselves in Love's Baby Soft and putting on mascara on the school bus in an effort to get the attention of their teacher-crushes. At the time, flirting that way had felt just as harmless as a game of tag.

Mr. Barr interrupted her thoughts. "I'm so sorry. This is all on me."

"Actually, I'm pretty sure it's all on me. I'm the one who started this whole game back then to begin with. I would go on and on about how immature the boys in our grade were who were interested in me just to avoid things I wasn't ready for. And to make matters worse, this whole time, since I've been back, I've probably been stirring it all up again, going on and on about you—about this." She motioned to the space between them and started to cry.

Mr. Barr went to wipe her tears and she jumped back.

"I can't," she said. It was obvious that all that was sweet between them had instantly soured.

"I understand." He paused and added sadly, "I don't think I can either."

Amanda was relieved that they were both on the same page. He continued. "I'm going to speak to the principal about taking that goddamn plaque down before the show. I should have brought up my suspicions before."

"Well, I hope they believe you. I can't imagine Eliza finally opening up about this and then having her integrity questioned. But it happens all the time."

"I'll let you know what the administrators say."

As Mandy turned to go back to the house, she saw Carson standing behind a tree smoking.

"You're smoking again?" she scoffed. When she got close, she could see he had tears on his face. She had only seen him cry at the movies, and not on account of the drama, on account of the box office. She was dumbfounded, yet without sympathy. She knew what Eliza had said was hard for *everyone* to hear, and how it had affected her was even harder to witness. But Carson deserved to hear it—and see it. She was not going to comfort him. He saw that.

"Tell the kids I say goodbye, and that I'll see them on Sunday at the show."

Luke came to the front door and called out to Mandy.

"OK. I have to go," she said.

"Tell Eliza—um—forget it," he mumbled and left.

Luke sat down on the front step. Mandy sat down next to him.

"She's asleep," he said. "I gave her a Valium that we had in the medicine cabinet from somewhere." He began to cry. "When we got upstairs, I sat her down on the bed and I lifted off her sweater to put on her nightgown. Her arms were cut up. She's been cutting herself. When she saw that I saw, she said, 'I'm sorry, I just wanted to feel something.'"

Mandy started to cry, too. "She hasn't been leaving the house. I should have told you, but I couldn't betray her."

"What?"

"She's barely left the house since the twins' graduation. It's when they announced that honor for that horrible man."

Luke filled her in on what had occurred at the ceremony. "They made a speech about him and had a slideshow. I feel sick that she had to sit through that, with everyone clapping and singing his praises."

"It must have triggered her, Luke. She didn't leave the house for four months in high school. We never knew why, but it must have been . . ."

She didn't complete her sentence. She couldn't bear to say it out loud, to hear it out loud again.

Luke wiped his eyes with the palms of his hands. "I don't know where the hell I've been. How could I have missed this? It's crazy—now, looking back, I see it. I see it all. I feel like such a self-absorbed idiot."

He put his head in his hands for a minute before making an attempt to shake it off. As if things weren't bad enough, a car pulled up to the house carrying Eliza's parents.

"Oh my God," Mandy exclaimed. "This can't be happening."

"And yet there they are—the ice queen, Birdie Reinhart, and her spineless husband, Herb." Mandy recognized that Luke was in no state to deal with his in-laws.

"OK, Luke, I think you should go check on your family and leave this to me."

"You would do that?"

"I got it. Go."

Luke made a run for it while Mandy approached the car.

It had been years since she had seen Eliza's parents, and their faces both lit up at the sight of her. She hated to have to break their hearts, but this secret had been kept long enough.

CHAPTER 43

Alison

Alison and Olivia walked to their cars. They were tired and hungry and emotionally spent and Lily was being unusually fussy. They hugged goodbye without exchanging a single word. There was nothing to say.

The whole evening had been heartbreaking, especially, Alison thought, the tears from Eliza's children. It always blew her mind how women have the ability to bury things away in order to survive. Never telling anyone for years and years—their mothers, their best friends, all in the dark; carrying the weight and the shame alone. Her own mother had been no different.

When she got into her car, she started to cry. She thought back to her conversations with Jackie on the bulletin board and with Jack in real life. She realized that the only person she wanted to talk to after this brutal night was him. She wanted to feel the safety she had when he hugged her at the fair, before it all came crashing down. For that brief moment she had felt something that she never had before.

She thought again of Jackie's wayward dating advice: *Follow your heart.*

As she came upon Jack's house, she filled with the anticipation of seeing him again. Zach was already asleep in his car seat, and she wrestled with what to do with him, one of those first-time parenting situations that always left her second-guessing herself. She went with taking him out in the car seat and grabbing her diaper bag, in case they were invited in. As soon as she got to the door, she wished she hadn't. It felt presumptuous.

Her empty belly filled with nerves as she rang the bell. In her mind, he would probably apologize again upon seeing her. And this time she would accept it. Despite her hardened, law-honed tendencies, she trusted him. After the parade of god-awful men she had just experienced, Jack's crimes felt more like misdemeanors. After several minutes passed, Alison felt a wave of disappointment. He wasn't home.

She was about to give up when the driveway filled with the light of a car turning in.

Jana got out first and walked over to Alison, looking at her suspiciously. Between bearing witness to her father moping around after their last date, and being front and center for today's discussion regarding Alison's presumed love triangle, she was not a fan.

"Can I help you?" she said with an extra dose of teenage sass.

"Hi, yes, we met at the fair. I'm Alison Le."

"I know who you are, thanks."

Alison seriously considered running. This was not the welcome she had anticipated.

Jack walked up looking gorgeous in a cable-knit sweater and jeans. Her heart dropped at the sight of him. She didn't remember ever feeling that way before. She smiled. He didn't. He instructed

Jana to go inside, and she did, slamming the door quite purpose-fully behind her, an action that quickly doused the warm feeling in Alison's belly and replaced it with dread.

"Well, I guess your daughter hates me," she said, wishing again that she had run.

"A little. She's very overprotective of me and she knows I *was* down about blowing it with you."

He said it in a way that emphasized the past tense.

"Well, you didn't completely blow it," she said with a cautious smile.

Alison grappled with what to say next. He didn't.

"I saw the press conference, and at first I didn't believe you were with that guy, but I realize now . . ." He paused and shook his head, in a way that made him seem so vulnerable and contin-ued. "I may look like a strong, tough guy, but it's been a long time since I've felt anything close to what I did for you. I'm not the kind who would do well with one of those open relationships people do now. That's not my style. Especially not one where your picture would be flashed in all the papers with the would-be mayor."

"But I'm not with him. Not that way."

He looked at her skeptically.

"Well, in what way are you with him?"

"We are nothing. He is Zach's father. That's it. I don't like him that way."

Jackie actually took a step back from her, his body language reeking of uncertainty. She felt an unfamiliar pull in her stomach, possibly desperation.

"I like you that way, though," she said, hoping so badly to turn things around.

He smiled and took a step toward her. "You do?"

She breathed a slight sigh of relief from the warmth in his tone.

"Yes, very much so."

"And you are sure—there's nothing more between you and Marc Sugarman?"

"Nothing. I thought maybe there was, but I'm sure—very sure."

His smile grew. "When you didn't take his hand, right? At the press conference—that's when you were sure?"

She laughed. "Yes—that's when I was sure. You are unbelievable!"

"Actually, I am believable. Very, very believable."

He apologized again for misrepresenting himself. "I'm really sorry for not being up-front with you. Please know that's not who I am. I can show you who I am—if you want."

She smiled cheerfully. "I want."

He leaned in to kiss her. She leaned in to meet him. Just as their lips were about to touch, she noticed something move in the bushes. Her eyes widened.

"Don't move," she whispered.

Though confused, he listened. Two eyes looked out at her, then moved back into the shadow. From its brief appearance, she was pretty sure that it was the lost dog from the bulletin board.

"I think that lost dog is in your bushes."

"Who? Truffles Goldstein?"

After all of the awfulness of the night, the mere fact that this sweet, eager man knew the missing dog's full name really sealed the deal.

"I think so."

"OK, what should we do? He's very skittish, right?"

"Yes. They said he always runs when spotted."

"Should I get him a treat? I have chocolate inside."

"That would be good if you want to kill him."

"Sorry. I never had a dog."

"Wait." She reached into her diaper bag. "I have turkey."

"Great. Call out 'treat' with the turkey, and I will grab him from behind. Go slow."

"OK."

Alison carefully unwrapped the turkey and put it in front of her on the ground. It smelled so good, this dog had better appreciate it, she thought as her empty stomach rumbled.

"Treat! Here, Truffles. Here, boy," she said calmly and took two steps back. After a moment, Truffles crept out and cautiously sniffed the turkey. As he gulped it down, Jackie reached out and grabbed him by the collar. The dog flinched, but didn't even stop eating.

"We did it!" Alison cheered.

"My car is right there. Should we take him home?" she added.

"Yes. Let's do it."

"I can watch the baby!" Jana called out from the window. They all laughed, realizing she'd been eavesdropping the whole time. Alison was glad she'd been listening, happy to have gained her approval.

They climbed into Alison's car and messaged Truffles's owner, who tearfully gave them her address. Once there, Truffles raced to the door, crying and jumping up and down as they rang the bell. He knew he was home. He barreled in, nearly taking Jackie down with him.

The reunion was right out of the movies, with Truffles taking turns licking the tears from everyone's faces, Jackie's and Alison's included. Outside, Alison was feeling quite thankful.

"You saved Thanksgiving," she said.

He didn't understand why, but he took it with pride. "Can we kiss and make up now?"

"If you don't mind, first, I could really use a hug."

As he wrapped his arms around her, they both sensed that it would be a long, long time until they would let each other go.

CHAPTER 44

Eliza

Eliza woke up at 3:00 a.m. with a fuzzy memory of what had
happened the night before. She went downstairs and got herself a glass of water. The fridge was filled to the brim with leftovers. Or actually, now that it came back to her, with uneaten
Thanksgiving dinner. She pulled out a turkey leg and headed back
upstairs to her computer. She actually felt lighter. Not good, but
certainly less dead inside. She sat down at the computer, opened
up the bulletin board, and wrote. She knew enough about triggering events to begin with a warning:

THE FOLLOWING POST CONTAINS DETAILS OF SEXUAL ASSAULT

The pent-up words flew out of her:

My name is Eliza Hunt. You may know me as a mom in the
neighborhood. Maybe you grew up with me, or maybe you just know me

as the moderator of this bulletin board. What you don't know is that I
am a rape survivor.

Thirty years ago a shop teacher at Hudson Valley High, Roy DeLuca,
raped me in the musty basement of the school. I can still smell that
room. I was a virgin. In fact, I had kissed a boy only once, twice if you
count Spin the Bottle. I was too ashamed and too afraid to tell anyone,
and I never told a soul until tonight. It has been the deepest, darkest
secret of my life.

I thought it was my fault because I often smiled at him and was
wearing a short skirt and carrying a copy of *Lolita* from English class.
He asked me to climb up on the table, so that he could see how pretty
I was up close. I was flattered that a grown man thought I was pretty.
No one had called me that before. And then he forced himself on me,
forced himself into me. The pain was intense, but I didn't cry out for
help. I didn't say no, I didn't say stop, I just lay there voiceless, in
shock and pain. Afterward he pulled up his pants and said, "Did you
like that?" Sometimes I think that was the worst part.

I am coming forward now, for myself, because this toxic secret has
persistently eaten away at me for thirty years; for my children,
especially my daughter; and for other women in this group that I lead,
as an example. I'm ashamed that I kept it quiet for all of this time. I
pray nightly that in doing so I didn't cause other women to suffer the
same fate. I know many people will be surprised by my admission,
surprised that I bore this alone for so long. There is a reason that Roy
DeLuca was given such an honor of having the auditorium named for
him at Hudson Valley High, and I know that his many fans will possibly
try to discredit me. I know from watching other women come forward
that my memory and my integrity will come into question. And I know
that Mr. DeLuca, who is now dead, will not be able to defend himself or

deny my claims. It doesn't matter to me. I am glad he cannot defend himself. A defense of any kind would be as damaging as the act itself.

I mourn the person I may have been if this hadn't happened to me. The price that I have paid for it is immeasurable. The price that the people that love me have paid for it is also immeasurable.

Roy DeLuca raped me. I am happy that he is dead. I hope it was as slow and painful as my life has been on account of his disgusting actions.

She pressed Post without even reading it over and went back to bed.

At around ten o'clock in the morning, Luke came into their room and sat next to Eliza, lovingly nudging her awake. He had a cup of coffee for her and some toast and jam that he placed on her nightstand.

"Kayla wants to show you something, if you're up to it," he said.

Eliza sat up and pushed herself back against the headboard. She took a sip of her coffee before speaking. "Are the kids OK?"

"Yes. Upset, but doing OK. They are proud of you."

"Proud of me? What for?"

"Hold on."

He opened the door for Kayla to come in. She entered clutching her laptop.

"I have to show you something, Mom," she said.

She opened up to the post that Eliza had written in the middle of the night. There were already 487 likes.

"Look what you've done for all of these women. You have inspired them to speak out. Some even name names."

She began to scroll through the comments. Kevin came to the door.

"Come in," she said, patting the bed. "I am so sorry for putting you through that last night."

"Mom, I love you so much."

"I'm going to be OK. I promise. I will go for help and make sure of it."

"We know you will," Kevin said.

"I love you, Mom," Kayla said, hugging her.

It broke Eliza's heart to see her children in this reversed position, comforting her. She hugged them tightly, hoping they would recognize her strength.

Under her post the comments flowed, each more painful than the next, with new ones arriving every minute. In between words of encouragement, like, "Thank you, Eliza Hunt. Your courage is remarkable," and hashtag slogans from the "Time's Up" movement like #believewomen and #metoo, came heartbreaking confessions from women with their own painful narratives. Eliza had unknowingly created a safe space—providing the perfect pulpit to trade secrets for absolution. All of these women expelling a rage that had been bottled up for years. Finally heard, finally free.

She and the twins read through them together.

I was always told to be polite. That's what I was thinking when my dad's uncle stuck his hand in my bathing suit bottom in our pool.

In my head I slapped him and ran from his office, but in reality I sat paralyzed while he forced himself on me. I was too frozen to even form the word "no."

My mother's boyfriend molested me. I never said a word because she was finally happy. When I saw him eyeing my sister I spoke up. She threw him out, but I know she resented me for it.

I was young like you were. I have never told anyone. You are very brave.

In college the cutest guy on campus asked me to an away-weekend formal. Back at the room he pulled out rubbers. I said they wouldn't be necessary. He said why, are you on the pill? I laughed; no, I'm a virgin. He said, not after tonight you're not. I still can't speak the rest.

I was in camp. I was 16. My dad had died the winter before and I missed him terribly. An older man at camp paid a lot of attention to me. I let him. I'm still ashamed.

I was also raped at 17. I have never written those words before. Though I still think of it every single day. I am 67.

In eighth grade I was babysitting for a family down the street. One night it was raining, and the dad insisted on driving me home. He pulled over and asked if I had ever seen a man's penis before. I ran home and never told a soul. His name was Jim McClusky. Fuck you, Jim McClusky.

It seemed to be endless—endless women had buried their pain deep enough to keep hidden, but not deep enough to keep it from eating away at their souls. It was too much for Eliza to take in all at once. Her eyes felt heavy. She closed Kayla's laptop and told everyone she needed to sleep a little more.

Luke realized that Eliza had forgotten all about her parents' visit. He broke it to her gently. "Honey, your mom and dad arrived last night. Mandy explained the whole thing to them. Your mom really wants to see you. Should I tell her to wait?"

That the whole town now knew what had happened to Eliza was one thing; that her parents knew felt infinitely worse.

"No, just send her in." She turned to the kids. "Give me a few minutes with Grandma, OK?"

They were both happy to escape that conversation.

As Birdie sat at the end of the bed, visibly rattled, Eliza noticed that her once-glamorous thinness now came across as fragility. She actually felt bad for her. If anything remotely approaching her experience had happened to Kayla, Eliza knew she would have been enraged beyond imagination. So she was surprised her mother's first reaction was one of guilt.

"I'm so sorry, so, so sorry," Birdie said, unfamiliar tears escaping down her face. Eliza's eyes welled up in response.

"Don't blame yourself, Mom. How could you have known if I never told you?"

"But . . ." She cried some more, swallowing her words.

"Kids hide things from their parents all the time. It's not your fault, Mom, really."

But there was something that was very much Birdie's fault, and they both knew it.

"Please, Eliza, let me say what I have to." It was so hard for her to speak that she couldn't meet her daughter's eyes. She looked down at the tissue that she was twisting in her hand and continued. "Daddy and I read what you wrote on the Interweb. The part about no one saying you were pretty before then. I'm sorry that I was always so critical of you, Eliza. I just wanted the best for you, but your father said that maybe if I had told you that you were beautiful you wouldn't have looked for that attention somewhere else."

Her father finally stood up to her mother, but it was way too late in life to matter really—and his blaming her mother for what happened was as ridiculous as blaming her seventeen-year-old self. Eliza had accepted her mother's limitations long ago. She had come to terms with the incessant criticism and knew that her mother couldn't see beyond her own vision of what her daughter should be like to see her for who she was. She chose to put Birdie out of her misery and responded generously.

"Mom, stop. That's not why this happened. It happened because a man was a monster. It's not your fault any more than it's mine. I know that, and so should you."

More tears trickled from Birdie's eyes and she was having trouble catching her breath.

"You look tired, Mom. Want to lie down a bit? Rest your eyes?"

She patted Luke's side of the bed and her mother looked at her as if she'd suggested they share a Whopper with fries. The disparity between her relationship with Birdie and the mother-daughter relationship she shared with Kayla was never more evident. Lying in bed with her daughter, chatting or napping or watching TV, was second nature for Eliza, while this scenario felt completely foreign. To her surprise, Birdie pushed through her discomfort, walked around the bed, and lay down. She rested her hand on her daughter's, and although it felt more awkward than comforting to Eliza, as they both drifted off, she felt loved by her mother. It may have been the first time.

CHAPTER 45

Amanda & Eliza

By the time the play rolled around on Sunday, the whole town knew of Roy DeLuca's horrific actions, and as is typically the case with such predators, more women had already come forward with similar accusations. The school board called an emergency meeting and voted to take down the dedication plaque and open up an investigation into the charges against Mr. DeLuca.

At the start of the play, Mr. Barr gave his own soliloquy:

"Tonight the Hudson Valley High Shakespeare Troupe presents its thirtieth annual production, *Measure for Measure*. This play was first performed in 1603, yet ironically it represents many of the same troubles and power struggles found in our society today. While at first, I thought it might be too racy for high school students, I'm now confident that there is no better age to point out its ideals. I hope it leads to further discussion in your homes. This play was written over four hundred years ago, and I believe William

Shakespeare would agree that time is most definitely up! Without further ado, I present *Measure for Measure*."

While Amanda had been present at many rehearsals, it was only when watching it now that she saw the parallels between men like her husband and Mr. DeLuca with Angelo, the play's villain.

Determined to enforce a law regarding immorality, Angelo sentenced a man named Claudio to death for impregnating his fiancée. Claudio's sister, Isabella, who was about to become a nun, begged Angelo to spare her brother's life. At first, he flatly denied her request—the law, he said, required an execution. But Angelo was overcome by lust for Isabella. He threatened that he would only pardon her brother if she had sex with him.

Even in the dark, with Sadie sitting between them as a buffer, Amanda could tell that Carson was struggling with the play's content. Clearly he had made the connection between himself and Angelo, and to make matters worse, his very own daughter was playing Angelo's prey, Isabella. Seeing her placed in the same position in a power struggle that his victims had experienced was a head trip of epic proportions—though that was not how Shakespeare would have described it. When Isabella (Pippa) swore to tell the world that Angelo wanted to trade sex in exchange for releasing her brother from prison, Angelo responded with:

Who will believe thee, Isabel?
My unsoil'd name, the austereness of my life,
My vouch against you, and my place i' the state.

You didn't need SparkNotes to interpret this one:

Who will believe you?
My good name, my austere life,
My word against yours, and my place in Hollywood.

Between the play and the real-life drama at Thanksgiving, Carson was overwhelmed by the need to right his wrongs. When the applause subsided, he pulled Amanda aside. She was anxious to find Pippa, but it looked like waiting a minute for the crowd to disperse might be prudent anyway.

"What is it?" she asked.

Carson had prepared a monologue as well.

"I'm going to head back to LA in the morning. You've tolerated me long enough. I'm beyond sorry for the pain I caused you and the girls. I don't deserve you, Amanda. I don't deserve them either, but they are stuck with me. I will give you a divorce, even the house if you want it. I hope that you do. I'm sorry."

He was right in that she had tolerated him long enough. The rest was suspect—typical remorseful words in Carson's cycle of abuse. She was proud of herself that she had gotten to a place to question that. Pippa bounded up full of love for both of them. Flowers and accolades were exchanged, but nothing more was said.

That night, back at his hotel, Carson called each one of his accusers and apologized. He was open and honest and said simply, "I am very sorry for what I did to you. I now realize that consent is not viable when there is such an unequal division of power. I hope that my apology gives you some form of peace."

Some of the women just hung up on him, some said thank you and hung up, but one of the women, Cathy Lingstrom, whom he imagined had suffered the greatest betrayal on account of being their close family friend, made a public statement about it.

She began by saying:

> Carson Cole called me last night to apologize and to take responsibility for his actions. Today I feel as if I have set down a weight that I have been carrying around

for years. There is a reason it is called the burden of
proof. I am thankful to be relieved of that burden.

As Amanda sat at her father's kitchen table reading Cathy's
words, she wanted to put down that weight, too, but she still felt
skeptical. Her father entered the kitchen and, as if reading her
mind, said, "You read it, I see. Do you think he's sincere?"

"Possibly. But he always acts remorseful for a period of time. I
hate to say it, but it's more likely a great big public manipulation."

He kissed her on the top of her head. "I'm happy to hear you
say that. The fact that you are questioning him and not taking him
at his word, that makes me know you are going to be OK."

"Thanks, Daddy. I am."

The girls scampered into the kitchen. Amanda pulled them
toward her and added, "We are."

"We are what, Mommy?" Sadie asked with a smile.

"We are going home. What do you think about finishing up the
semester here and heading back home before Christmas?" Amanda
asked.

"I would love that," Sadie said. Amanda knew she missed her
room and her friends.

Pippa did as well, but added with a maturity that surprised
Amanda, "If it's OK for you, that would be nice."

"It is. I miss home, too." Amanda hugged them both and added,
more for Sadie than Pippa, "Daddy won't be living with us, but
you will see him as much as you want. OK?"

"OK," Sadie said, hugging her again.

The next day Amanda and Luke drove Eliza up to a residential
treatment program specializing in overcoming trauma and
anxiety. Eliza had found it herself and jumped when they said they

had an empty bed. She knew it would take her longer than the twenty-eight days that insurance pays for to unpack thirty years of baggage, but she wanted to begin with an intense program. She couldn't bear the fear she saw in the eyes of Luke and her kids and was determined to ease their burden. While a cloud had been lifted, the fog was still very much there. She was still filled with fear when attempting to leave the house—so the fact that she had left the house to get better was already a bigger step than she could have imagined taking just a week earlier.

Before leaving, Eliza asked Olivia to take over as moderator of the Hudson Valley Ladies' Bulletin Board. Olivia protested.

"But it's yours. I will just fill in until you come back."

Eliza had other ideas for her future. "I'm hoping to be able to do something outside of the house, maybe catering."

Olivia agreed. Actually, she happily agreed, but just for the time being. She knew she had a long healing process in front of her as well and would have to learn how to navigate dealing with Spencer and his family. Running the bulletin board would supply a much-needed distraction.

CHAPTER 46

Eliza & Amanda & Alison & Olivia

28 DAYS LATER

As the first snow dusted Hudson Valley, Eliza Hunt sat in the lobby of Crossroads Village, the treatment facility that had been her home for the past twenty-eight days, waiting for Luke to pick her up. He was due to arrive at eleven, but she was eager to go home and had been sitting there waiting since ten. She was excited to escape the monotony, the food, and the same faces day in and day out. She was also nervous—nervous to reconnect with Luke and deconstruct the wall that had grown between them. Thankfully, that process was well under way for both of them.

She had learned so much about herself over the past month. She learned why she was hyper vigilant and startled so easily that her kids nicknamed her Jumpy, why she tensed up if Luke looked at her a certain way and got nervous if she ever felt sexy. And of course, all of the reasons behind her cutting herself. It was mostly textbook stuff—she checked nearly every box on the checklist for survivors of sexual assault and trauma.

Luke had come to visit for four days during "family week" and it had been tough for them both. Being forced to talk about the ugliest things in her life in front of strangers was very heavy and extremely uncomfortable. Talking about them in front of her husband felt even worse for Eliza. The pain she saw in his eyes when she described what had happened to her was not something she would soon forget. While they both felt they had been rubbed raw, it was a necessary step toward her recovery.

The process had seemed to work well for Eliza. The doctors put her on an antidepressant that tapered both her lows and her highs, allowing her to examine her issues in neutral. She was by no means cured, if such a thing were even possible, but she'd been given the tools to live her best life, as they liked to call it in rehab. The psychiatrist there connected her to a local therapist whom she had already met and bonded with over Skype. She was set to see her twice a week to start.

She also felt physically healthier, which went a long way toward feeling good about oneself. The forced walks outside and daily yoga classes were beneficial in more ways than one, and she committed to continue exercising at home.

The clientele at Crossroads was partially made up of women and teenage girls with anorexia. Eliza saw so much of her mother in these women. It brought her new ways to understand her and put a different lens on her childhood.

Luke arrived a few minutes before eleven and she could see from his face that he was nervous as well. It made her wonder, would they still fit together? He didn't really know the real Eliza—neither did she; she'd been gone for so long. He hugged her tentatively and she responded longer and stronger than she ever had before. It surprised him, and he responded with tears—lots of them, more than she had collectively seen come from his eyes in their lifetime together. She knew from that quick display of emotion that their particular love could mend anything—even layers upon layers of anything. She was excited to begin a journey that felt much more promising than the one she had left, both hers and theirs.

The first question Eliza asked when they pulled off the exit for home was, "So, is there any food in the house?"

Luke answered sheepishly. "Well, yes, if by food you mean six different kinds of cereal and ramen."

It was oddly satisfying to hear that he suffered in that department. *Everyone likes to feel needed*, she thought when she felt bad for feeling that way.

"Do you mind if I drop you off and head over to the Stop & Shop?"

"We could go together," Luke volunteered. She could tell he was worried about leaving her alone. That would never work, she thought.

"No thanks. I want to go on my own, test out my sea legs."

As soon as she dropped Luke at home, she called Amanda. She had spoken to her briefly during her stay, begging them to let her make a call to check on her. Amanda and the girls had been settling back in in LA, and things were quiet, which was exactly what she had hoped for. Carson had continued down the remorseful path, treating Amanda with respect and coming to terms with his accusers. He was one of the few men to really speak up about the culture he subscribed to and take responsibility for his actions. It didn't negate what he'd done at all, but it did teach his children the power of forgiveness.

Amanda was thrilled to see Eliza's number pop up on her phone. "Eliza!" she shouted. "Did they spring you loose, or did you escape?"

"I'm out! Good to gallivant through the real world on my own."

"That's great! How are you feeling?"

"I'm really excited to be home. I feel strong and more empowered, for sure. How are you guys doing?"

"All good. You won't believe it, but I'm coming from an audition."

"That's amazing. How did it go?"

"All right. My agent thinks I'm getting calls due to curiosity more than talent. But whatever gets me in the door, right?"

"Right for you. In my case, it's out the door!"

"Exactly." Mandy laughed, happy to have her old friend back.

Eliza arrived at the Stop & Shop and the two women hung up, but not before promising to speak with each other at least once a week going forward.

Eliza pushed her cart down aisle four, sashaying right past the donuts without stopping, and headed toward the produce department. Once there, a McIntosh apple flew past her face, just missing her nose. She picked up the apple and handed it back to the embarrassed mom, pushing the redheaded culprit in her shopping cart.

"I think this belongs to you."

"I'm so sorry," the mortified mother responded. "I'm at my wit's end with this one."

"He has a good arm. Maybe you should sign him up for Little League. The Pee Wee group always begins in the spring," Eliza offered.

"That's so funny. I posted my troubles on a local moms' group and that's what a lot of the women suggested."

"Oh. That is funny," Eliza said, remembering the last time she had encountered a young mother at the Stop & Shop. "Which group was that? Valley Girls?"

"No," she said with a hint of disdain. "If you need real answers you have to go to the Hudson Valley Ladies' Bulletin Board."

"I'll be sure to check it out," Eliza responded with a smile.

Before heading home, Eliza took a moment in the car to text Olivia the directive she had thoroughly thought through while she was away. It was time to pass the torch and move on to the next chapter of her life.

Olivia was thrilled to receive Eliza's message. She was just up the road at the Café Karma Sutra with Alison when it came through. They were waiting on line to order, each with a receptacle in hand.

"Look!" Olivia held up her phone. "Eliza is back and wants me to officially announce my position as the new moderator of the bulletin board!"

"That's great, Olivia!"

Eliza's prior posts, both the original, fictional ones and the heartbreakingly true ones, had changed the tone of the bulletin board and pushed its membership north of ten thousand, spreading to towns on either side. With these growing numbers she would soon need to enlist help. There was an increasingly strong feeling of community and support among the members. Olivia was excited to take it to new heights.

Alison had news as well, hidden in a folder of legal papers regarding Olivia's divorce. When they sat down, Olivia opened up the folder with dread, but soon her face lit up.

"What do you think?" Alison asked, as Olivia studied the words on the page. It was copy for an ad that Alison wanted to put in the local paper. At the top it read:

Alison Le, Country Lawyer

"Would you design the ad for me? And my letterhead? And a shingle for my front lawn?" Alison asked with unusual exuberance.

"You're staying? For me and Jackie?" she squealed, semi-seriously. Alison and Jackie had been inseparable since Thanksgiving.

"Ha-ha. You should know me better than that. I'm staying for me and Zachary."

"Either way, I love it!"

Alison was excited to become a small-town lawyer. She would pay her bills with things like matrimonial and estate law while offering herself pro bono for immigration cases. Olivia promised to promote her new venture on the bulletin board, as she was, after all, a very satisfied client.

That afternoon, while Lily napped, Olivia proudly built her inaugural fire in the living room fireplace. Out the window the first snowfall was gaining momentum. She was looking forward to the panorama of white it would leave in its wake. She sat down and wrote an official introductory post.

Hello, ladies of Hudson Valley. My name is Olivia York, and I am the new moderator of the Hudson Valley Ladies' Bulletin Board.

I have big plans for us all, including book clubs, charitable drives, and meet-ups. Please feel free to comment with any and all suggestions and ideas. I can't wait to see what the future of the Hudson Valley Ladies' Bulletin Board brings!

The fire was slowly dying, and Olivia was out of logs. The rest of the bundle sat outside within sight but would take some wrapping up on her part to get to. She didn't feel like leaving the warm, cozy house. She looked up above the fireplace, at the painting of her and Spencer—the last remaining remnant of her marriage. She thought back to an art history class at Wellesley, to stories of Impressionists burning the canvases of works they weren't happy with. She wasn't happy with this one, that was for sure.

Without much thought, Olivia took the painting down from the wall. She placed it on the floor and pummeled it with both of her feet, ripping right through the canvas itself. It was liberating. She pressed all her weight on one side of the frame while lifting up the other, snapping it in two, then she snapped those pieces in two again. With each snap she felt calmer and more collected. Within a few minutes, the anniversary present was unrecognizable. Though not completely worthless, she thought, as she tossed the pieces into the fire. She felt oddly at peace as she watched the colors dance through the flames. It was beautiful, like some sort of sacrificial celebration.

"*The Rebirth of Venus,*" she said out loud with a smile, as the fire caught her marital image and slowly curled it to ash.

She looked back at the bulletin board. Comments were pouring in. Her first post was on its way to becoming an epic thread. She heard Lily on the baby monitor and scurried to her room to get her. As she scooped her up in her arms, she told her, "It's you and me, baby girl. Everything is going to be all right."

ACKNOWLEDGMENTS

Thank you to my agent, friend, and greatest ally, Eve MacSweeney. Your brilliance, thoughtfulness, and hands-on approach have me counting my blessings daily. Thank you as well to Christy Fletcher for always lending your ear and expertise, and to Anita Zabludowicz for the wonderful introduction.

To my smart, talented, and visionary editor, Amanda Bergeron, thank you for believing in me so wholeheartedly. There are no words to describe what that means to me. And to Claire Zion and the rest of the team at Berkley, Jin Yu, and Diana Franco, for welcoming me aboard so graciously and for all of your hard work on my book.

To my sister-in-law Andrea Levenbaum for never letting my participles dangle and, more importantly, for always having my back.

For Linda Coppola, thank you for allowing me to fill your commute with the sound of my reading and rereading and reading again. How lucky am I that my husband chose you as his best friend all of those years ago at Camp Roosevelt.

For Phoebe and Valerie Cates, I feel so fortunate to be on the receiving end of those intuitive, confident, and creative Cates genes. Thank you for being there for me from the first draft to the final touches.

There are some difficult topics discussed in this book. A few amazing women shared their stories with me, giving me great insight into the pain and recovery associated with both sexual abuse and infidelity. Thank you for your strength and courage. I hope my readers will benefit from your journeys.

To my own personal sisterhood, many of whom have been by my side for life. I'm afraid if I list you all I will leave someone out, but I think you know who you are and how much I count on your love and laughter and support. I am blessed to have you in my life and hope I am a blessing to you in return. And to all of my family, friends, and readers who showed up for me before and I know will again: Thank you. I loved sharing my last book journey with you and look forward to doing it all again this go-round.

For all of the women throughout the world who have embraced online forums with candor, support, and humor, I salute you. At times it may have seemed like I am making fun, but believe me, I am laughing with you, not at you, and have often benefited from your advice, bravery, humor, and introspection.

A special shout-out to the fabulous collection of Bookstagrammers on Instagram: Your talent, dedication, and selfless love and support of the book community is extraordinary.

And last but certainty most, my family. To my very fit (argh), very loving husband, Warren—you are my heart, soul, and very best friend. To Raechel, your dedication to your art and beliefs inspire me daily. I am so proud of the delightful and beautiful woman you have become. To Talia, courageous, funny, and wise beyond your years, you fill my heart with hope and pride. And to Melodie, your help with this project has been immeasurable. Your editing, insights, and remarkable ability to do just about anything has been invaluable. To me, you are perfect. Collectively, to the whole lot of you: I see you gingerly trying to escape out the porch door in Fire Island before I shout, "Wait, how does this sound?" Or, "Look at this sentence, does it need a comma?" Or the dreaded, "What's that word that I'm thinking of—you know the one?" Yet you always stop, think, and thoughtfully answer, barely ever rolling your eyes. Thank you for toasting and smiling and congratulating me when I say, "I finished my book today!" even though you know I will make that same enthusiastic announcement a dozen more times. And lastly for the endless love, laughs, encouragement, and most importantly, for all of the dancing!

Eliza Starts a Rumor

JANE L. ROSEN

BEHIND THE BOOK

Eliza Starts a Rumor begins with Nora Ephron's famous words: "Above all, be the heroine of your life, not the victim." The quote not only sums up the journey of my four protagonists, but my own journey as well, because writing this book actually helped me to be my own hero.

When I began working on *Eliza*, I was at a very low point in my life. My family and I were set to travel to the Florida Keys, but ended up spending spring break at Memorial Sloan Kettering hospital, where my youngest daughter was being treated for a recurrence of thyroid cancer. Then my mother had heart surgery. Although it had seemed to be successful, she passed away two weeks later, leaving us all heartbroken. It was a dire time in my life, both personally and professionally. I was suffering from an awful case of writer's block. It was something that had never happened to me before or since, but was obviously a byproduct of all I was going through. Like Eliza, I was feeling quite desperate.

A week after my mom passed, I was scheduled to give a talk about my first novel, *Nine Women, One Dress*. I was tired of giving the same old speech I had presented a dozen times before, so I decided to change things up. Following a question from someone in the audience, the conversation turned to the subject of online mothers' groups. Suddenly, the energy in the room quadrupled right in front of me. Everyone started laughing and chatting and raising their hands to share stories and confessions. As I stood up there, taking it all in, I realized that I had the basis for a new novel. Unblocked, I began writing it the next day.

I was mourning my mother, worrying about my daughter, and perseverating about my career—no one would have blamed me if I'd done nothing but hide under the covers and feed myself a steady diet of carbs and Bravo TV. But instead of sinking into my world that was spiraling out of control, I found a lifeline on the page. I concentrated on the various challenges Eliza, Amanda, Alison, and Olivia faced. With Amanda, I explored the plight of the innocent spouse in the #MeToo movement, with Olivia, the horror of a new mother worrying about whether her husband is being faithful. Through Alison I delved into the particular stresses of being a single parent, and through Eliza, the way that the wounds of childhood trauma can rear up in adulthood and have to be confronted in order to live a healthy life. I created women who became their own heroes and, in doing so, helped to squash the sense of despair that was threatening to engulf me as well.

The feeling of control a writer has in resolving her characters' issues was satisfying to me in a very personal way as I embarked on this novel. While teaching my characters to put themselves first, I put myself first. I did what I needed to do to climb out of my hole. Of course I still miss my mother every day and I still worry about my daughter, now thankfully happy and healthy, but I no longer let my grief and worry define me. I choose resilience and created characters who did the same.

For women, especially, I think that's a very hard thing to do. We are mothers, daughters, spouses, employers and employees. When we face a tragedy, we are expected to bounce back quickly, because other people are depending on us. It's often said that we should heed the wisdom of a flight attendant's instructions: secure your own oxygen mask first before helping others with theirs. It's good advice. We are our own saviors. Every life has its own unique struggles, and every woman's life certainly does. It's how we *face* our struggles that gives us a path forward, that lets us take control when we can. This is how we become the heroes of our own stories.

DISCUSSION QUESTIONS

1. The four women in *Eliza Starts a Rumor* are quite different from one another. Which of the women did you most connect with?

2. Do you belong to any online women's groups? What have they given you that you couldn't find elsewhere? Have you ever posted or commented on something online that you regret?

3. Jackie freaks out when his daughter Jana wants to use a tampon. How did your mother handle this? Was it different than how you would?

4. Like Eliza, we all stayed home for a long period of time, but due to COVID-19. What was this experience like for you? Do you think the accessibility of the Internet and the aftereffects of COVID-19 will spur more agoraphobia in the world?

5. This book celebrates the value of community and friendship among women. In what ways do you feel the opportunities to

create community have changed over the past ten years? Do you find it easier or harder to sustain friendships?

6. Do you think Eliza's actions of posting the rumor came in part because of her feelings of inadequacy surrounding becoming an empty nester? If you have children, do you worry about that time in your life, whether it's in front of you or behind you?

7. Do you agree with Alison's life choices? Why or why not?

8. Did you find how Olivia went about catching Spencer cheating to be satisfying? Do you think you would have had the strength, courage, and patience to wait it out like she did?

9. When Olivia's crisis comes to a head Amanda points out how she still has time for a do-over. How do you think the #MeToo environment is affecting women's choices and actions today? Do you think how Eliza and Amanda originally dealt with their adversities would be different in the current environment?

10. Do you believe that Carson was sincere in his remorse or do you think it was a publicity stunt? Do you think men like him are capable of change?

11. Near the end of the book Eliza's mother, Birdie, guiltily apologizes for never calling Eliza pretty as a child. Do you understand her guilt? Do you think it's valid?

12. Were you surprised by the ending of the book? Were you satisfied with each of the women's transformations and trajectories?

WHAT'S ON JANE'S READING LIST?

FICTION

The Cider House Rules by John Irving
Mila 18 by Leon Uris
The Prince of Tides by Pat Conroy
Amy and Isabelle by Elizabeth Strout
Swing Time by Zadie Smith
The Story of Ferdinand by Munro Leaf

NONFICTION

Caste by Isabel Wilkerson
To Begin Again by Naomi Levy
Between the World and Me by Ta-Nehisi Coates
Nobody Will Tell You This But Me by Bess Kalb

Author photo © Lori Berkowitz

Jane L. Rosen is an author and screenwriter whose critically acclaimed first novel, *Nine Women, One Dress*, has been translated into ten languages. She lives in New York City and Fire Island with her husband and three daughters.

CONNECT ONLINE

○ JaneLRosen
⬛ JaneLRosenAuthor
🐦 JaneLRosen1